The Connector

The Connector

Tony Williamson

STEIN AND DAY/*Publishers*/New York

For Lisbet, who put it all together

First published in the United States of America, 1976
Copyright © 1976 by Tony Williamson Productions Limited
All rights reserved
Printed in the United States of America
Stein and Day/*Publishers*/Scarborough House,
Briarcliff Manor, N.Y. 10510

Library of Congress Cataloging in Publication Data

Williamson, Tony.
The connector.

I. Title.

PZ4.W7297Co3   (PR6073.I43344)   823'.9'14
ISBN 0-8128-1930-6   75-34348

One

Paul Ryker reclined contentedly on the rooftop terrace of his villa. Above, the sun burned ferociously against a steel-blue sky; below, the narrow streets of Algiers crawled down towards the cluttered confusion of the harbour. A seagull swam lethargically above the shimmering rooftops, its shadow passing briefly over the squat, dark figure of Ryker.

It was two o'clock, September 24th, and on Ny Vestergade, in Copenhagen's commercial district, a small blue van and a grey Mercedes took up positions on either side of the Jansen Diamond Corporation. No one got out. The four men just sat and waited, looking at their watches.

On the rooftop in Algiers, Ryker opened his eyes and considered the dark blue window of his gold Omega. Pressing the button which illuminated the red digits, he watched the seconds flick away, visualizing the scene in Copenhagen, feeling the throbbing sense of power that always came at this time. He was a short, thickset man with a thin, often cruel mouth, and dark, cold eyes that might as well have been empty sockets for all they said about the mind they served. He reached languidly for the tall glass, grimaced with annoyance when he found the Collins slightly warm, and sipped it briefly, without enthusiasm.

It was three minutes past two. The driver of the blue van, a fair-haired, square-jawed man in his early thirties, moved to the rear doors. He was wearing a dark blue coverall and a small, flat cap. His name was Lee Corey. Across the road the doors of the Mercedes opened and three men stepped out. They paused, a casual group, before crossing to the van.

The most imposing member of the trio was Hans Kerstan,

196621

a tall, ungainly man with large hands and craggy features. As he reached the rear of the van, he was already removing the stained tan raincoat, revealing a dark blue coverall beneath. Without a word Lee passed him a cap and a heavy canvas bag.

Janos Loron remained at the front of the van, casually lighting a cigarette, eyes moving constantly up and down the street. A car came into view and he paused, whistled softly. Lee and Kerstan immediately stepped away from the van, carrying the bulky canvas bags, and began strolling towards the gates of the Jansen Corporation.

The car drove past, its driver oblivious to the fact that he was being scrutinized by four pairs of eyes, his registration noted, his description studied and filed for possible future action.

Chris Holgar, the fourth member of the group, stepped out from behind the van, opened the rear doors and removed his raincoat. He was quickly joined by Loron who threw his coat into the rear, donned a cap and picked up a canvas bag. Within seconds Loron and Holgar were strolling towards the gates, their dark blue coveralls and canvas bags identical to those of Kerstan and Corey.

It was five minutes past two.

The phone buzzed softly beside Ryker and he considered it with a curious, detached expression, before lifting the receiver. 'What is it, Milena?'

The voice that answered was soft, sensual. 'Miss Delar has arrived, Paul. She's waiting in the study.'

Ryker's mouth tightened and when he spoke there was a thin edge of anger in his voice. 'I said I would see her at two thirty.'

'She has a rehearsal at the club this afternoon. She hoped you might see her earlier.'

He considered the phone with distaste. 'Tell her to wait.'

Ryker leaned back, adjusted his sunglasses, then closed his eyes and thought of Copenhagen.

The duty security officer on the gate that day was Karl Nielsen. He was a square, solid man in his early forties. The job didn't pay that much, but there were no pressures and no responsibilities and that's the way he liked it. He ate reasonably well and lived, with reasonable comfort, in a small apartment on the east side of the city. His wife, Gerda, would like a house, but as he so often told her, why hang a mortgage

6

round their necks when all they needed were four rooms and a balcony.

Karl turned from filling out the morning report to see four men gazing at him through the reception window. He noted their blue coveralls, the fact that they appeared to be carrying tool bags. As he slid the glass open, the tall, ungainly man pushed an identification card at him. 'Wienstadt Maintenance. We're due to service the air conditioners.'

Karl took the card, noted the name of the firm, the photograph, then crossed to the appointments book. Sure enough, Wienstadt Maintenance was written in for three o'clock. He frowned, glanced at the clock over his desk, moved back to the window.

'You're not due until three,' he said.

The ungainly man considered him with a disgusted expression, turned and looked at his companions. 'He wants us to wait until three.'

Karl shuffled uncomfortably as they considered him with quiet contempt. The ungainly man turned back: 'Listen, we've got two more jobs to do this afternoon. If you don't want us to come today that's all right by me.'

Karl forced a quick, apologetic smile. 'I didn't say that, but we have to be careful. Your appointment is three, and it's only five past two.'

The ungainly man swung his heavy canvas bag into the window, holding it there with his huge, hairy hands. 'Open it,' he said harshly.

Karl smiled again, gave an awkward, uncomfortable shrug. 'Just doing my job.'

'Then search the bags and let us get on with ours!'

The smile thinned and Karl reached forward, opened the canvas bag. He went through it with a smooth efficiency, finding nothing but the tools and various types of filters he would expect to find. He nodded finally, allowing the man to take it back and step away.

The second bag contained cleaning fluids, more tools and various types of hose. The third was mainly electrical and included a heavy drill, coils of wire and boxes of fuses. He nodded and waved it away. The last man was small, lean and contemptuous, slamming down the heavy bag. Karl gave him an angry look, opened it and laboriously began to check the contents. The tools and wadding didn't surprise him, but in the bottom of the bag were four breathing masks. He took one out, frowned at it for a moment, then held it up.

7

'What's this for?' he asked.

The small, lean man looked up at the sky as though asking his Maker why he should be subjected to such imbecilic behaviour. The big, ungainly man leaned forward. 'We use them to breathe through, darlin'. You know, if we have to crawl about in the air ducts, it stops us getting a load of shit up our nostrils!'

Karl reddened angrily, pushed the bag back across the counter. 'All right. Get on with it.'

With various expressions of studied contempt, the group strolled casually towards the main block. Karl Nielsen watched them go, promising himself that next time . . . next time he'd give them one hell of a rough ride.

The time was nine minutes past two and Karl Nielsen had exactly fourteen minutes to live.

Suzanne Delar sat uncomfortably in the black leather armchair facing the narrow Moorish windows which looked out over the faded coloured roofs of Algiers. She was a slim, attractive girl, barely twenty-one, with black hair that fell in soft waves around her shoulders. She wore white slacks which hid legs she was convinced were too thin, but accentuated the rounded hips and narrow waist. The blouse she wore was a vivid red, open at the neck about which hung a delicate golden pendant framing a single pearl.

She was nervous and desperately hoping it didn't show. The house, the name of Ryker, even this room made her nervous. There was a ponderous quality about it, an overpowering arrogance in the ornate tables and bookcases, in the heavy black leather and gilded paintings. It was a room that reeked of cold and ruthless energy, that exuded the power and wealth of Paul Ryker.

She jumped nervously as the door opened behind her, rose quickly to her feet to face the man she had seen only once before and disliked intensely ever since.

'My dear Miss Delar, how flattering that your eagerness to join me could not wait a further hour.' He smiled mockingly, took her hand briefly, then moved to the heavy oak desk which dominated the room.

She remained on her feet, wanting to get this over as soon as possible, trying to ignore the cold knot in her stomach. Ryker considered two letters on his desk, placed them carefully to one side, then studied her for a moment.

'You know why I wanted to see you,' she said.

'I had a visit from that little fag you laughingly call a

manager.' He smiled, dark eyes gleaming.

Her smile grew strained around the edges. 'About my brother. He's not bad really, it's just that he got in with a rough bunch and then they . . . they held up a bank.'

Ryker leaned back in his chair, laughing softly. Suzanne suddenly had to sit down, knowing her hands were clenched, knowing she couldn't help it. Ryker picked up a fly switch from his desk. It was a long, elegant affair in black tooled leather with a swathe of white horsehair at the end. He flicked it idly at an imaginary fly.

'You mean they tried, rather badly, to hold up a bank. They got caught and the judge threw the book at them.'

She swallowed, nodded. 'Harold got ten years. He'd only met them a month before. He didn't know what he was getting into.'

'Do you?'

Ryker was suddenly still, eyes fixed on her intently. She hesitated for a brief moment, then nodded. 'I think so.'

He smiled slowly, without any warmth or humour. 'You want me to get him out?'

She nodded again. 'I heard that you have contacts, know an organization in Britain. If Harold could only get to Algeria I could help him to start a new life.'

'Hold up a new bank?' The eyes gleamed, the cold, thin mouth widening as he chuckled softly.

She shook her head quickly. 'No. No, nothing like that.'

The laughter stopped and Ryker stood up, moving round his desk, stepping lightly despite his bulk, until he stood behind her. A hand rested briefly on her shoulder, the short, stubby fingers moving slowly, delicately, to her neck.

'Have you any idea how much that organization would charge?'

She turned round, eyes wide, pleading. 'I've saved a thousand pounds.'

'A thousand!' He gave a short, explosive laugh, moving away towards the narrow windows. 'They wouldn't look at ten thousand. And even if you took to whoring that would take quite a bit of saving.'

A nerve in her forehead was tying itself into knots. She stared at him coldly, repelled yet strangely fascinated by the total arrogance of the man. 'I've no intention of taking to whoring.'

Ryker turned from the window, eyes hooded, black. 'The organization you speak of owes me a favour. If I collected, your brother would be in Algiers within a month.'

9

She sat looking at him, suddenly and shockingly aware that she should never have come here. But now it was too late. The offer was there, bleak and empty, and all she had to do was nod her head.

Ryker watched her with idle curiosity. She was attractive, but that wasn't why he had decided to have her. It was the helpless quality in her eyes, the open hunger for sympathy, for comfort. She used her body the way she used her mind, he decided. For basics.

Slowly Suzanne nodded her head. Ryker's expression didn't change. 'You realize I shall need certain guarantees of your . . . sincerity.'

She nodded, mouth suddenly dry, the room around her a lofty chamber in which the voice seemed to echo from every side. 'Now?' she asked.

He nodded, flicking the horsehair switch lightly, but with a more deliberate, menacing air.

She stood up, waiting for him to tell her where to go. His eyes gleamed and the thin mouth curved. He gestured with the switch. A quick, imperative movement. 'Your clothes. Take them off.'

She wanted to turn and run. She wanted to be away from here, to be far from this house and this coldly-smiling ape of a man. Instead she unbuttoned her blouse and slipped it off her shoulders. Unzipped the white slacks, stepped out of them. Unfastened the bra, then slid the briefs down to her knees and let them fall to the floor. At that moment Suzanne Delar hated her brother with all the fury of her being.

Ryker stood before her, the switch moving constantly, hypnotically, flicking at the desk, at the air before him, at his hand. It made a soft, whispering sound.

'Well,' she said, trying to put a defiant note into her voice.

He smiled, gestured to the large, black leather couch against the wall. 'On there.'

She crossed to it, started to stretch out on her back. Suddenly he was standing over her, shaking his head, eyes boring into her, the switch moving steadily in a rising rhythm. 'On your stomach,' he said, softly. 'First you must be taught obedience.'

It was fifteen minutes past two on the Vestergade. Traffic was quiet at this time of day, the occasional truck moving towards the bridge across Frederiksholms Canal, which intersects the end of the street. From here you could see the

10

green-roofed buildings of the Christiansburg Parliament, and beyond the four coiled dragons that crowned the Stock Exchange.

In the Jansen Diamond Corporation four men were grouped around the heavy pump and ventilators of the air conditioning unit, located in the basement of the building. Air ducts ran away in different directions, the large, square tunnels vibrating constantly with the endless rush of air.

Kerstan was unscrewing the last bolt that held the inspection panel on the main air duct. He removed it, passing it silently to Lee Corey, who placed it against the wall. Holgar passed out the breathing masks, then took up a position beside the door. There was a gun in his hand now – a snubnosed Walther PPK automatic. He nodded to Kerstan who took two canisters marked cleaning fluid from his bag. He glanced briefly at Corey and Loron, checking that their masks were in place, then twisted the cap on the first canister. There was a hissing of gas, a cloud of white vapour, then he tossed it through the inspection hatch into the main air duct. The second canister followed, then Lee handed him the panel which he quickly bolted back into position.

The diamond processing section was contained in a low wing extending from the main block. In here the rough diamonds were sorted, graded, then distributed to the various polishers and cutters. At a dozen benches the spinning discs of the polishing machines clung precisely to the gleaming facets of a diamond. Air ducts hung above each bench, sucking away the abrasive dust that is a constant hazard of the industry. At various points other ducts fed a steady flow of clean air into the room.

Two security guards were on permanent duty at the entrance to the processing wing, one at a desk, the other in a small office facing the door. At seventeen minutes past two both guards became aware of a sharp acrid odour in the air. The guard in the office, a man with some twenty years' experience in security, reacted instantly. On the wall of the office, beside the keyboard, was the red-handled switch of the alarm system.

He was four paces away when he became aware of the gas, two paces away when his vision blurred, one pace when he hit the floor.

Outside the processing wing the second security post was a glass-walled cubicle that provided a clear view of the main block and the wide windows of the processing plant. The security guard on duty was leaning back in his chair, admir-

11

ing the view on the second floor. It was his favourite diversion. In the third office on the right there was a certain Miss Lieberson whose desk was beside the window and who invariably wore the kind of mini-skirt which left very little to the imagination, especially when she leaned across her desk to speak to one of the other girls. Dan Larsen was enjoying a particularly extravagant view of long, slim legs and pale blue briefs on this sunny afternoon, until it occurred to him that there was something rather odd about the way Miss Lieberson was leaning across her desk.

Even as he came to the conclusion that she was not just leaning, she was sprawling, her slim figure slid slowly, limply, from the desk and vanished from view. With growing alarm he scanned the other windows. No one was in view. Usually he could see people moving, working at desks.

As he reached for the telephone there was a sharp tap on the window behind him. He turned to see a man wearing a breathing mask looking in at him. His mouth was suddenly dry as he saw the gun in the man's hand, knew that he could not trip the alarm system. Not if he wanted to stay alive.

The eyes above the mask bored into him. He sighed, shook his head, kept his hands clearly in view. The man stepped into the cubicle and gestured for him to turn round. The blow was a sudden, brief agony, and then he knew no more.

Lee checked his watch as they entered the processing wing. It was two nineteen, right on schedule. Kerstan led the way, gesturing at the various benches. Loron cleared the left side, Holgar the right. Kerstan went straight to the cutting section, stepping over the sprawled bodies of two elderly men in white coats. Beyond them, laid out in trays, were the blue diamonds that had taken weeks of careful cutting and polishing to perfect. It took thirty seconds for Kerstan to empty the trays into the small cloth bag, and then he was stepping out, checking his watch, gesturing to the others.

It was two twenty and the biggest diamond robbery in the country's history had just taken place.

Karl Nielsen was debating whether to make a fresh jug of coffee when he saw the four maintenance men strolling casually towards the gate. He glanced at the clock, surprised that they had taken so little time. The big, ungainly man was moving towards him, reaching casually inside his coverall. A vague note of warning sounded in Karl's mind. They had been too quick. There was something about this man, a coldness in his face. But even as the warning grew into fear, the man's hand was coming into view.

Karl stared at the gun, a sick, empty fear coalescing inside him. There was a numbness in his legs, a dryness in his mouth and an idiot voice in his mind was recording the fact that the gun was a 7.65mm. Walther PPK automatic. It fired and a small hammer hit him in the chest. There was no pain, and with a kind of detached curiosity he watched the room revolve around him, felt the shuddering blow as he hit the floor. His head rolled to the right and he saw the man looking down at him, then turning away.

The cold hand of fear went away to be replaced by a hot, burning anger. Lying there, feeling the beginning of the pain, the pulsing of blood, the anger turned to rage. The room was getting dark and there seemed to be no sound any more. Slowly, forcing back the sickness in his throat, the waves of darkness that kept pressing in, he pulled himself up the side of the chair and gripped the desk with a ferocious determination. On the wall the red switch of the alarm swam before him, a thousand miles away. There was a pounding in his head now, a ball of ice in his chest, and even as the rush of blood spurted from a ruptured lung into his throat, he gripped the switch and pulled it down. He died hearing the bells, knowing that Gerda would be proud of him.

Lee was locking the rear doors of the van, Holgar and Loron already getting into the Mercedes. Kerstan checked his watch: 'You lead.'

Lee nodded. 'I know. Why kill the guard? It's bound to mean trouble.'

Kerstan gave him a quick, contemptuous look. 'He was the only one who could identify us.'

Lee shrugged, his face devoid of expression, and moved towards the driving seat. It was two twenty-three, and then they heard the alarm bells.

'Shit!' said Kerstan, and ran for the Mercedes. Lee jumped into the van, fumbled the keys and cursed briefly. Then the engine roared into life and he pulled away from the kerb, going fast through the gears as he approached the end of Vestergade. In the side mirror he could see the big Mercedes close behind, Loron at the wheel, his small black eyes gleaming like a frightened rabbit. He smiled with bleak satisfaction, slowing deliberately to take the corner into Frederiksholms Canal.

Traffic was light at this time of day, and he picked up speed along the side of the narrow canal, heading for the main Christiansgade and the Langebro Bridge. A taxi cut across

13

in front of him and he stabbed the horn, swinging out, ignoring the gesticulating hand of the taxi driver. Then he was sliding into the main street, the bridge four hundred metres ahead. It better be down, he thought. By God it better be down.

The police car turned into Christiansgade north of the bridge, lights flashing and siren sounding. It hurtled along the side of the main canal, scattering traffic, intent on blocking the entrance to the bridge in the shortest possible time.

Lee watched it coming with a cold, angry disgust. The chances of a patrol car being this close were a thousand to one. Today they had to hit the jackpot.

The Mercedes was still close behind, Loron swinging out, wondering if he could get past. Lee swung out also, knowing neither of them could make the bridge unless somehow they stopped the patrol car. His foot went down hard on the accelerator, and he swung wide over the crown of the road, eyes fixed on the police car as they approached the bridge from equal distances. Seconds ticked away. His hands were moist, light on the wheel, the bridge almost on them now.

The patrol car flashed its headlights, telling him to stay clear, and then the driver was braking hard, realizing too late that the small blue van had no intention of stopping. Lee slid the door open, then gripped the handbrake as he swung the wheel, stamping down on the brake at the same time as he pulled on the handbrake.

The van spun, tyres screaming, sliding broadside at the police car. They collided on the ramp to the bridge, but Lee was already hitting the road, rolling limply to cushion the impact.

The police car smashed into the van, carrying it across the ramp to explode in a cloud of steam and mangled steel against the concrete pillars. The driver was slumped over the wheel with fractured ribs and concussion. His companion was weakly trying to unfasten his safety harness, blood pouring down his face from a dozen lacerations.

Lee came to his feet, breathing a sigh of relief when nothing gave way. The Mercedes was reversing to get round the wreckage, Kerstan holding the rear door open and bellowing something at him. He lunged for it, gripping Kerstan's huge hand which jerked him inside as Loron accelerated for the bridge. But already the red light was flashing, and the barrier coming down. The alert bridge engineer had taken in the situation and pulled the lifting

14

bar. Beneath the bridge huge cogs began to turn, heavy steel hawsers tightened, and the twin sections of the bridge began to rise.

Kerstan stared bleakly at the barrier ahead. 'Take it,' he said.

Loron's mouth tightened into a thin, frightened line, but his foot went down hard and they smashed through the barrier, on to the rising bridge, hurtling at the widening gap ahead. The car took off at an angle of forty-five degrees, clearing the six feet with the brown waters of the canal widening beneath them, then slammed down on the opposite side with a scream of tortured steel as the chassis took the impact. Then the spinning rear tyres gripped the rim of the bridge and they hurtled down to smash through the last barrier.

It was 2.25 and beyond lay the harbour area, the labyrinth of narrow streets around the warehouses where they could lose themselves and the Mercedes.

The phone buzzed softly in Ryker's study. He moved towards it without haste, plucking at the white shirt now dark with perspiration. Before picking up the phone he selected a short black cigar, lit it from a slim gold lighter.

'Yes, Milena?' His voice was cool and remote.

'We have the call from Copenhagen.'

He smiled briefly. 'All right. You can come in now. I think Miss Delar requires some assistance.'

There was a soft laugh on the phone, then a click as she connected him to the outside line. 'Mr Ryker?' said the voice. 'This is Copenhagen.'

Suzanne lay on the black leather couch, her face turned to the wall, her eyes staring blankly at the cool white plaster. Behind her she could hear Ryker talking on the phone, asking sharp, meaningless questions. But all she could comprehend was the burning of her back and buttocks, the sick humiliation inside her. Someone came and knelt beside her. She turned, knowing it could not be Ryker, because he was still talking, and he would never kneel.

She recognized the girl as the secretary who had shown her into the study. She was slim, olive-skinned, with a wide, sensual mouth that was smiling at her mockingly. She was opening a jar of cream and as Suzanne started to sit up, she shook her head, pushed her firmly down. 'You stay,' she said. 'You must stay.'

Ryker listened to the voice as it described the robbery and the escape, his eyes on the two girls as Milena began to work

15

the cream into Suzanne's back and buttocks. Occasionally he asked brief questions, but his eyes never left the girls.

At first the relief provided by the cool cream made Suzanne relax and give way to the pleasurable sensations. The girl's touch was gentle, soothing, but gradually she became aware that it was also something else. The hands were probing, pressing, sliding with increased intimacy. Almost before she realized it, her pulse was racing, her breath quickening, and a warm, sensual glow suffused her body. She turned her head, looking at the girl in astonishment. Milena was watching her, and as their eyes met she smiled and her hand slid deeper, probing blatantly now.

Ryker chuckled softly, said something into the phone and put it down, then moved towards them. Suzanne stared up at him with horrified eyes, unable to stop the sensations that were twisting her round, causing the blood to pound in her throat. She was dimly aware that Milena was moving, that the sensations were becoming sharper, more urgent, and then she was moaning, feeling the surging need, knowing that Ryker was still watching . . . but not caring any more.

Two

Along Copenhagen's Istedgade the neon lights spell out every form of sexual activity known to man. Tourists crowd the street, moving from sex shop to porno shop, staring self-consciously at a thousand magazines dealing with only one subject. For half a mile sex is a commodity as profitable as baked beans, whether it comes in a can or in the glaring spotlight of a nightclub.

On the stage of Club 69 a lethargic couple were removing the last of their garments and beginning to get in the mood for what the programme chose to call 'straight intercourse'. At the moment at least one of the partners was anything but straight, and a few derisive hoots and whistles were beginning to make themselves heard. With a rather anxious look, the young blonde girl decided that discretion was not the better part of valour and departed from the set routine, moving into a position more appropriate to the setting. A moment later her partner was perking up a bit and the waiters decided it was time to stop taking orders.

Lee Corey sat at a centre table, watching the performance with rapidly diminishing interest. The casual blue slacks, open silk shirt and dark blue blazer, were drawing a line of limpid looks from the girls at the tables along the wall. He ignored them, glancing at his watch for the third time and wondering what was keeping Kerstan. It was a week since the robbery and the Press were beginning to run out of excuses for repeating the story. Copenhagen's CID were still 'following leads' and finding people who were 'helping enquiries', but today's quote from the Assistant Commissioner suggested that hope was not burning too brightly at the 'Politi'.

He described the robbery as a highly organized, professionally executed operation, which had clearly been planned many weeks in advance. He added ominously, that such a

17

well planned operation would almost certainly have an equally well planned escape route.

Lee smiled bleakly. Within an hour of the robbery the diamonds were on a train heading for Hamburg; Holgar was taking the hydrofoil trip to Malmo in Sweden, and Loron was driving back to his garage in Zealand.

With half a million tourists moving in and out of Copenhagen, the police might just as well have gone home and watched TV.

A middle-aged American woman giggled nervously at the table next to him, and on the stage the man paused in the middle of his stroke to glare down at her furiously. His injured pride was so comical that Lee almost choked on his beer. There was a movement beside him and he glanced up to see the tall, ungainly figure of Kerstan settling into a chair.

'How's the show?' he asked.

Lee grimaced at the stage where the quite attractive blonde was being bounced energetically on the water bed and trying very hard not to look sea-sick. 'You're just in time for the climax,' he drawled, mockingly.

Kerstan grinned, took an envelope from his pocket and slid it across the table. Lee looked surprised: 'I thought it was being paid straight into my bank?'

'It is,' said Kerstan. 'That's a ticket for tomorrow's flight to Algiers.'

Lee frowned, studying the man. He knew very little about Hans Kerstan. He had met him in Stockholm a month before whilst trying to get rid of 50,000 dollars in counterfeit hundred dollar bills. Kerstan took them off his hands at forty per cent face value, then spent a week trying to discover how he got them. Lee let him amuse himself until he started dropping heavy hints about insurance and unfortunate accidents, then took him back to his room and stuck a gun up his nose. After that they seemed to get on very well together, and Kerstan told him to buy a small blue van.

'I like it here in Copenhagen,' he said mildly. A ripple of applause was rising around them and on the stage the performers were bowing with relieved expressions.

'Algiers is a great town,' said Kerstan.

'What are you with? The tourist board?'

Kerstan grinned, beckoned to a waiter and ordered a Tuborg. As the waiter moved away he turned back, leaning across the table. 'You drove that van like a natural. It was appreciated.'

'By whom?'

Kerstan shrugged. 'My people – and a man who likes to live in Algiers.'

Lee sipped his beer and considered him without expression. 'I don't take trips to places I don't like unless I know a hell of a lot more.'

'This trip you take,' said Kerstan, his eyes suddenly hard. Lee stiffened angrily, starting to lean towards him. Kerstan sighed, waved one of his huge hands. 'Look, Lee, if you hadn't pulled that crazy stunt the chances are we'd all have ended up in the canal. I'm doing you a favour.'

'Then do me another and tell me who, where and why?'

Kerstan accepted the beer from the waiter and put a ten kroner note on his tray. He thought it out, watching Lee's studied disinterest. Finally he nodded. 'All right, but all you got from me was the ticket?'

Lee gave a brief nod, waiting.

'The job we did was planned to the last detail, the last second, right?'

Lee shrugged. 'You went over it so many times I was beginning to think I'd seen the movie.'

'Right.' Kerstan sipped his beer, eyes moving casually over the nearby tables. 'Now the man who planned it lives in Algiers. That's all he does. Just plans jobs and takes a fee or a percentage, depending on how he feels that day.'

Lee raised a sceptical eyebrow. 'What's he got out there? A crystal ball?'

Kerstan smiled bleakly. 'A lot of people who feed him information, and one of the sharpest minds in the business. He's never wrong, that's why he's always busy. That's why he's called the *"Connector"*.'

Lee allowed himself to look slightly impressed. 'And he wants to see me?'

Kerstan nodded emphatically. 'Tomorrow. Don't ask me why, but he got a full report on the job so he must know the way you worked out.'

Lee stared at him for a moment, then shrugged and picked up the envelope. He tore it open at one end, pulled out the air ticket and a folded sheet of paper. It simply told him that he would be met at the airport in Algiers. He put the ticket in his pocket, crumpled the note into a ball and left it in the ashtray.

'All right,' he said. 'But this Connector of yours better have something interesting to say, or I get the next plane back.'

Kerstan smiled bleakly, 'He will.'

Kerstan finished his beer, stood up and held out his hand. 'Take care, American,' he said.

Lee watched him go, seeing again the tall, ungainly figure in dark blue coveralls as he aimed the automatic without thought, without emotion, and blew a hole in the security guard's chest. It had meant nothing to Kerstan. It was something that had to be done – like stubbing out a cigarette.

On the stage two attractive blondes were coming on with enough equipment to start a small gymnasium. He drained his glass and left, his mind already ticking off the various things he would have to do before catching the plane tomorrow. Outside he waved down a taxi and told the driver to take him to the Sheraton. The gun would have to go, he decided. He could probably get it through Copenhagen's airport, but he would have to change flights at Orly and nothing got through there any more.

It was a few minutes after midnight when the taxi dropped him at the Sheraton. He paid the driver, then entered the main hall and crossed to the bank of elevators. The elevator to the Penthouse Discotheque was busy as usual and he waited until the cheerful group of Danes had packed themselves in, then took the next elevator to the thirteenth floor. Once there he let the doors open, then close, and pressed the button for the lobby.

In the lobby he stepped out, casually lighting a cigarette, his eyes moving left and right. A young couple were waiting for the penthouse elevator, but there was no one else. He strolled round the corner into a dimly lit vestibule and stepped into the public phone booth. He dialled the number and waited, facing the entrance to the lobby. A crisp, feminine voice answered: 'United States Embassy.'

'C-2,' he said.

A young man and a girl in sweater and jeans strolled across the vestibule towards the lobby. He watched them intently, but neither of them glanced back.

'C-2,' said a voice.

'Blue index,' he said softly. There was a brief pause, then: 'You have it. Go ahead.'

'I have contact,' Lee said. 'I'll be taking the morning flight to Paris, connecting for Algiers. No information, but the instructions come from a man they call the Connector.'

'Did they give you a name?' asked the voice.

Lee grimaced, wondering who the hell was on duty tonight. Probably Patterson. He pictured him sweating on the phone, making notes although the tape and back-up tape were running.

'Do we need a name?' he asked bleakly.

'No,' said the voice. 'No, I guess not.'

Lee put the phone down and strolled back into the lobby. There was a short, stocky man waiting for an elevator. Lee stubbed his cigarette out, waiting until the doors had closed, then caught the next elevator to the thirteenth floor.

Three

Suzanne opened her eyes and lay staring at the domed ceiling above. The faint sounds of traffic drifted up from the street below. She turned her head, seeing the sleeping figure of Milena beside her. She realized that Ryker had left, and the knowledge allowed her to relax briefly between the cool silk sheets. The figured marble clock on the bedside table showed five minutes past ten. She stretched luxuriously, looking around the cool white room with its heavy, ornate furniture. Her gaze crossed the dress and underclothes lying in the centre of the tiled floor, and then the memories came flooding back.

She stared at the ceiling, letting the sick loathing well up inside her. She tried, as she had tried so often in the past week, to understand the person she had become. At first it had been easy to imagine that if it meant freedom for Harry, a new life, then nothing else mattered. But she knew now that it was not that simple. Each morning she told herself it would be the last time. Each day she convinced herself that tonight she would go back to her own flat, to her own bed and the collection of little figures that looked down from the shelves and made her glow with warm memories of the house in England and the golden days, when she knew so little and dreamt so much. But when the club was closing, Bruno would be outside with the big white car, holding open the door, and the excitement would start to burn inside her. It would pulse and quicken all the way to the house, building to a hot, throbbing need as Ryker and Milena led her up the stairs.

She tried to understand the strange hunger that drove all resolve from her mind, turned her into a moaning, writhing, eager victim of their desires. She sighed. It was beyond understanding.

There was a movement beside her and she turned to see that Milena was awake, her dark eyes gazing at her intently. The wide, full mouth curved in a mocking smile, but she said nothing. Suzanne stared at her coldly, then began to get out of bed. Milena laughed softly, reached out and caught her round the waist, cupping her breasts in her hands as she sat up. Suzanne tried to pull them away, shaking her head quickly. 'No. I don't want that.'

Milena shrugged and lay back on the pillows, watching her with a quiet smile. Suzanne crossed to her clothes, aware that her cheeks were burning, that her pulse was racing. She had begun to pull on her briefs when Milena came up behind her and slid her hands around her waist, briefly touching her breasts, then pulling her back towards the bed. 'I could always ask Paul for assistance,' she said softly.

'Please don't,' said Suzanne, hating the weakness in her voice. 'I have to go out.' Milena looked at her for a moment, her eyes shrewd and calculating, then she shook her head and smiled confidently.

'Later,' she said.

Four

Lee Corey stepped into the harsh sunlight outside the air terminal and took his first look at Algiers. Beyond the cracked and dusty concourse, waves of heat shimmered over a flat, barren landscape of thorny shrubs and bleak, faded buildings. In the distance the orange groves climbed the hillside towards the city, a confusion of red, white and yellow buildings that leaned together listlessly in the sun.

A group of battered taxis were parked outside the terminal, the drivers slumped lethargically behind the fly-stained windscreens. No one showed any inclination to fight over his fare, so he picked up the suitcase the Algerians had managed to lose for thirty minutes in the short journey from the plane to the baggage chute, and started towards the nearest car.

A policeman leaned drowsily against a concrete pillar, the submachine-gun drooping impotently in his arms. Across the concourse, in the meagre shade of the only palm tree, a gleaming white Cadillac purred softly into life and swept round to stop beside him. Behind the wheel was a large bull of a man whose thick, muscular neck bulged around the dark blue chauffeur's tunic. His skin was dark, and from the wide nostrils and thick lips, Lee decided he owed more to the Negro than the Arab.

'Mr Corey?' he said, in a voice that grated with disinterest.

'Who else comes here on Tuesdays?' Lee answered bleakly, and threw his case into the back.

They drove away from the terminal at a smooth and steady sixty, past the faded hoardings advertising everything from yoghurt to Y-fronts, and began to rise up through the dreary decay of the Algerian suburbs.

'I know you hate to talk and drive,' Lee said drily, 'but if you feel like mentioning one or two names I've no objection.'

The chauffeur looked at him briefly, then shrugged. 'I'm Bruno.'

'Hi, Bruno. Who are we going to see?'

He had the grace to look surprised. 'Mr Ryker, of course.'

'Of course,' Lee said drily. 'It's painted along the side of the car and embroidered in gold thread on the hat, you're not wearing.'

He leaned back in his seat, staring bleakly at the bulging neck, trying to decide how much of it was fat and how much was muscle. He came to the conclusion that he did not want to find out.

Ryker's house, with its black-barred windows and white, studded walls, was located in a narrow street behind the colourful bazaars along the Bab-el-Oaud. The heavy black oak door was set with a small grille which slid open at Lee's persistent pressure on the bell. The eyes that looked out at him were large, brown and impassive. They gazed at him for a moment, then the grille closed and the door opened.

He stepped into a small, cool hall with wide arches leading off on three sides. The tiles were black on white, aggressively Greek against the sweeping Moorish arches and high domed ceiling. The girl who was closing the door, was tall, dark-haired and slender, but there was a cool edge to her voice that did not encourage long conversations.

'Mr Corey,' she said, 'as you are thirty-five minutes late, Mr Ryker would rather see you immediately.'

'Rather than what?' asked Lee.

'Rather than wait until you have bathed and changed.'

He smiled bleakly and shook his head. 'I'll take a shower, change my clothes, have a large rye on the rocks with a cold beer on the side, and then – only then – I may decide whether to meet your Mr Ryker today or tomorrow.'

Some of the cool assurance went out of her, and she glanced instinctively towards the door on the left. Lee grinned, stepped through the arch into a large, deeply carpeted room, where a short, thickset man stared at him coldly from beside a glass-topped table.

'It's entirely up to you, Mr Corey, but I have an appointment in half an hour.'

'That's okay,' Lee said casually. 'Cancel it.'

Ryker laughed softly, without any humour. 'You have no need to impress me, Mr Corey. After reading the report from Copenhagen I am quite convinced. Sit down, please.'

He waved casually at a chair, gestured to Milena, who crossed to a recessed bar and began pouring rye into a very long glass. Lee shrugged, sat down and watched Ryker sip his frosted Collins.

'You are probably wondering why you're here,' said Ryker.

'Let me put it another way. I'm beginning to wonder why the hell I came!'

'I doubt it.'

The man exuded power and confidence. From his perfectly-tooled sandals to the gold-figured belt and flowered shirt, he radiated success and arrogance. But his eyes were the most impressive feature. Dark, almost black, they bored into Lee with a remorseless intensity.

Milena handed Lee the drink and vanished silently. He took a long drink, stared back into the eyes. 'All right. I'm here, so let's talk.'

Ryker nodded. 'Good. You are probably aware that I'm called the Connector.'

'You put things together,' said Lee, with studied indifference.

'So does a mechanic! I create opportunities for people like you. Greedy, ruthless people who aren't afraid to take what they want.' The black eyes gleamed with a fanatical light. 'There are many like you, searching for the perfect opportunity. I supply it . . . for a price. I connect men, equipment and events so that the chances of failure are reduced to the absolute minimum.'

'Like Copenhagen,' said Lee, bleakly.

Ryker's mouth tightened. 'Kerstan is one of the best men in Scandinavia. He rarely makes mistakes. On that occasion he failed to ensure that the security guard was dead. If it hadn't been for your skilful improvisation, I don't believe any of you would have got across that bridge.'

Lee shrugged. 'So?'

'So men like you I need from time to time. Men who can operate in the field with initiative.' He considered him bleakly. 'Men I can trust completely.'

Lee took a long drink, rattled the ice in his glass and looked up into the cold black eyes. 'I do all right the way things are.'

'You have fifteen thousand two hundred dollars in your bank account, with a further ten thousand due from the diamond robbery. The way you spend, that will last you about three months and then you'll take anything going.'

'You sound like my accountant,' said Lee drily. 'Who gave you the figures?'

26

Ryker gestured impatiently. 'Information is my business. In the last three days I have obtained copies of your bank statement, your birth certificate, your FBI file and the report from New York State Penitentiary, where you served two years out of five for armed robbery. Now let's not waste time, Mr Corey. Do you want to work for me?'

Lee nodded. 'If the money is right.'

Ryker smiled. 'If you are the man I need, your bank account will show a credit balance of more than a quarter of a million dollars in less than a month from now.'

Lee stared at him for a long moment. There was no doubt that he was perfectly serious. He shook his head in disbelief. 'What's your game, Ryker? Nobody pays that kind of money.'

'Except me.'

'The percentage man,' said Lee, cynically.

Ryker shrugged. 'Sometimes it's just a percentage, sometimes more. On this occasion I need very special people for an operation that is far too good for the common herd.'

'So you're pulling the job yourself?'

He chuckled, amused by the idea. 'Don't be naive, Mr Corey. There are far too many policemen all over the world just waiting for that day. No. I shall be here, as always, but this time the key people in the operation will be carrying out my orders. My plan.'

'For a quarter of a million? Each?'

'At least,' Ryker said softly. 'At the very least.'

The only sound in the room was the soft whisper of the fan that revolved on the ceiling above. The black eyes bored into Lee, unblinking, cold and dispassionate. After a moment he nodded and took a drink of rye. 'That sounds like my kind of game. When do we play?'

Ryker leaned back, apparently satisfied with the response. 'That's all for the moment, Mr Corey,' he said, in a voice that signified the interview was at an end. Milena seemed to appear out of nowhere, so he took the hint and finished his drink.

As they crossed to the hall, a girl entered the room, pausing uncertainly as she saw Lee. She wore a white tailored suit, dark blue shirt with a pale blue silk scarf knotted round the slim throat. Her dark hair fell in soft waves around her shoulders and the eyes, large and brown, gazed briefly into his before glancing quickly towards Ryker. There was a nervous quality about her that intrigued him. A tightness in her as she looked at Ryker.

27

'It's time I left for the club,' she said.

Ryker rose, smiling. 'So soon, my dear? That's a pity, I was hoping you might entertain Mr Corey for a while.'

There was a subtle inflection on the words that caused the girl to flush with embarrassment. She forced a small, tight smile, and again Lee was aware of the tensions in her. He gave her a casual grin, then moved on with Milena. As they crossed the hall, he heard her voice, sharp with anger, but strangely afraid. The words depressed him.

'I'm not your whore,' she was saying. 'Don't ever treat me like one.' And he could hear Ryker's mocking laughter all the way up the stairs.

The sun was touching the ragged peaks of the Atlas Mountains by the time Lee had bathed and changed. He stretched out on the bed, enjoying the cool breeze that was beginning to blow down from the mountains. The room was large and airy, the narrow windows set high in the walls. Ornamental grilles across the windows made it impossible to look down to the street below, so he had been unable to get a look at the visitor who had arrived an hour before. He debated going down on some pretext, but decided that the last thing he wanted to suggest at this stage was curiosity.

He thought again of the dark-haired girl. According to Milena her name was Suzanne Delar, but despite the French flavour, he felt sure she was British. He wondered why she was here. Obviously she was involved with Ryker, but it seemed unlikely that their interests would be anything more than social. Somehow the thought depressed him.

There was a brief knock at the door, then it opened to admit Milena. She placed a tray with rye and a bowl of ice on the table by the bed, asking him with cool disinterest if he was comfortable. Lee nodded, dropping ice into a glass and submerging it in whisky. There was something about the woman that grated on his nerves. A surprising fact, as she was extremely attractive in a darkly sensual way. She stood by the bed, watching him impassively. He ignored her and tasted the drink.

'We will be eating at seven o'clock,' she said, finally.

'Who's we?' he asked. 'Ryker and guests, or you, me and the rest of the hired help?'

Her mouth compressed into a thin line. 'We will both be dining with Mr Ryker. There is a man he wishes you to meet.'

'What's his name?' he asked casually.

'Werner Borsch,' she said, watching his face intently for

some sign of recognition.

He kept it calm, expressionless, but in his mind he was clicking through the files, stopping at Borsch. It had carried the red symbol, the one they put on files belonging to those with a permanent warrant out for them. He could only dimly recollect the face, but the German nationality triggered off the rest of it:

Borsch, Werner, born Munich, 1929. Professional hit man, operating on the Continent but known to have carried out two contracts in the States in 1971 and 1973. Since 1970 believed to be associated with the Baader-Meinhof movement in Munich
Note: This man is armed and dangerous. Approach with caution.

Lee frowned, as though trying to recall the name. 'Borsch? I've got the feeling I should know him.'

'You could do,' she said. 'It doesn't matter. You will know him soon enough.'

She turned and left. Lee took a long drink of the rye, wondering what kind of chaos Ryker was planning to have a man like Borsch along.

Five

Werner Borsch was a square, stocky man with close-cropped fair hair and pale blue eyes. The planes of his face were flat and uninteresting, the mouth a hard, thin line. Even his voice had an empty, remote quality, as though the thoughts which activated the words reposed in a vacuum somewhere. There was a sallowness to his complexion, a paleness to his hands, that made Lee think instinctively of the walking dead.

Ryker's introduction had been brief and casual. 'Lee Corey, Werner Borsch. You'll be working together.'

Borsch had nodded, already aware of the fact, and his pale eyes had moved slowly, deliberately over Lee. His words were flat and emotionless: 'You handled the Copenhagen business.'

Lee shrugged. 'I was part of the help.'

'I read your file. How come they know so much about you?'

Lee stared at him coldly: 'I talk in my sleep!'

Ryker gave one of his short, throaty laughs and led them to the table.

The meal was a desultory affair. Milena served the shish kebab of beef, kidney and lamb on a bed of saffron rice, then ate in silence. Occasionally she would glance at Ryker with large luminous eyes which seemed aware of his slightest need. Borsch put food in his mouth, chewed and swallowed, then repeated the process with about as much enthusiasm as a camel chewing its own droppings. Only Ryker showed any inclination to talk, describing the various attractions of Algiers as an endless permutation of sun and sin.

In this city, he told them expansively, you could buy anything or anyone. The only question to be decided was the currency.

Borsch considered Ryker with his flat, pale eyes. 'Death is the only currency worth bargaining with.'

Ryker nodded in agreement. 'True, but even the assassin expects to be paid.' He looked around the table and chuckled softly. 'Though not always in the agreed manner.'

Borsch stopped chewing, his eyes suddenly cold. 'A dangerous assumption, Paul,' he said quietly.

Lee watched with amusement as Ryker tried to hide his sudden alarm. He forced a shaky laugh. 'Not you, Werner. Never with you.'

The chewing started again, but the eyes stayed on Ryker. There was a chill in the room and Lee was aware that, for a moment, the Connector had lost control of a very dangerous piece of equipment. In an attempt to recover his composure, he turned to Lee, producing a thin smile.

'What do you know of the Baader-Meinhof, Mr Corey?'

Lee shrugged. 'No more than I read. A bunch of political extremists.'

'Extremists, yes,' Ryker agreed, 'but not entirely political. They have been known to temper idealism with opportunism.'

Lee looked bored and helped himself to wine, aware that Borsch was watching him intently now.

'Who the hell cares,' he said. 'Most of them are dead or in gaol.'

'Some,' said Borsch, bleakly. 'Not most. Some.'

'Okay,' Lee acknowledged. 'Some.'

'Including Janos Lodtz,' said Ryker.

Lee gazed at them for a moment without expression, then shrugged. 'So?'

Borsch's mouth twisted contemptuously and he went back to eating. Ryker allowed himself a brief smile, unaware that behind Lee's expression of bored indifference his mind was flicking through the files of Central Registry.

Lodtz, Janos, born Warsaw, 1925. Committed first criminal offence at age of 13. From 1939 to 1945 continued criminal activities under guise of collaborator. As Gestapo informant was responsible for more than a hundred executions, whilst personal activities ranged from blackmail to robbery and murder. When Russia moved into Poland subject fled to Germany.

Lee could see the dark red folder now, with its symbols in black, yellow and blue, signifying that the subject was listed for political anarchy and murder. Between 1945 and 1960 Lodtz had worked for both Eastern and Western Intelligence, blossoming as the years went by into a highly trained and totally ruthless killer. Eventually he was too hot for even the KGB to handle and wisely removed himself to Brazil until 1965 when he met one of Andreas Baader's lieutenants. It was the Baader-Meinhof philosophy of urban anarchy that intrigued Lodtz, for he knew that within such a political organization there would be ample opportunity for his own less idealistic pursuits.

He returned to Germany and, as the extremist group edged further into the field of terrorism, Lodtz expanded into such lucrative sidelines as robbery, narcotics and murder. By 1972 he was one of the most feared men in Europe, commanding some twenty fanatical killers. Only a bullet in the leg prevented him from evading arrest; and only the mysterious disappearance of two key witnesses enabled him to escape the death penalty.

Milena was serving the coffee before Ryker enlarged on his reference to Lodtz. Pouring large brandies and passing them to Borsch and Corey, he explained that Lodtz was currently serving a life sentence in a maximum security penitentiary on the outskirts of Munich. He was undoubtedly a powerful influence in the Baader-Meinhof organization, perhaps the only man who could gather support for Baader himself.

Lee frowned. 'I don't get it,' he said, finally. 'Pulling a job is one thing, but messing about with political fanatics is something else.'

'It is indeed,' said Ryker. 'That's why we need them. Police understand crime and the cruder motives behind it, but give them a politically motivated fanatic and they are lost. Give them a dozen, with machine-guns and hand-grenades and they panic.' The black eyes gleamed. 'They always panic.'

'I still don't see where that gets us?'

Ryker sighed patiently. 'Of course you don't, Mr Corey, but you will – in time. For the moment, all you need to know is that Janos Lodtz is serving no useful purpose in gaol. Therefore, we must remove him!'

Lee's astonishment was genuine. 'From the maximum security cell? You're crazy!'

Ryker chuckled softly, then rose and moved to his desk. Unlocking a drawer he took out a large manila envelope and returned to the table.

'The plan is quite simple, and most effective,' he said, passing the envelope to Borsch. 'You will both leave for Munich tomorrow afternoon, spend a day making the necessary preparations, then put it into operation on the night of the seventeenth.'

Borsch had removed a sheaf of closely-typed pages and was glancing through them. Lee hesitated, wondering how far he could go with Ryker. Reaching a decision he shook his head and stood up.

'No dice, Ryker. That's not my scene.'

Borsch stirred, his dead eyes lifting from the page he was reading and boring into the American. 'It became your scene when you sat down to dinner,' he said bleakly.

Ryker chuckled softly, but there was no humour in the sound. 'I suggest you reconsider,' he said, 'Otherwise I will find it impossible to include you in the main operation at the end of the month.'

Borsch changed his position slightly. A movement of his legs, an angling of shoulders, the right hand moving across casually to stroke a lapel. There was little doubt in Lee's mind that the pale fingers were only inches from the butt of a pistol.

'Well, that would be a pity,' said Lee drily. 'But that's the way it's going to be unless you come up with a better reason for breaking into jail than the fact that Lodtz is feeling lonely.'

Ryker glanced at Borsch, whose empty eyes were riveted on the American. 'Would fifty thousand dollars be sufficient reason?'

Lee smiled. 'I'll say one thing for you, Ryker. When it comes to making up people's minds, you don't screw around.'

After dinner Lee strolled through the narrow streets of the old town, leaving Ryker and Borsch to discuss the Munich operation. They had made it clear that his presence would not be required, and his brief attempt to learn more about the plan met with instant suspicion from the German. Rather than press the issue, he had shrugged it off with casual disinterest.

He turned on to Bab-el-Ouad, which runs north through the old city below the Kasbah, the ancient fortress of the deys.

The cry of a muezzin floated through the still air, calling the faithful to the last devotions of the day. He picked out the slender tower of the mosque, gleaming in the harsh moon-

33

light above the flat-roofed houses that descended in terraced confusion towards the harbour below. There were a few Europeans on the street, but the majority of people were Arabs or Kabyles, moving lethargically in their galabias. Small cafés, reeking of spices and Turkish tobacco, rubbed shoulders with sophisticated French restaurants and fashionable stores.

Lee turned into the street named after the Kasbah, descending in narrow, jagged turns to the new city. This was an area of clubs and bars, of beggars, pimps and whores who seemed to inhabit every shadowed doorway, calling softly to the passer-by in a litany of sensual promise.

Lee's bleak smile gave no encouragement and even the horde of Arab children crowding his heels with cries of baksheesh, soon lost enthusiasm and dwindled away. Halfway down the street he stopped outside the Club Arabesque, his eye caught by the cabaret photographs on a board outside. The shapely brunette billed as an exotic dancer looked familiar. He moved closer and realized, with some surprise, that this was the girl he had met in Ryker's house earlier. The doorman, looking like something out of a lion's cage, was beckoning him over. He shrugged and entered, descending narrow stairs to an arched doorway leading into the smoke-filled room.

Although it was early yet, the club was quite crowded. A small group provided the music for a girl who appeared to be giving her own interpretation of the dance of the seven veils – only the veils consisted of faded gauze handkerchiefs dangling from a G string. Lee slipped a ten dollar bill into the sweaty hand of the head waiter and they immediately embarked on a voyage through the dimly-lit sea of tables. He found himself on the edge of the dance floor, eyeball to navel with the gyrating houri who at this range smelled of garlic and olive oil. He beamed at her, hoping she was better at cooking than dancing. She smiled back and flicked a nipple the size of a cherry, so he decided that the kitchen was probably not the best place to judge her talents.

A waiter arrived and put a bottle of bourbon and a glass beside him. He waited until Lee had slipped a bill across the table, then gestured hopefully towards the line of girls at the bar.

'A little company, monsieur,' he said.

'Maybe later,' said Lee, just to keep him on his toes.

The waiter beamed and nodded, moving to another table. The music reached a discordant climax with much banging of cymbals and rattling of maracas in time to the shaking of the dancer's ample bosom, which was now spraying perspiration over the front three rows. Lee poured a glass of dubious bourbon and drank a silent toast to her stamina. She could probably earn more, and work less, in any office – and lay the boss into the bargain.

The lights came on long enough for the manager of the club to announce, with much rolling of eyes and licking of lips, that it was now time for the fabulous Suzanne. There was some scattered applause, then the group went into a slow beat number and the spotlight picked out the slim figure of Suzanne Delar.

Unlike the previous number, her performance was sensitive and skilful. Wearing a costume of flowing blue veils which billowed around her as she turned and twisted to the beat of the music, she built to a sensual and abandoned climax which ended with her prostrate on the floor. As the applause showered around her, she rose to her feet, smiling coolly. As she turned to leave she saw Lee. For a moment her eyes widened with surprise, then she nodded briefly and moved off towards the dressing-room.

The image of the girl stayed with Lee a long time after she had gone. Again he wondered how, and why, she had become involved with Ryker. The simplest way to find out, he decided, was to ask. Glancing round he located the head waiter and raised an index finger. He moved towards him, beaming happily.

'*Oui, monsieur?*'

'The dancer, Suzanne Delar,' said Lee. 'Find out if she'll join me for a drink.'

The smile vanished and was replaced by nervous disappointment. 'I'm sorry, monsieur, but Miss Delar does not normally drink with the patrons.'

Lee slid a twenty dollar bill across the table and the waiter looked even more unhappy. He folded it nervously, glancing towards the line of girls at the bar. 'Perhaps someone else would . . .?'

Lee shook his head, 'Miss Delar.'

He sighed and put the money in his pocket, 'I will do what I can, monsieur, but . . . he shrugged.

Lee gave him a reassuring smile. 'Tell her I'm a friend of the family.'

The waiter nodded unhappily and moved off on what he obviously considered was a futile errand. Lee poured another measure of bourbon and settled back to wait. The club was really getting crowded now. A group of Americans, looking as though they had just stepped out of a package tour, were being settled down at a table nearby. Most of the tables were occupied by groups or couples, any unaccompanied men being quickly provided with one of the well-endowed girls from the apparently endless supply at the bar.

Across the floor the head waiter had reappeared with the slim figure of Suzanne Delar. She was wearing a simple white dress, her dark hair resting in soft waves on her shoulders. As she reached the table Lee rose, smiling, and offered her a chair. The waiter, glowing with pride at having accomplished the impossible, held the chair for her while giving Lee the knowingest of smiles.

'What'll you have?' asked Lee. 'Champagne?'

She shook her head and the waiter's face fell. It fell even further when she suggested martini and lemonade. He leaned forward to put an ashtray beside her, whispering something in her ear. Suzanne gave him a cold look that withered him where he stood. 'Just a martini and lemonade,' she said crisply.

Lee grinned as the man moved away. 'I don't mind buying champagne if it keeps the management happy.'

She gave him a cool, level look. 'I work as a dancer. Nothing else.'

'It's enough,' he answered. 'But right now you're not working, so relax.'

She smiled briefly and inclined her head. 'All right, Mr Corey.'

'Lee,' he corrected her. 'What time do you go on again?'

'Just after midnight. That's when I do two numbers.'

'And then home to mummy?'

She looked at him for a long moment, then shook her head. 'No. Home to Paul Ryker.'

He smiled easily, noting the defensive tone in her voice. 'He's a lucky guy.'

The waiter arrived with her drink and she sipped it silently for a while. Lee took the opportunity of studying her, trying to work out why she was so tense. It showed in the tightness round her mouth, the constant movements of her hands. If she wasn't lifting the glass she was rubbing a finger, touching her hair, playing with the clasp of her handbag. Finally it got too much for him.

'Look, if you don't relax I'm going to have to drag you out on the floor for a dance. And dancing with me is only slightly more enjoyable than waltzing with a Watusi!'

She smiled. The effect was definitely worth the effort.

'I'm sorry. It's been a difficult day.'

'Yeah, I caught part of it.'

Suzanne felt herself blushing. 'Paul can be a bit of a bastard at times,' she said, wondering what kind of man lay behind the mocking smile and clear blue eyes. If he was involved with Ryker the chances were he was just as ruthless and cruel, but somehow he did not seem that type. There was an air of calm assurance about him, but also a boyish exuberance in his quick grin.

'How close are you to Paul?' she asked finally.

Lee grinned. 'About as close as you are to that Watusi I was talking about.'

She could not help smiling. 'Will you be there for long?'

He shrugged. 'It's too soon to say. We're involved in a business deal that might take some time.'

She nodded politely, hiding her disappointment. She knew the kind of business deals Ryker would get involved in.

'I hope it works out for you both.'

'And for you,' said Lee lightly. 'Or is that up to Ryker?'

Her face tightened. 'I hope not,' she said, quietly.

'He's not really your type, is he?' Lee asked.

She shrugged. 'Type? Do any of us know the way we really are?'

He grimaced. 'If you're going to get philosophical I'm going home.'

She smiled. 'Paul Ryker is a very influential man.'

'He's also an arrogant bastard with about as much respect for human dignity as a Watusi with a hangover!'

'You seem terribly close to the Watusi,' she said, laughing now.

'I spent a month with them once. Apart from teaching me to eat with my right hand and scratch my – chin – with my left, they showed me a very simple way of appreciating people.' He considered her seriously. 'If they look up when you enter a room, they have respect. If they don't, they're only concerened with themselves and they'll screw you the first chance they get.'

'Ryker is like that,' she said.

'And you're not worried?'

'Sometimes.' She hesitated, watching him uncertainly. 'I suppose I can always get out if I don't like the rules.'

'Maybe.'

'It's not your concern,' she said, quickly defensive.

Lee nodded. 'That's right.'

They considered each other warily for a while, the room

around them heavy with smoke and the sound of a dozen languages that blended into an endless chorus of inanity. Across the room a large, heavy-jowled man in a loud tropical shirt was weaving an uncertain course to an empty table nearby. He stabbed a stubby cigar towards the bar girls and the accompanying waiter beamed happily and snapped imperative fingers. A tall, olive-skinned girl with enough of everything, rose languidly from her stool and headed towards the table.

The man ordered champagne in a voice already slurred by alchohol, but sufficiently intelligible to reveal his American origin. Lee glanced towards him with casual interest. Their eyes met briefly and for a moment the American was still, his gaze sharp, intense, and then he was rising clumsily to greet the girl.

Lee turned back to Suzanne, smiling easily. 'Dance?' he said.

She hesitated, then nodded, glancing at her watch. 'I'll have to get ready for my next number soon.'

'I can hardly wait.'

She was warm and soft in his arms, moving with a relaxed and easy grace. It was hard to imagine the girl with a man like Ryker. He grimaced; one of the few lessons life had managed to hammer home was that women were about as logical as lemmings in the suicide season.

'What made you choose Algiers?' he asked.

'A man.' She smiled quickly at his look. 'He talked me into a contract with a club in Spain, then took off with all our wages. There were six of us stranded, flat broke and owing four weeks' back rent.' She grimaced. 'If we could have got our hands on him he would have been minus one or two very important assets.'

Lee chuckled. 'I'll bet.'

'After that I worked as a waitress until this job came up. It wasn't exactly my idea of show business, but the pay was good.'

'No family?'

Her face clouded briefly. 'A brother.'

He waited, but she didn't seem inclined to enlarge on the subject. 'In England?' he asked, finally.

She nodded, eyes dark and sad. Suddenly she seemed so small and lost that he instinctively drew her closer. She moved against him, closing her eyes and resting her head on his shoulder. Again he wondered about Ryker, but now there was anger in the thought. The slim, strangely defenceless girl, had no place in this menagerie.

The music stopped and she was smiling up at him, reminding him that it was time for her to get changed.

'How about later?' he asked casually.

She looked doubtful. 'Bruno usually collects me at twelve thirty.'

'That's all right,' he drawled. 'Tonight he can collect me too.'

At the table Lee signalled for another rye and settled down to watch the ice cubes melt. There was a harsh bellow of laughter from the next table and he glanced round to see the American slapping his thigh enthusiastically as the girl giggled into her champagne. Casually he let his glance wander over the other tables. There were two groups of four and a number of attached, or semi-attached couples. No one seemed to be paying any particular attention to either Lee or the American.

He fished the last cigarette from the packet, crumpled it into a ball and dropped it in the ashtray. His eyes briefly held the American's as he lit the cigarette, then rose and moved towards the bar. As he passed their table the girl was announcing in a soft, sultry voice that she loved aggressive men. The man in question gave a loud, booming laugh, and told her in a voice that carried half-way to the bar, that talk was cheap. The girl raised a mocking eyebrow and mentally doubled her fee.

The bar was crowded, the air thick with smoke and limpid looks. Lee asked for a packet of Gauloises, staring down half a dozen blatant promises before strolling towards the men's room. Inside he checked the four cubicles, then proceeded to wash his hands until the door opened and the American stepped inside.

'It's clear,' said Lee.

'Hannigan,' he said, moving to a stall and unzipping his flies. 'I've got you on a Blue Index. What's the score?'

'Ryker,' said Lee. 'He's got some kind of party set for the end of the month. One of the guests is a man called Janos Lodtz.'

'Lodtz?' Hannigan frowned. 'Isn't he one of the Baader-Meinhof mob doing time in the . . .?'

'The very same,' said Lee. 'I'm leaving for Munich tomorrow.'

'Christ!' Hannigan exclaimed. 'I've only just got here.'

'You stay. I'll be back in about three days. Just tell C-2 to put a discreet tail on me in Munich.'

'Check,' said Hannigan, zipping himself up and moving to the washbasin. 'Does that tie in with Lodtz?'

'It should do,' said Lee drily. 'I'm planning to break him out of gaol tomorrow night!'

'Jeez! Washington isn't going to like that.'

'I'm not exactly mad about the idea myself,' Lee murmured, 'but unless they want me to blow a six-month cover, I intend to get him out!'

'Rather you than me, fella.' Hannigan dried his hands. 'The guards in those German pens don't screw around. And you'll never get co-operation for a hardcase like Lodtz.'

'You're such a comfort,' said Lee, heading for the door. He paused, glancing back with a mocking grin. 'And aggressive with it!'

Lee had a drink at the bar to give Hannigan time to return to his table, then made his way back as the lights dimmed for the floor show to begin. The first two acts were about as subtle as a drunken Samurai, but Suzanne's appearance drew a burst of enthusiastic applause followed by an even more appreciative silence.

She danced with slow, sensual, languid movements that seemed oblivious to the audience around her. With eyes closed she swayed to the pulsing rhythm, the dark hair swinging across smooth ivory shoulders, the hands moving sensuously from firm, full breasts to the rounded hips and slender thighs. She was at once a child of innocence and a woman of sensual promise, building with increasing abandon to the throbbing climax of the music.

Considering that the previous performers had left the spotlight with nothing more than their ear-rings, Suzanne's clinging white gown owed little, if anything, to local convention, yet succeeded in being twice as erotic. With the final crescendo she froze in the spotlight, opening her eyes at last to break the spell and acknowledge the enthusiastic applause.

Lee found his own response as enthusiastic as the rest of the customers, aware with some surprise that the girl was a lot better than she realized. She didn't need Ryker. She didn't need anything more than a ticket to Paris.

As she was leaving the floor, Lee recognized the squat figure of Bruno cutting across to the dressing-room behind the stage. It was only just midnight. He wondered casually what the chauffeur was doing here so early. After a moment Bruno reappeared, pushing his way towards the exit. As he cleared the last of the tables his small, black eyes cut through the smoke to hold briefly on Lee. There was no sign of recognition, but he knew that his presence had been duly noted and would be part of Bruno's report.

Lee smiled bleakly to himself. He'd take short odds that Suzanne had just been given the elbow for the night. Ryker and Borsch would be burning the midnight oil, reviewing every step of the Munich operation. He would have given a great deal to be in on that meeting, but knew that his tenacious link with the Connector had a long way to go before he would be invited to a conference of chiefs of staff. There were compensations, he told himslf, and settled down to wait for Suzanne to dance her final number.

The ice-blue African moon gave the streets of the Old Town a deceptive air of cleanliness in the early hours of the morning; an antiseptic glitter that even made the rotting garbage seem like pop art. Unfortunately the odour was as obtrusive as ever and destroyed the whole effect.

They managed to find a taxi lurking lethargically in the shadows of the Kasbah, and Suzanne gave the driver her address in a complicated mixture of French and Arabic.

She was silent for most of the journey, already regretting the impulse which had made her accept Lee's offer to take her home.

He stirred beside her, gesturing at the harbour which appeared briefly between terraced mounds of apartments. 'You'd expect a man like Ryker to put a yacht in the middle of that.'

'I believe he used to have one,' she answered. 'But it sank or something.'

Lee chuckled, 'Or something is probably right.'

She regarded him with some bewilderment. 'For someone who's in business with him, you're not exactly falling about with enthusiasm.'

Lee grinned at her in the shadows, casually draping an arm around her shoulders. 'You don't do business with Ryker. You just allow him to use you for a while – at a price.'

Her face burned in the darkness. Despite his mocking tone, there was a grim and pointed warning in the words. She wondered how much he knew, then felt again the searing shame that smouldered in the corners of her mind. Angrily she tried to tell herself that she didn't care, that he was probably no better than Ryker. The mere fact that he was here proved he was some cheap, vicious crook with a smooth tongue and dirty mind. The arm around her shoulders pressed gently, insistently, and she glanced at him to see the slow, warm smile.

'God, but you're beautiful,' he drawled, the words both mocking and sincere.

She smiled. The bitter anger dissolved and she was only aware of his eyes, calm and deep, and knew finally that he was one of the dangerous kind. And knowing it made her twice as vulnerable.

The apartment was small and totally feminine. Whilst Suzanne set about preparing coffee, Lee wandered around the room, admiring the collection of tiny figures that lined almost every shelf. Fuzzy warriors and grinning gonks vied with pink rabbits and glass horses. In a corner a collection of glazed clay figures glowered at the narrow windows looking out across the domed white roofs of the city. Suzanne returned with the coffee to find him trying to impale an orange on Don Quixote's spear.

'My toys are in the bedroom,' she said sternly.

'Fine with me,' he grinned. 'Let's go play!'

'Coffee, then straight back to uncle.'

He shrugged with mock dejection, waiting while she poured the coffee. They sat together on the sofa, silent now. He looked around the room with slow deliberation, and then his eyes were on her and she knew the question although it never came.

'You need friends in a place like Algiers, Lee.'

He nodded, accepting it. But there were other questions in him that she didn't want to answer. She tried to rush her coffee and only succeeded in burning her mouth, then spilling some in the saucer. Covering her irritation she put the cup and saucer on the coffee table, starting to get up for a napkin.

Lee caught her hand and without any haste, or apparent effort, drew her back to the sofa and kissed her gently, but firmly. His mouth was warm and deeply disturbing. She pulled away, her face tight and angry.

'Aren't you forgetting something?'

'You mean Ryker?' he asked bleakly.

She hadn't meant Ryker, but before the thought even surfaced she had retorted angrily. 'I mean I'm not part of the hospitality!'

Lee stood up slowly, his eyes cold. 'I wasn't looking for any handouts. Especially from Ryker's pocket!'

He moved purposefully towards the door. She watched him go with a helpless exasperation, knowing he wasn't the kind who would ever turn back. His hand was on the door before she spoke.

'Lee.'

He turned back, waiting.

'At least drink your coffee.'

He stared at her for a long, thoughtful moment, then nodded and moved back to the sofa. 'I thought you'd never ask,' he said coolly, but before the anger could rise in her he was laughing softly, his arms going round her, his warm mouth searching hers with a slow, deliberate urgency. Long before the kiss had ended she knew that there was no point in resisting. His hands were too sure, his mouth too knowing, and his touch so softly insistent it was impossible to ignore.

They made love slowly, languorously, in the small bed with the rows of fluffy figures on the shelves above. At first she was only aware of the gentle magic in his hands, the touches that came and went, building a throbbing, aching void inside her. But then his mouth was following the same path and silken fingers were slipping gently into the void, and there was only a breathless infinity of time until he was there and she was exploding into a blind, endless shuddering release.

Afterwards she cried softly in the darkness. He turned to her, touching the wetness of her cheek.

'Ryker?' he asked gently.

She loved him then. She loved him for his understanding, his wisdom, his strength.

Six

The Caravelle touched down at Munich's busy Reim Airport at 5.15, but by the time they had collected their bags and cleared customs it was almost six o'clock. The flight had been smooth and pleasantly devoid of conversation. Borsch had settled down beside the window, his pale blue eyes staring intently at two hours of unchanging cloud.

Any attempt to start a conversation received a bleak gaze and after the third attempt Lee conceded defeat and turned to the stewardess for light relief. No, they didn't have vodka Martinis ready mixed; and no, a bucket of crushed ice was not available. Lee looked suitably shocked and ordered a dozen miniatures of vodka and vermouth, sweet and dry. The stewardess clearly thought she had a lush on her hands, but brought them together with a plastic beaker and some ice cubes.

With extreme care Lee poured two of the small bottles of vodka into the beaker, followed by half a bottle of sweet vermouth and one-and-a-half of dry. He stirred them busily for three minutes, before sampling the mixture with care. The stewardess moving back along the cabin, paused to enquire with just the right touch of sarcasm if everything was satisfactory.

Lee shook his head, worried. 'Not really. What altitude are we flying at?'

She looked slightly bewildered. 'Twenty-nine thousand feet, sir.'

'Ah' said Lee gravely, 'that explains it. It's definitely affecting the conditions.'

'Conditions, sir?' She was clearly baffled now.

'The alcohol isn't mixing. It's always difficult between twenty and thirty thousand feet. Something to do with barometric pressure.'

She managed to hold a tight smile and prepared to move on.

'I'm sorry, sir, but there's nothing we can do about that.' Lee let her get two strides away before correcting her. 'Oh, but there is.'

She turned back, allowing herself to look slightly bored. 'Really, sir?'

'You could just ask the pilot to take us up a couple of thousand feet,' he grinned. 'Over thirty thousand it all settles down.'

She took a deep breath, striving for control, before telling him that the pilot would not be prepared to change his flight plan just to suit the drinking habits of a passenger.

'All I want is a civilized altitude,' said Lee. 'Just ask him to go to Martini height. I'm sure he'll understand.'

The girl was beginning to look harassed. Lee's polite insistence and apparent knowledge of the behaviour of Martinis at given altitudes was sufficiently plausible to raise an element of doubt.

'I'm sorry, sir,' she said finally. 'It's out of the question.'

Lee sighed, looking dejectedly at the Martini.. 'Well, in that case we'll have to compromise. Do you have a couple of olives?'

'I'm afraid not, sir.'

Lee nodded. 'That figures. If we're not flying at Martini height, you're hardly likely to bring along a barrel of olives. How about a maraschino cherry?'

The stewardess was close to despair. She shook her head.

'A slice of lemon?'

She nodded with relief and almost ran for the service hatch. Lee chuckled and settled back with his drink.

A moment later she returned with the lemon and an icy glare which suggested that she had conferred with the other stewardesses and was no longer in any doubt about Martini heights.

Borsch maintained his remote silence throughout the flight, turning from his vigil at the window only long enough to eat. It was not until they were outside the airport that Lee observed drily that if he was not such an argumentative bastard they'd get on quite well. Borsch regarded him with his cold fish eyes, allowed his thin mouth to twist into something resembling a smile, then hailed a taxi.

It took them only fifteen minutes to cover the busy stretch of autobahn between the airport and the city centre, and throughout the journey Lee saw no sign of the car he knew would be following. It wasn't until they had entered Buerger-strasse and stopped outside the Pension Ernst that he caught his first glimpse of a possible candidate. A white Volkswagen went by, turning almost immediately into a nearby side street. Lee glanced idly at Borsch, but the man was paying off the taxi and showed no interest in the car. Lee relaxed and collected his suitcase, reasonably sure that the same white Volkswagen had been parked outside the air terminal.

Pension Ernst turned out to be a bleak, unprepossessing hotel where a thickset woman answering to the name of Frau Schultz glared at them over a dog-eared register.

'How long?' she asked, with pointed disinterest.

'Two nights,' said Borsch.

She nodded, collecting their passports and providing them with keys to their rooms. As they turned to leave she displayed a flicker of interest by asking if they were there for the Oktoberfest. Borsch considered her bleakly until her mouth tightened, then he nodded and uttered a single 'Ja.'

Lee found his room as depressing as the rest of the place. He unpacked quickly, then moved to a window that had a surprisingly impressive view of the Frauen Cathedral which dominated the wide elegance of Munich's famous pedestrian street. It didn't take long to locate the Volkswagen. It was now parked some fifty yards across the street from the hotel, the driver leaning casually in a doorway reading a copy of *Stern*. After a few minutes he gave up trying to place the man, although there was something distinctly familiar in the way he carried himself. The lapse annoyed Lee intensely. After spending years training his memory to the point where he could pluck out facts and faces at will, the figure across the street should not have eluded him. He had come to the conclusion that the man was wearing a disguise, probably a hairpiece, when there was a tap at the door and Borsch entered.

'You ready?' he said.

'For what?' replied Lee, with equal brevity.

'We have a meeting.'

'You know something, Borsch? You're about as communicative as a pregnant gorilla – and the resemblance doesn't end there.'

Borsch shrugged off the insult and turned towards the door. 'We'll go over it all later.'

'Why later?' Lee pressed. 'For all I know this might be my lucky day and you're going to fall under a bus or something.'

Lee grinned, enjoying the thought. Borsch led the way from the hotel to the nearby rank. As they got into the taxi Lee glanced across the street. The casual figure still reclined in the doorway, his face effectively hidden by the magazine. He made no move towards his car as they pulled away and Lee wondered if they were doing a double-ended surveillance; the anchor man covering the hotel with the chain man cruising in a radio car.

Borsch had told the driver to take them to the Theresien Wiese, a choice which surprised Lee. The Wiese was a large exhibition ground, and the traditional venue for the city's Oktoberfest; about the last but one place to go for a quiet bit of conspiracy – the other place being the general office of Munich's police headquarters.

The festive spirit was in full cry when they reached the large open area dominated by huge beer tents and the noisy throng of early evening revellers. They picked their way across ground turned into quagmire by the procession of pilgrims in search of the perfect brew, past the appetizing stalls with the endless supplies of spicy white sausages and sauerkraut, to the third beer tent on the right. Borsch paused, checking the location, then nodding a bleak head towards the smoke and a deafening roar inside.

'Look,' said Lee helpfully. 'If you want a beer I know a dozen within spitting distance.'

'Listen, Corey,' Borsch grated. 'You're a pain, but I'm trying to live with it. If I were you I'd keep my mouth shut and do what I'm told.'

'Or else?' Lee asked, helpfully.

Borsch's face tightened, but he refused to be drawn and moved into the beer tent. Inside it was even worse than it sounded on the outside. The long wooden tables were lined with drinkers in various stages of inebriation. The air was heavy with smoke, laughter and stale beer, and at least a dozen groups were competing from various points with their favourite beer songs. The effect was overwhelming – even the echoes were slurred.

They took a table at the rear, Borsch beckoning to one of the ample-bosomed German waitresses who was passing with ten tankards of beer held effortlessly in her hands. He ordered two Mass beers and she slopped the tankards on the table already floating with beer, accepted the mark pieces, and vanished into the gloom.

'Okay,' said Lee. 'Who do we meet?'

Borsch shrugged. 'I don't know.'

47

The situation was so incongruous that Lee had no hesitation in believing him.

'I've got to hand it to you, Werner. Only a genius would have thought of choosing a place like this for the rendezvous. Now me, I'd have picked somewhere stupid – like an empty office or the back seat of a car doing a ton down an autobahn.'

Borsch lifted a froth-covered nose from his beer.

'The choice was made for us. In a place like this we can be watched by a dozen people – until they're sure we're genuine.'

'What kind of people?'

'The dangerous kind. The kind the police would give a lot to get hold of.'

Lee nodded, thoughtfully.

'The Baader-Meinhof people.'

Borsch's gimlet eyes bored into him.

'If you want some advice, Corey, you forget about that name while you're here. I'm one of the few they trust – but even I couldn't save you if they thought you knew too much.'

'Werner, you've got me scared to death,' Lee said, letting an edge of contempt sharpen the words.

Borsch smiled bleakly and turned away, sipping his beer and gazing over the rows of crowded tables. Across the room a couple in faded jeans and stained T-shirts were moving unsteadily towards the door.

The girl was in her early twenties, her thin blonde hair straggling across her face as she giggled happily and hung on to her companion. The man was a few years older, with a beard and long greasy hair. They looked like low-flying drop-outs on a bad trip, and by the time they had covered half the distance to the table Lee had them marked out and labelled.

'Five will get you ten that your contact has a beard and big tits!' Lee drawled casually.

Borsch glanced towards the couple who were moving unsteadily past. They paused, laughing loudly, then turned and lurched to the table. Borsch glanced across at Lee, a grudging respect in the look.

'You don't miss much, Corey.'

The bearded man turned from the girl, his cold eyes pausing briefly on Corey before settling on Borsch. He spoke quickly in German. Borsch nodded, took a folded sheet of paper and handed it to the German. He glanced at it, whilst the girl lolled limply in her seat. She was apparently in an alcoholic haze, but her eyes were constantly roving the room, returning frequently to Lee with a cold hypnotic gaze. Suddenly she let out a gurgling laugh, punched her companion lightly on the shoulder and staggered to her feet. He rose to join her, speaking softly to Borsch in a voice lost beneath the noise around them. Then they were gone. A happy, inconspicuous couple without a care in the world. Except one – they were both war.ted for murder.

Lee turned to Borsch. 'What now?'

'I have to see someone on the other side, alone.'

Lee shrugged. 'Be my guest.'

'There are other people here,' Borsch said slowly. 'If you move, or get curious, they might get the wrong idea.'

Lee grinned and toasted him mockingly with his beer.

'The only thing I'm curious about is when you and your friends are going to stop screwing around and get down to basics!'

Borsch, for the first time since he had met Lee, made some attempt at apology.

'It's necessary,' he said awkwardly. 'The people we need for this job can't afford to take any chances.'

The German rose and moved away, losing himself in the crowd milling around the bar that went the entire length of the tent. Lee settled back, sipping his beer and letting his gaze wander casually over the crowded tables in a futile attempt to spot the tail he was sure they would have planted. It could have been any one of a dozen people. The old man sitting alone, his head sagging drunkenly on his chest. The young couple in jeans holding hands and sharing a cigarette. The tall, saturnine character with a copy of the *Süddeutsche* propped against his beer – he was the most obvious choice and therefore the least likely.

Lee gave up. All he did know was that someone in the noise and the smoke was watching. He could feel the eyes, stabbing icy fingers into the back of his neck. It didn't really matter, he decided. However good they were, his local contact would be better.

He picked up his tankard, drawing consolation from the thought, and was about to take a drink when someone hit him a jarring blow in the back that sent a good half litre of Munich's finest slopping across the table. He turned with quick anger to find himself staring into a round, unshaven face with a wide, thin mouth and red-rimmed eyes. He looked as though he was working his way through his third hangover, but when he spoke German it carried an unmistakeable American accent. It was also the last voice he expected to hear in Munich.

'My apologies, friend, that was very stupid of me,' he said, sitting unsteadily beside him, 'Allow me to buy you another.'

'I was enjoying the one I had.'

The man grinned nervously and held up two dirty fingers to a passing waitress.

'It tastes better when it's free.'

Lee nodded coldly and turned away, ignoring him. The couple in jeans were still holding hands. The old man had stirred long enough to slop beer down his well-stained rain-coat. The lone drinker had turned to the sports page of the paper.

'What the hell are you doing here, Max?' Lee asked keeping his lip movement to the absolute minimum.

'I felt like a beer,' he answered drily, pitching his voice low and staring down at the table.

'Christ!' Lee murmured. 'I've got so many people watching me I feel like selling tickets!'

Max chuckled softly as a jovial German frau with legs like pit props swooped down on them with fistfuls of beer. He dropped the marks in her apron pocket as she set the two tankards in front of them, beaming a cheerful *'danke'* before moving on. Max turned with his beer, raising it to Lee.

'Prosit, friend.'

Lee adopted a mollified expression and returned the toast, still recovering from the shock of seeing him. Max Weller could normally be found on the third floor of a steel and glass complex in the centre of downtown Washington. The office itself had certain unusual features that people tended not to talk about. The floor was covered in rubber tiles reputed to be nine inches thick. The walls were tastefully decorated with what looked like hessian, but was actually a space-age material that carried a constant electrical charge. The same material covered walls and ceiling, turning the office into a bug-proof cage resting on an insulating rubber cushion. Even the tinted glass windows were wired to detect the delicate touch of a laser beam capable of picking up the most minute vibrations.

Weller had every reason to want total security. As head of C-2 he walked a narrow and lonely path between the jealously guarded jurisdictions of the FBI, the Secret Service and the CIA. Ever since Edgar Hoover had declared that the fight against crime was no longer national, but global, the need for an international arm of the FBI had been clear. The solution was C-2, ostensibly a department created to liaise between Interpol and the FBI, but in reality a small unit of undercover agents operating against organized crime on a world-wide front.

Although Weller worked closely with Interpol 1, the Washington arm of the world police network, he was also able to use the full facilities of the FBI and utilize agents based at every major American Embassy in the world, ostensibly legal attachés with full diplomatic immunity. Weller was, in effect, able to use a clandestine force second only to the CIA as back-up to his own C-2 operatives in the field. The result was a formidable force using undercover techniques to strike at the heart of organized crime across the world.

The fact that the neat, wiry American had left the secure confines of his office in Washington was astonishing. The fact that he was sitting, with a two-day stubble, in a beer tent in Munich was shattering.

Lee stared abstractly into his beer, hoping the observers would fail to detect the movement of his lips.

'Are you covered?'

'There's a man at the bar trying to work out who's covering you.'

'Any ideas?'

'Could be the guy with the paper, but we favour the two kids playing footsy.'

'You're out of your mind,' Lee said. 'If the Bureau knew you'd gone into the field they'd have a seizure!'

Max leaned back, taking a long drink of beer, then wiping his mouth on a sleeve before fumbling for a cigarette. When he finally got it out he turned to Lee and asked him for a light, the hard, grey eyes meeting his for the first time. They bored into him with the blunt impact of a stone axe.

'We're getting out of our depth on this one, Lee.'

'Is that all you came to say?'

'If Ryker is planning to use the Baader-Meinhof, then its got to be the biggest thing he's ever set up. We have to know where and how, and if possible to involve Ryker himself.'

'Check,' murmured Lee.

'So that means protecting your cover at all costs, even if it means going right out on the proverbial limb.'

'Including pulling a gaol break that could involve killings?'

Max was silent for so long that Lee began to think they'd been spotted. He glanced round casually, but there was no sign of Borsch or any activity around the bar. Max was hunched

51

over his tankard, blowing smoke at the table. When he spoke his voice was thin and weary.

'If the Germans ever got a whiff that we had prior knowledge of a break, let alone an active part in it, the blast would shake every window in the White House. It'd be worse than Watergate. Much worse.'

'But if we pull out, or tip off the federal police, we lose Ryker.'

'That's about the size of it. You know why I'm here. If you go into it, you go on your own. The prison guards will be shooting to kill if they get the chance, and if you're caught . . . I never even heard your name!'

Max drained his glass, stubbed out the cigarette and rose unsteadily to his feet. He paused to grin crookedly at Lee, giving him a friendly slap on the back.

'See you, friend,' he said, and weaved his way towards the exit.

The beer tent was suddenly a very lonely place, the noise and laughter seemed remote, distant, like echoes from another room. Even the beer had lost its taste. Lee knew that, even as Max was making an inconspicuous withdrawal, his own cover would be pulling out. Within the hour the Bureau would be cancelling the local surveillance order, the day file heading for the oblivion of an incinerator. From now on, at least until he was back in Algiers, Lee Corey was on his own. Expendable.

He smiled drily as he remembered one of Max's own cynical observations. 'Sooner or later, everyone becomes expendable.'

Seven

It was a further half-hour before Borsch emerged from the crowded rear of the tent, ordering another round of the potent Mass beer, then drinking it silently. It was almost ten o'clock and Lee stirred restlessly.

'If you're through here, I'd just as soon find a bar with a piece of action.'

'You'll get all the action you need, Corey. We're in business. Tonight!'

A fine cold drizzle of rain was falling as they left the beer tents and pushed their way through the milling crowds to the west corner of the Wiese. A dark blue Mercedes detached itself from the shadows and purred softly up to them. The driver, Lee noted, was the bearded young man who made the first contact. He said nothing, keeping his eyes firmly on the road as they pulled out into the busy traffic and headed for Maximilian Strasse through the centre of the city. Borsch leaned back in the deep leather upholstery, his eyes glazed with disinterest.

'Does it have to be a mystery tour?' Lee asked mildly.

'Why not, Corey? You're a bit of a mystery yourself.'

Lee considered the man carefully. The chances of him knowing anything were remote. Even if they had noticed Max beside him, it was too early to start flinging innuendoes around. Lee gave a casual shrug, confident that Borsch was bluffing.

'Maybe I should get a publicity man and wear yellow socks?'

The pale, empty eyes gaped at him. 'Who was the man who spoke to you in the tent?'

Lee ignored the tight knot in his stomach and managed to look amused. So they *had* spotted Max. That meant they were tailing him now. He considered the possibility of Max showing his hand, but rejected it almost immediately. The head of C-2 was too sharp a fox to let himself be run to ground. He would give them the grand tour until they got bored and went home.

Borsch was waiting, his mouth tightening angrily as Lee continued to grin.

'Well?' he rasped.

'You sound like a jealous frau!' Lee replied mockingly. 'Who the hell do you think he was?'

'I'm asking you!'

'Then find him and get his autograph! He didn't bother to tell me, and if he had I wouldn't have given a damn!'

The German considered him for a few seconds, then turned and looked out of the window. They were leaving the city on the south-east autobahn, picking up speed as the dark waters of the River Isar appeared on their left. The last of the suburbs soon dropped behind and were replaced by rolling countryside and gentle, tree-covered hills. The sign ahead announced the exit for the town of Rosenheim as the driver flicked his indicator and pulled over to the right, beginning to decelerate.

Lee estimated that they had travelled some forty kilo-metres, far enough from Munich to make any tail con-spicuous. As they pulled off the autobahn the driver slowed to a crawl, his eyes watching the rearview mirror for any car coming off behind them. A moment later a Volkswagen swung towards the access road, its headlights flashing briefly as it climbed towards them. Their driver acknowledged, dip-ping his lights, then accelerated towards the lights of Rosen-heim.

Lee breathed a sigh of relief. If the Bureau had kept a cover on him, there would have been no chance of avoiding the neat trap they had set. Borsch stirred beside him and he turned to find the German looking at him with a strangely contorted expression. After a moment he realized it was meant to be a friendly grin.

'You must excuse our caution, Lee, but we are not in the habit of taking chances.'

'That's okay, Werner,' said Lee, smiling at the German's use of his first name. 'I get nervous myself now and then. Especially when the people I'm working with don't seem to know what the hell they're up to!'

Borsch's mouth tightened briefly at the implied insult, but he decided to let it pass.

'There'll be a detailed briefing when the rest of the group

join us, but if your German isn't good enough we can go over it again later.'

'I'll get by,' said Lee. 'But if you're planning this for tonight it doesn't leave us much time to get all the equipment we'll need.'

'The meeting place also serves as a supply depot.'

'For whom?'

The German's eyes gleamed coldly in the shadows, then he turned back to the window. End of conversation.

The Mercedes parted company with the Volkswagen on the outskirts of Rosenheim, making a complicated detour through a dozen side streets before emerging finally on a narrow track at the southern edge of the town. The Volkswagen was parked in the yard of a disused farmhouse, the jean-clad couple from the beer tent waiting beside it. Lee nodded casually as he went past them, entering the farmhouse through a door that seemed ready to fall from its hinges, but was actually strong enough to hold its own against anything less than a battering ram.

They gathered in the stone-floored kitchen beneath smoke-blackened beams. An oil lamp shed a flickering light over the group as Borsch took a seat at the head of the sagging oak table. Beside him was the driver of the Mercedes, a man he now introduced as Heinz Rimmer. The young couple lounged beside Lee, looking slightly bored with it all. Their names were Gunther Stoltz and Sigrid Wentner. No one bothered to speak, so Lee lit a cigarette and ran his eyes up and down the girl's lanky figure. She ignored him the first time, but on the second run began to get interested.

Any further developments were curtailed by the arrival of a small van. A moment later a short, stocky man with iron-grey hair and shaggy eyebrows strode into the room. He surveyed them with an unmistakeable air of authority and when he spoke his voice was clipped, hard, and carried a strong East German accent. He shook Borsch warmly by the hand whilst giving Lee a cool, thoughtful look, then introduced himself simply as Carl.

Borsch had taken a large sheet of paper from his pocket and was spreading it carefully on the table. It showed a detailed plan of the prison and grounds with an inset layout of one of the blocks. Carl glanced at it briefly and gave a satisfied nod.

'You all know Stadelheim Prison,' began Borsch.

'I don't,' said Lee mildly.

Borsch gave him a sharp, irritated look.

'No matter, you'll be going in with me.'

Carl was leaning back in his chair, fingers delicately steepled, his cold grey eyes unwaveringly on Lee. There was enough quiet menace in the glance to bring the perspiration through the palms of his hands. Again he wondered how much they knew. If the Bureau had managed to foul it up after all . . .?

'Our plan depends on split-second timing,' Borsch was saying. 'The guards at Stadelheim are keen, efficient and they don't panic. That means we can count on two minutes, maybe three, during which we can wrong-foot them. After that they'll be back on their toes and ready for anything.'

He paused, glancing at Carl. The leader of the group made a small, approving gesture and carefully took out a folded sheet of paper which Lee had last seen in the beer tent in Munich. Carl opened it and studied the typed list of equipment as though he had never seen it before.

'There is nothing very difficult on your list. We have a Soviet RPG 7 rocket launcher which will do a better job than the bazooka. Unfortunately we only have two missiles for it.'

'We only need two,' said Borsch.

Carl gazed at him with a patient expression. Borsch shrugged defensively.

'You can always buy more rockets.'

Carl nodded slowly, his eyes moving again to Lee.

'Perhaps the American can get some for us?'

'Sure thing,' Lee replied drily. 'Just let me have a list and I'll cable the Kremlin first thing in the morning!'

Heinz Rimmer started to chuckle, but cut if off quickly when he saw Carl was not amused. Borsch began to look mildly exasperated.

'Carl, I don't care whether you use a bazooka or an RPG, but we must have something with that kind of kick. Now either Lodtz is worth using what you've got, or he isn't.'

Borsch leaned back in his seat and waited. After a moment the leader of the group sighed and nodded, folding the list of equipment and replacing it in his pocket.

'It will still cost you fifty thousand dollars.'

'Fine,' said Borsch, turning back to the plan and stabbing a finger at the main entrance. 'That's where you use them. At one a.m. you will fire a missile at the gates. The blast will blow them apart, leaving you a clear field to place the second missile here.'

Borsch indicated the main prison block. The remainder of the group leaned forward, beginning to look interested.

'By putting the second missile through the ground floor window you should destroy the main communication centre and eliminate the guards on night duty. You will then have a maximum of three minutes in which to move. Don't waste it. Go in through the smoke and create as much confusion as you can. Use incendiary grenades and CE canisters in the security quarters, the main compound and prison Block A.'

He considered them, his eyes cold and remote, choosing his words carefully.

'The chances are that the guards won't know what's hit them until you are out and clear, but if you meet any kind of resistance you had better wipe it out. Understood?'

They nodded. Lee watched without expression, but a kilo of ice was doing a slow somersault in his stomach. Borsch had gone through the briefing with no more emotion than the local vicar rehearsing a wedding, but what he was describing was sheer, bloody chaos. With growing alarm he listened to the group enthusiastically discussing how many incendiary grenades and CE canisters they would require, the fire power they would need to deal with any guards who survived the holocaust.

'I'll take the Mauser machine pistol,' Rimmer said, looking across at Sigrid as though he expected an argument. 'Gunther is happy with the Schmeisser.'

'I want an automatic,' said Sigrid crisply.

'A Walther PPK?' Carl suggested.

She gave him a scornful look as though she wouldn't be seen dead carrying a PPK. He shrugged, slightly apologetic.

'The 9 millimetres are a bit heavy for you.'

'Crap!' she said. 'I'll take a Luger.'

'It's too heavy. You haven't the arm for it.'

The group watched with various grins of anticipation. Sigrid was obviously a girl who knew her own bloodthirsty little mind, but Carl was used to dealing with it. He gave her a wintry smile.

'If you don't want the PPK, then it'll be the Beretta.'

'Christ, Carl!' She glared at him furiously. 'I've been using a Luger since . . .'

She stopped suddenly, her face paling as she saw the anger in him. His mouth was a thin line and his hand made a short, chopping movement.

'You will take the Beretta .38,' he said in a quiet voice, then turned to Borsch. 'You will require a fitted silencer?'

'That's right. On a Luger.'

Carl nodded and glanced at Lee.

'The same for you?'

'I prefer the Walther P.38 with the collapsible stock, snail drum magazine, telescopic sight and extended silencer.'

Carl didn't even blink.

'That's settled then,' he said, and turned back to the plan.

Eight

They left the farm shortly after midnight in three vehicles, separating on the outskirts of Rosenheim to make their own way along the autobahn into Munich. It was a cold, windy night with the moon appearing occasionally from behind heavy, brooding clouds. The wind was stripping the last of the summer leaves from the trees, swirling them in dark, oily patches across the roads, and from the low hills in the south there was a distant rumble of thunder. It had a distinctly Wagnerian air about it and the effect was depressing.

Lee sat beside Borsch in the Mercedes, racking his brain for some way of getting a warning to Max Weller. Taking part in a gaol break was bad enough. This was insane. He checked through the schedule again, knowing it was futile. He would be with Borsch every second of the way, and even if he found an opportunity to overpower him, there would be no time to stop the massacre at the main gate.

He thought of Sigrid and Rimmer in the other car. They had all taken a drink of Corn before leaving, toasting each other with the potent spirit, their faces already stained dark beneath black woollen caps. The girl had raised her glass, eyes blazing like some demented Joan of Arc, her voice thick with the lust for battle.

'Death,' she had said. 'I drink to death.'

He had drunk the toast, hoping fervently that she would be the first to go. They were picking up speed on the autobahn now, Borsch leaning back in his seat, eyes closed, face impassive.

'What kind of group is this?' Lee asked curiously.

'Political extremists who believe in the doctrine of Baader and Meinhof. Like so many groups they've given up trying to beat the system, to create a climate of change within

59

the present political structure. The only answer is extreme activism, urban guerrillas sabotaging anything connected with government.

'Ever since the purge of the Baader-Meinhof movement there have been a number of fringe groups building up supplies of weapons, establishing contact, formulating a unified plan. But they'll never get the support of radicals unless they can produce a leader – someone who can bring the extremists together.'

'Like Baader?'

'Or Meinhof.' Borsch shrugged. It didn't matter to him.

'And how good are they?'

'Good enough. The girl, Sigrid, killed two American army drivers who gave her a lift, then drove their truck and its load of arms three hundred kilometres.'

'Nice girl,' Lee said softly. But the chill down his back didn't come from the knowledge that she was a killer. It came from memories less than an hour old.

After the meeting had broken up he strolled around the farm, ostensibly for a breath of fresh air, but in reality trying to get a line on the hidden armoury that had to be somewhere close. He was lighting a cigarette beside the ramshackle barn, wondering how far he would get if he tried to reach a phone, when Sigrid moved up silently out of the darkness.

'Not really your scene,' she said softly.

'You mean this?' he asked, waving a hand. 'Or the job in town?'

'All of it.' She shrugged, her mouth twisting with contempt. 'We're not exactly in your league.'

Lee wondered what kind of league she thought he was in. Even the Mafia would get the shudders with this crowd. 'I'm not complaining,' he said generously.

'We'll get better, once Janos is out and we can build up the group.'

'Sure you will.'

'Not that you need worry,' she said, quickly. 'Heinz and Gunther will be all right, and nothing ever shakes Carl.'

Lee nodded, smiling politely. It was nice to know. She had turned casually, pushing open the door of the barn. Now she stepped into the shadows, glancing back, her eyes holding his briefly. 'Let's talk in here,' she said.

They picked their way across the barn, avoiding bales of rotting hay, a rusting plough and a stack of old oil drums. She stopped in deep shadows at the rear of the barn, turning to face him with wide, hot eyes, which narrowed with disappointment when he offered her a cigarette. She shook her head, watching as he lit one for himself.

'Tell me about Janos,' he said, casually.

She shrugged. 'We need him. He knows key people in the Baader-Meinhof. People the police never caught.'

'Is that important?'

She looked at him in astonishment. 'How else can we start again? Janos knows the way, the things we should be doing and how they should be done.'

'You mean the political side?'

She nodded, a fanatical light in her eyes now. 'Of course. Carl only wants to train, to build up our strength. But how can we do that if Germany thinks we're afraid to move?'

'Nobody's going to think that after tonight.'

'True,' she said, 'but so much time has been lost. Every month the capitalists get fatter, stronger. The pigs in Government pass new laws, make new deals, build their industrial machine on the backs of the people.'

'So what's the answer?' Lee asked, casually.

'Death!' she said, with quiet conviction. 'Kill the fat pigs who hold the power, and keep on killing them until they stop and give it back to the people.'

Watching her Lee was astounded by her naivety, yet shocked by the ruthless finality of the philosophy. This was the ultimate weapon of the political extremist, the urban guerrilla, using death and destruction to bring a government to its knees. From the Black September movement to the IRA, the philosophy had paid off. You can't negotiate with a bomb. The Baader-Meinhof had been stopped in mid-stride, but if this girl was anything to go by, the race wasn't over yet.

'So Janos makes that possible?' Lee asked mildly.

'Of course. He's the only man who can lead the big operation.' She stopped, looking at him in surprise. 'Surely you can see that?'

Lee didn't see it at all, but he was beginning to get the idea. 'You mean at the end of the month?' he asked lightly.

She nodded, eyes shining. 'That's when the whole world will know we mean business.' She moved closer to him, her breathing noticeably faster now. 'I may not see you until then.'

There were a dozen questions he wanted to ask, but if she began to realize how little he knew it could create complications – and complications with these people would tend to be basic and final. He stubbed his cigarette out, looking at her bleakly. 'Maybe that's just as well.'

Her mouth tightened with quick anger. 'What's that supposed to mean?'

He shrugged, letting his eyes move over her with casual assurance. 'The first rule of survival. Don't get involved.'

The frustration stretched skin-tight around eyes and mouth, but his logic was the kind she could understand. With a short, abrupt nod, she accepted rejection. 'All right, Lee,' she said slowly. 'Until Rome.'

He gave her an easy smile and ran his hand lightly over her buttocks. 'Until Rome.'

Long after Sigrid had left he was still standing in the darkness of the barn, trying to put the facts together and getting nowhere. The Baader-Meinhof were concerned with Germans and Germany, and yet Sigrid had distinctly referred to Rome. Eventually he returned to the farmhouse, unable to shake off the feeling that C-2 was getting into something much bigger than robbery and Max's trap to catch Ryker could turn into a pit that would engulf them all.

They came off the autobahn on to the Inner Ring road which took them across the John F. Kennedy Bridge and down the Richard Strauss Strasse to Ostbanhof railway station. Here Gunther parked in the main square facing the station until the Volkswagen and the van arrived. It was now five minutes to one and Borsch was getting impatient. He waved Carl ahead in the van and they moved off together through the sparse traffic down Innsbrucker Strasse, turning right at the intersection with Sohliersee. This led them directly to the Perlacher Cemetery, set in a small wood which backed on to Stadelheim Prison.

Gunther parked the car behind trees beside the main gate, then ran back to the road to be picked up by Heinz in the Volkswagen. They moved off towards the intersection with Lincoln Strasse that would take them round to the main entrance of the prison.

Borsch checked his watch. It was five minutes before Carl was due to fire the first missile. 'Ready?' he asked.

Lee slipped the coil of thin nylon rope around his shoulders, pushing the collapsible steel grappling hook into his belt. 'You call it,' he said bleakly.

Borsch glanced round, his face gaunt in the moonlight. Beyond the trees the ranks of ornate gravestones made ghostly fingers in the night. Nothing moved, the only sound the distant hum of traffic from the autobahn. The German nodded and they moved forward, vaulting the low railings and moving into the trees that stretched in landscaped terraces along the avenues of the cemetery. They covered the ground quickly, using the neat paths between the graves until they were close to the crematorium. Here Borsch turned left, crossing to a thickly wooded area. In the dark shadows among the trees they stopped, listening. For a full minute Borsch made no movement, then satisfied he gestured silently and they moved on through the trees until they gave way to an open grassy bank and the heavy steel fence which separated them from the gaunt walls of the prison.

Crouching low, they ran the twenty yards of open ground to the fence where Lee, using powerful cutters, quickly removed a three-foot section. Again they paused, listening, watching the grey walls of the prison. Nothing moved. Lee ducked through the hole in the fence, Borsch following, and together they ran for the wall. Once in its shadow they relaxed, Lee uncoiling the rope and opening the grappling iron. He glanced at Borsch, a frozen figure, his gaunt face impassive as he watched the second finger of his watch.

'Now,' he said, softly, and Lee swung the grapple and sent it soaring up, over the wall.

At precisely 1.15 a.m. Carl parked his delapidated van in Amerstortfer Strasse and casually lit a cigarette. From the corner of the street he was able to look directly at the entrance to Stadelheim Prison. The heavy, metal-studded doors were closed and no light showed in the window above. He nodded with satisfaction. During the day the room above was manned by a guard, but at night the room was normally unoccupied. The lights of the Volkswagen swept into view, then snapped out as it stopped across the road from the gates. Carl checked his watch. It was time.

In the Volkswagen Heinz and Gunther checked their weapons, touched the cold, round incendiary grenades for the hundredth time. It was a cold night, but perspiration glistened on both their faces. In the rear Sigrid saw the gleam of sweat and smiled with quiet contempt. The small Beretta was a pulsing dynamo, sending wave after wave of delicious energy up her arm and through her body until every nerve seemed to tingle and glow. A light winked from the street behind them and she knew the wait was almost over.

Carl lay in the back of the van, nestling the rocket launcher in a bed of sandbags, its blunt snout raised over the tail gate and sighting on the prison gates. Missing was impossible, he knew, yet there was still the moment of tension, the fear that now something would go wrong. He pressed the trigger, turning his face from the blast as the missile fired, then quickly back to the night scope.

It seemed an age before the missile struck, although it was less than one and a half seconds. With a thunderous roar the entire entrance was engulfed in smoke and flame, part of the lodge house collapsing in the blast. The smoke cleared to show a massive, jagged hole where the gates had been. Beyond was the inner courtyard with the main block on the far side, the windows of the guardhouse brightly lit. A siren started, wailing into the night, but Carl was already loading the second missile, checking guidance and ignition, then sighting on the guardhouse. He pressed the trigger, the missile roaring into the night as the door to the guardhouse opened and a figure was silhouetted against the light. The guard stood, frozen, staring at the ruins of the gates as Carl angled the missile down a fraction, then laughed softly as man and missile blended into a ball of fire.

Before the echoes of the second explosion had faded, Gunther, Sigrid and Heinz were running through the gates, across the courtyard for the main block. A door opened to their right and a guard staggered out, still buckling on his pistol. Sigrid turned with Gunther, holding the Beretta in both hands, squeezing the trigger and gurgling happily as the bullet took the man in mid-stride and slammed him to the ground. Gunther glanced at her, mouth tight, then ran after Heinz who was already tossing a grenade into the wrecked shambles of the guard quarters. Sigrid pulled the tapes on two CE canisters and tossed them across the yard, then ran towards the end of the main prison block.

There was pandemonium in the cell blocks as a thousand prisoners began shouting and banging on the bars of their cells. On the ground floor guards tumbled out of their beds, grabbing guns and running for the corridor to the cell block, only to be met by a blazing inferno that had been the guard quarters and office complex. The only other way to reach the prison wing was across the courtyard, and here they were met by a hail of bullets and CE gas.

Sigrid had found herself a perfect vantage point on the far corner of the courtyard. Facing her was the rear door to C Block, and sooner or later she knew the night guards on duty in the block would have to come through that door. A cloud of gas from the canisters was being blown gently into the block, whilst at the other end of the courtyard Heinz and Gunther were still lobbing grenades through windows and pinning the guards down with a murderous crossfire. She didn't have to wait for long. The door burst open and two guards staggered out, their guns useless as they retched and vomited from the effects of the gas. Sigrid crouched before them, the Beretta extended in both hands, centring on the first man, squeezing one shot that took him in the stomach, then another that caught him in the chest as he was flung back against the wall. The second guard, lunging to one side, tried to see where she was with red, tear-filled eyes. Sigrid laughed softly. It was almost too much. The guard had his gun raised, could almost see her now. She let him fire, hearing the bullet sing off the concrete beside her, before pressing the trigger and watching with a cold, tight smile, as the red flowers blossomed on his shirt as the hammer blows slammed him back against the wall.

With the explosions Lee and Borsch dropped from the boundary wall to the exercise yard at the rear of the prison. Ahead of them lay Blocks D and E, the latter containing the maximum security cells on its second floor. They ran quickly to the door of the block, then waited for a full minute to give the guards time to react to the explosions and gunfire.

Crouching by the door, Lee felt a sick frustration as he visualized the carnage at the front of the prison. There was nothing he could do, nothing he could ever have done. Borsch, acting out of a natural caution, had made sure that there had never been an opportunity for him to get to a phone. Max had made the decision to stay out, but he could never have known the kind of hell that Borsch and Ryker had in mind. There was a cold metallic click beside him as Borsch cocked the heavy Luger, gesturing for Lee to enter first. He pushed open the door, stepping silently into a long, white-walled corridor lit at intervals by security lights. Borsch had been confident that the TV monitoring system was only installed on the second floor. He had been right. The long corridor showed no signs of the miniature cameras. He crossed swiftly to the stairs leading up, pausing there until Borsch joined him. A glance at his watch showed that they had two minutes of what Ryker considered to be safe time. In the distance a rattle of gunfire sounded. Heinz with the Schmeisser, he concluded. Borsch slipped ahead, the light canvas shoes making no sound on the steel stairs.

At the first floor they paused to glance along a corridor

lined with cells. Apart from the clamour of the prisoners, there was no sign of any guards. During the night there would normally be at least two guards, but by now they would have rushed to the scene of the fighting. Borsch allowed himself a bleak smile of satisfaction as they moved on, taking the stairs to the second floor.

The maximum security wing at Stadelheim consisted of two parallel corridors joined by three connecting passages. The cells were locked electronically from a control room at the far end of the corridor. Each intersection was covered by TV cameras which slowly scanned the cells and corridors. The guardroom itself had a heavy steel door which could be closed electronically by the guard monitoring the cameras. A second guard constantly patrolled the floor, passing each cell once every ten minutes. At that precise moment he was moving along the main corridor towards the stairs, a pistol cocked and ready in his hand.

His name was Jorgen Gischner, a man in his early forties with twenty years in the prison service. The explosions and gunfire from the main block left no doubt in his mind that a breakout was in progress, but he had begun to tell himself that whatever was happening could hardly effect them here. The corridors were deserted, the prisoners quiet now after their initial demands for information. He had been involved in two prison riots over the years and he was just as happy to be out of it this time. A phone bleeped ahead of him and he moved to it, knowing it would be Kestner in the control room.

'Yes, Hans?' he said quietly, proud of his calm, level tone when all hell was breaking loose somewhere over towards C Block.

'I still can't contact the front office,' said Hans, a sharp note of tension in his voice.

'They've probably got their hands full. They'll contact us when they feel like it.'

'I suppose so,' Hans said, doubtfully. 'Maybe you should come back and we can close the security doors?'

'You know the form. As long as the prisoners see us around they won't start getting ideas.'

'What the hell can they do?' Hans asked nervously. 'If they want to smash their beds up, let them.'

Jorgen hesitated, glancing back along the corridor. Nothing moved, but in the distance there was another rattle of gunfire. He recognized the sharp chatter of a sub-machine gun and he felt a brief spasm of fear. If the guards over at C

Block were using the Schmeissers, then things must be very bad.

'All right, Hans,' he said. 'I'm coming back now.'

Borsch placed one hand on the door, the Luger raised at shoulder height ready to fall and aim on the guard who was putting down the telephone. Lee tapped him on the arm, shaking his head. Borsch glanced at him, his thin mouth tightening angrily.

'Kill him and you blow everything,' Lee said, softly. 'His partner will be watching on the monitor. All he has to do is throw the switch and we might as well go home!'

'We can't let him get back,' Borsch said, tightly.

'All right. Give me ten yards, then put out that camera. I'll take care of the guard.'

The cold, empty eyes held him for a brief moment, then Borsch nodded and raised his gun again.

'Now,' he said.

Lee ran with long, loping strides that ate up the distance with the least possible sound. Ahead the guard was strolling back along the corridor in full view of the camera. Lee was banking on the fact that his partner would be watching the guard, not a fleeting figure just coming into the field of vision.

The guard was almost beneath the camera when the 9 mm. bullet smashed into the lens with a dull crack, showering glass to the floor. The guard looked up in astonishment, taking in the smoking ruin of the camera and momentarily believing that the equipment itself had blown up. Then his training took over and he whirled, dropping into a crouch, the pistol coming up in both hands, finger tightening on the trigger as Lee covered the last stride and kicked savagely at the gun. His foot took the guard across the wrists, knocking the gun aside before he could fire a shot, then his left hand was stabbing at the guard's diaphragm, doubling him forward to receive the slashing blow across the temple from the barrel of his gun. Even as the guard fell to the floor, Lee was moving on, knowing he had only seconds before the guard in the control room decided that the camera failure was no accident.

He turned the corner at the end of the corridor, the open steel door of the security quarters gaping before him. Inside the guard was frowning at the blank screen, trying the switch a second time, then rising from his seat and moving to the door. Beside it was the switch that would seal the room from the rest of the wing. He hesitated, listening. Jorgen should be coming round the corner any second. He couldn't very well close it in his face. Hans sighed and stepped into the doorway, turning towards the corner as Lee's stiff hand took him across the throat. He staggered back, gagging, getting only a fleeting glimpse of a slim man in black stepping lightly towards him – then a numbing blow behind the ear brought darkness.

Borsch stepped into the control room, taking in the unconscious guard with a look of grudging approval before moving to the array of keys on the wall. Lee glanced at his watch as Borsch took down number thirty-four. They had less than a minute.

'I'll collect Lodtz, you cover the stairs,' Borsch said, already heading for the cells.

'Make it fast,' said Lee.

The German didn't bother to glance back. Lee looked around the room, bent down to the guard and checked his breathing. He would be nursing a sore head for a day or two, but that was all. After loosening the man's tie he left the room and moved quickly down the main corridor to the stairs. The other guard was sleeping peacefully, but the sound of firing had stopped. It wouldn't be long before police and fire engines were converging on the prison, so Carl and his group would be pulling out, using the van and the Volkswagen to get away, before the police had time to set up road blocks.

Borsch appeared with Janos Lodtz exactly three minutes and thirty seconds after they dropped from the wall into the exercise yard. They were now into the time zone that Ryker had described as variable. From now on the prison guards could react in one of three ways, the most likely being close to panic as they tried to cope with fires and gas, organizing a police chase after Carl's group, and evacuating the prisoners and wounded from the main block. But the next logical step would be a phone check with the other blocks, particularly maximum security. When that happened they had to be clear of the cemetery, the logical route for the escape. The variable factor was the state of mind of the guard commander. If he was cool and alert he would first delegate someone to check out the rest of the prison.

They left the block by the rear door and crossed the exercise yard to the wall. The rope was still in place, so Lee went up first, straddling the wall and covering the yard as Lodtz started the climb. The speed with which he made the ascent showed that he had kept fit in prison and the quiet assurance of the man in what must have been a bewildering situation spoke volumes for his equanimity. Borsch joined them, pulling the rope up and dropping it on the other side of the wall. They slid down in seconds, pausing to free the rope before moving across the open ground to the shadows of the woods. In the distance the wail of approaching sirens rose up into the night. A sound as plaintive and as futile as the efforts the entire Munich police force would make for the rest of that long night.

Nine

Janos Lodtz looked younger than Lee expected. He was a tall, slim, intense man with thin features and piercing blue eyes. His blond, almost white hair, had been cropped short in prison and the regulation denim gave him a lean, hungry look that belied his fifty years. He had spoken only once since they reached the car: a terse demand for a gun which Borsch had silently passed him from the glove compartment. It was another of the heavy Lugers and Lodtz quickly checked the firing mechanism, working it rapidly and smoothly a dozen times before slapping the magazine into the butt. Then he settled back, the gun on his lap, his intent gaze checking out every street and car they passed. At one point, as they were travelling along Maximilian Strasse, two police cars howled by in the direction of Stadelheim. Lodtz sank back into the shadows in the rear of the car, the gun rising briefly, then falling back as the sirens faded behind them.

Lee watched him, acutely aware that this was the man who had trained and led a fanatical death squad. His escape was a disaster second only to the escape of Baader and Meinhof themselves, an eventuality that would no doubt be debated with vigour at government level that day. Again he wondered what kind of mayhem Ryker was planning. According to Sigrid, he had less than three weeks to find out.

Borsch took them along Leopold Strasse, then turned off into the Schwabing district of bars, nightclubs and discotheques. Most of the bars were closed, but the discos were still booming and couples strolled hand in hand along the narrow streets. Borsch drove the Mercedes along Wilhelm Strasse, turning into a narrow alley behind Schweizerhs Theatre, and stopped outside the Konigstaffen Bar. The place was in darkness, but Borsch had only to tap on the door before a light went on and it opened. Inside they were greeted by Franz Korton, a grey, wrinkled man in his sixties who pumped Lodtz's hand for a full minute before taking them through the bar to a dusty flight of stairs that led down into the beer cellar. Here Franz had laid out a heated tray of sausages with bowls of sauerkraut and mustard. They helped themselves to the food, washed down with tankards of ice-cold lager, while Lodtz changed into a light grey suit and conservative striped shirt.

'How long can you stay here?' Borsch asked him.

Lodtz looked at Franz for a moment, the old man shrugging awkwardly, not wanting to commit himself.

'Carl will be in touch within the next hour,' Lodtz said confidently.

The old man looked relieved. Borsch nodded, finished his beer and glanced across at Lee.

'Then we'll get back to the hotel. If we get in too late the police may have begun a check.'

'They'll check, all right,' said Lodtz, 'but not before morning. Is it a place you can trust?'

'Within reason,' Borsch replied. 'The woman who runs it has no reason to like the police. Her husband is serving two years for dope peddling.'

'Good,' said Lodtz, his piercing gaze shifting to Lee. 'And your friend?'

The question was gentle, almost indifferent, but the eyes held Lee's in an icy grip. Borsch hesitated, then made a flat, emphatic gesture.

'He's part of the big one. Without him, it would not have worked tonight.'

Lodtz relaxed, his thin mouth twisting into a bleak smile as he held out his hand.

'I don't have much time for Americans,' he said.

'I'm not crazy about Krauts,' drawled Lee. 'But I'm sure we'll get over it.'

Lodtz chuckled, then turned back to Borsch.

'When will you be back?'

'In seventeen days. Can you be ready by then?'

Lodtz nodded, pushing a sausage into his mouth and speaking round it.

'There will be people to contact, but there is time enough.' He smiled mirthlessly. 'At least Carl's group have had their initiation.'

'A good man,' agreed Borsch. 'And I'm sure Lee can vouch for the girl.'

71

'Show her your pistol and she'll follow you anywhere,' Lee said drily.

Borsch chuckled, leading the way to the stairs. They shook Lodtz's hand, then went out through the bar to the Mercedes. Borsch took the wheel and drove along Leopold Strasse to Marienplatz. He was relaxed and voluble for the first time, clearly delighted with the way the operation had gone.

'How come our friend Lodtz knows so much?' Lee asked. 'He's been in a maximum security cell for the past two years.'

Borsch shrugged. 'You know what it's like inside. Messages can be got through. Anyway, Lodtz is a professional. He only needs to know that there's something special laid on for the end of the month.'

Lee didn't believe him for a moment. Lodtz had talked about contacting people, getting things ready on time. That could only mean he knew a great deal more.

'He must trust you a hell of a lot more than you trust me,' Lee said, mildly.

'Listen, American, if I didn't trust you, I'd have put a bullet in your head back at Stadelheim.'

'That wouldn't have been very smart. They'd have traced me back to the hotel and tied you right in with the break-out.'

'True. Perhaps I would have given you to Sigrid and let her carry out the execution.' Borsch smiled slowly, amused by the thought.

'Anyone who thinks killing is fun is a bad risk.'

The German glanced at him, eyes narrow and shrewd. He nodded agreement.

'You're right, of course,' he said. 'But the next time that might be a good thing.'

'You mean the fact that she's unstable?'

'Exactly.'

They drove in silence for a while, the lights of the pedestrian street glowing ahead before Borsch spoke again.

'You have to understand that the people we are dealing with are motivated by idealism. Whatever they do must be part of the grand design by Baader and Meinhof. That is where Ryker's plan becomes a work of genius.'

'I'd have a better idea about that if I knew what his plan was,' Lee said.

'You'll be told when you need to know. Until then, relax and think of the money going into your bank account.'

'Maybe,' said Lee doubtfully. 'But if Lodtz knows it all, and the police pick him up first . . .?' He left the question hanging.

Borsch stopped the car in Marienplatz behind the twin towers of the church. He considered Lee thoughtfully for a moment. 'Lodtz knows only what Ryker wants him to know,' he said, finally. 'They are all so obsessed with the idea of freeing Baader and Meinhof that anything more mundane, more mercenary, is beyond their comprehension. Remember that next time you deal with these people. Now go back to the hotel. I'll see you in the morning.'

Lee got out of the car and watched him drive around the square towards the pedestrian street. He would probably abandon the car in one of the back streets, just in case the police found some tenuous link between the blue Mercedes and the prison break. He set off walking briskly towards the hotel, pausing after a few minutes to light a cigarette and check if he was being followed. He didn't trust Borsch, not for a moment, and the German's sudden change of attitude was the most disturbing development so far. It was possible that Lee's involvement in the prison break had convinced him that there was no longer any need for caution, but Borsch had been in the game too long to volunteer any information without a purpose. Lee crossed the pedestrian street debating whether to find a telephone and get word to Max at the Embassy. He finally decided against it, realizing that the head of C-2 was hardly likely to be in the office at this hour of the morning, and there was no one else he could risk talking to now.

He came out of a narrow street on to Buergerstrasse and walked the short distance to the hotel. Halfway down the street he paused, stubbing out his cigarette, letting his gaze rest briefly on a shadowed doorway facing the hotel. Then he moved on smiling bleakly to himself. The darker shadow in the doorway had forgotten the night was cold and heavy breathing makes a considerable cloud of vapour. Borsch must have got rid of the car, then run all the way to make sure he reached the hotel in time. If he'd been two or three minutes late, then the German would have known he'd been doing something else . . . like using a telephone.

Lee collected his key from the desk and went straight to his room, pouring himself a healthy measure of bourbon before going into the bathroom. The first thing he noticed was that the curtains were drawn across the shower cubicle, the next

73

that a pair of polished black shoes were showing beneath. He casually closed the door, then turned back fast with a gun in his hand.

'You've got three seconds,' he said softly.

'One will be enough,' said the voice, and the curtain was drawn back so that Max could step out.

'Where's Borsch?' he asked, crossing to the washbasin and turning on both taps.

'Playing games across the street.'

'I figured he'd let you show first,' Max said, staring at him with weary eyes.

'Let's hope he's satisfied and takes a sleeping pill.'

Max shrugged. 'There's a fire escape at the back. Not that I would mind cutting the bastard down.'

Lee waited, knowing what was coming. The lines of shock and exhaustion were etched deep into the man's face. 'Bad?' he asked.

'Seventeen killed, six seriously wounded.'

Lee stared at him in disbelief. 'Seventeen!'

'Two of the wounded will probably die before dawn. The main gate and administration area are completely gutted, half of C Block is still burning and three hundred prisoners are being evacuated.' Max stared at him with tight features. 'What in God's name were you doing, Lee?'

Lee shook his head slowly. 'I knew it was going to be rough, but that's insane. They must have gone berserk.'

'Then where the hell were you? When a bunch of animals go wild you turn your gun on them and to hell with Ryker, to hell with anything else.' He was staring at Lee with complete bewilderment. 'Okay, I said we'd play it their way. But not this. For Christ's sake, not this!'

'I went in the back way with Borsch,' Lee said quietly. 'I knew they planned to blow the main gate and start the fire, but there was every chance that the guards could have pinned them down, or at least taken cover.'

'Dammit, Lee, if anyone – including my own people – ever knew that I'd had a whiff of this, they'd crucify me!'

'There was nothing I could do,' said Lee, the initial shock giving way to anger. 'I didn't know the details until it was too late to stop it.'

'You could have done something!'

'What?' demanded Lee. 'Chop Borsch and press the panic button? He's not that easy to chop, and anyway there wouldn't have been time.'

Max stared at him with helpless anger. 'But seventeen.

Christ, it's a massacre!'

'Max, if I'd deviated from my plan at any time the only difference it would have made is one extra body.'

'I'll buy that,' he grated.

'All right,' Lee said coldly. 'Next time you decide to hook yourself a big fish, find another fly! When Ryker plays dirty he doesn't screw around, he just finds the experts and turns them loose. If it hadn't been Stadelheim it would have been somewhere else!'

Max took a deep breath and gestured helplessly.

'All right. You had to go along. But I want their names, Lee. I want to know who they are and where they are, and then it'll be my turn.'

'You'll get them,' said Lee quietly. 'In seventeen days you can have them on toast – with Ryker on the side!'

Ten

They landed at Algiers early the following afternoon to find an unusually attentive Bruno waiting to whisk them to Ryker's villa. He met them in the cool, vaulted hall, beaming happily and slapping them on the back as he led them through to the study. Milena preceded them, her slim figure encased in a dark green kaftan, and was ready with frosted glasses of Collins as Ryker sat them down.

'A triumph,' he proclaimed, enthusiastically. 'The latest report puts the operation down to the Black September organization.'

'They'll be pleased about that,' Lee said drily.

'Of course,' agreed Ryker. 'Naturally Kassim's people will issue a denial in a day or so, but that's the kind of publicity they need.'

'How about Lodtz?' asked Borsch. 'Did he get clear?'

'Completely. He's in a safe house well outside the search area.'

Lee sipped his drink, watching Ryker without expression as he continued enthusiastically about the clockwork precision of the operation; the effectiveness of Carl's diversion and the complete inability of the prison guards to cope with the attack. It wasn't until he referred to Rome that Lee showed a mild interest.

'Is that the big one?' he asked casually.

Ryker hesitated, then nodded brusquely.

'Rome is our target, but the operation there will make Stadelheim look like a tea party.' He grinned wolfishly. 'Lodtz will see to that.'

Lee glanced at Borsch, who showed only slight wariness at Ryker's revelation.

'So we both go in with Lodtz?'

The German shrugged, his pale, dead eyes giving nothing

away. 'He's a good man.'

Ryker chuckled softly, leaning back in his chair, amused by the German's caution. 'Come on, Werner,' he coaxed. 'Lee worked well, you said so yourself.'

'I have no complaints.'

'Thanks,' said Lee. 'A pity I can't say the same.'

The German's eyes burned with brief anger, then he relaxed and made a small, flat gesture.

'You were lucky. Maybe in Rome the luck will run out.'

'Nonsense,' said Ryker. 'The plan can't fail. Stadelheim proved that.' He paused, then stated firmly, 'I think it's time we put Lee in the picture.'

Lee waited, his face a mask of bland indifference, knowing that Borsch could still intervene. After six months of painstaking preparation, this was the moment he had worked for. Ever since the meeting with Max in Washington last spring, this had been the goal that was worth any price. But even as he waited for Ryker to speak, a part of his mind was cynically aware that already the price was too high for C-2, the FBI, and certainly every congressman in Washington.

The German's eyes stayed on Lee for a long moment before he nodded. Ryker beamed and held out his glass for Milena. She took it, her gaze resting briefly on Lee with a faint note of approval, then she was moving to the bar and Ryker was launching enthusiastically into his masterplan.

'The Italian economy has been taking quite a beating during the past two years. They've got roaring inflation, massive balance of payments deficit, national strikes and record unemployment. The country's about as close to bankruptcy as you can get and stay in business, and the only way they've been able to keep their Latin heads above water is by selling off their gold reserves on the world free market. Not exactly the done thing, of course, but at one hundred and forty dollars an ounce it's worth the effort.'

Ryker paused, his dark eyes gleaming, accepting his refilled glass from Milena before continuing.

'But this does mean that certain banks in Italy are having to ship out large amounts of gold bullion to the markets in Paris, London and New York. The gold is piped through private banks for conversion into dollars and sterling, but to get the free market price it must first be delivered. That's where we come in. They're planning to move the largest shipment of bullion ever to leave Europe from Rome's international airport on a Jumbo-jet bound for New York. We're going to see that it never reaches its destination.'

'How much?' asked Lee quietly.

Ryker paused, relishing the moment.

'Fifty million dollars. Ten tons of the stuff, all crated up in two hundred handy little cases.'

'And you just walk up and help yourself?'

'Not quite,' said Ryker smoothly, 'but almost. That's why I can afford to be generous. That's why I've already spent half a million dollars in preparation.'

'Okay,' said Lee, 'I buy all of that. What I'm not mad about is going into that airport with a bunch of trigger-happy nuts at my elbow.'

'You won't,' replied Ryker, simply. 'We needed a diversion at Stadelheim to get Lodtz out. In Rome we need Lodtz and the kind of people only he can find to create havoc. Not just a diversion. Total bloody havoc.'

Lee nodded, looking duly impressed, but it was hard to conceal the intense loathing he felt for the man. The black eyes gleamed with sadistic delight at the thought of the carnage to be unleashed in Rome, the havoc that Lodtz could wreak without thought, without feeling. And Ryker couldn't wait to let it happen. He leaned forward, the thin mouth twisting into a savage grin, his hands clawing at the air, his voice thick with emotion.

'It's the ultimate exercise in crime,' he said. 'They'll write books about it. Every security man in the airport will be guarding that gold shipment, but when all hell breaks loose they'll have a terrible dilemma. Do they guard the gold or do they protect the passengers?' He chuckled, relishing the thought. 'It has to be the passengers, of course. How can they stand by and watch Lodtz blow the airport apart?'

'What's in it for him?' asked Lee.

Ryker laughed harshly, nudging Borsch who allowed himself a bleak smile. 'Baader and Meinhof.'

Lee managed to look bewildered, but his mind was stunned by the simplicity of the idea. Lodtz was the most fanatical of Baader's disciples, a man with the power and will to lead any suicide mission if it meant a chance to free Baader and Meinhof. All Ryker had done was to present him with that opportunity, then use it for his own ends.

'It's worked in the past, and it'll work now,' said Ryker. 'The only difference is that while Lodtz is hijacking a Jumbo full of people, we'll be taking a Jumbo full of gold. A double killing.'

Lee nodded, apparently convinced, but he had not missed the quick look that had passed between Ryker and Borsch.

There was more, he realized. Much more. But further questions now would only destroy the delicate balance of trust he had established with them. Instead he raised his glass with a mocking smile.

'I'll bet when you were a kid you didn't just steal apples – you stole the orchard as well!'

Ryker allowed himself a modest smile, unaware that Lee knew perfectly well that he began life as a pimp in the backstreets of Hamburg during the Allied occupation of Germany in 1945 and 1946. At the tender age of twelve he was perfectly happy to sell his own sister, and frequently did. By the time he was sixteen both mother and sister had long since passed into drink-sodden oblivion, and pickings were thin in a country determined to drag itself out of the ruins of a war that had not only shattered its cities, but its very soul as well. Even the lucrative black market was becoming a dangerous pastime as self-appointed vigilantes held late night lynching sessions for the unconverted.

The immediate problem was to get rid of a German accent and change his name from Reichstadt to Ryker. This he did by informing on the black market dealings of a syndicate of American servicemen, thereby earning the gratitude of the occupying power and a work permit in the United States.

After two years with the Teamsters Union in New York he was back into prostitution, using the girls to buy contacts and favours, wheedling his way into the lower echelons of organized crime. By 1955 he had his own patch in Montreal, already acting as a link man between vice and narcotic operations on the Eastern seaboard and building a reputation for knowing how, where, and when to make crime pay. In the sixties he moved to Paris, then Marseilles, recruiting an army of pimps and petty crooks who kept him supplied with a constant stream of information. He was still a part of the American crime syndicate, the shadowy arm of the Mafia, but an increasing number of professional operators were coming to him for advice. The Ryker Connection was born, enabling him to live in the luxurious villa in Algiers, secure in the knowledge that he was above the law because he was never involved in the execution of a crime – only the conception.

Listening to him talking cheerfully about the death and destruction that would paralyse one of Europe's largest airports, Lee began to realize why this man had to be stopped at all costs. The bullion robbery would confirm his already considerable status throughout Europe. He would be in a position to dictate his own terms, create his own syndicates, build an organization that would dominate crime in Europe for decades. Yet the only way to stop Ryker was to catch him in the act, and that was about as easy as catching a piranha with your bare hands.

The conversation wandered in a desultory fashion to women and the varied attractions around the Kasbah. The subject appeared to bore the German, but before he could think of a reason to leave, Lee stood up and announced his intention of taking a shower. Ryker waved a magnanimous hand, turning back to Borsch to launch enthusiastically into his favourite diversion in the hashish-laden dens below Bab-Azoun. The days were gone, he reflected with some sadness, when you could beat a woman half to death for the price of a good meal. Borsch nodded, well used to Ryker's tastes, and remarked that if he needed a woman then the shape, colour and condition were immaterial – just so long as it took the shortest possible time and the minimum of effort.

'I'll keep it in mind. And by the way,' Hannigan said as cool draught of air informed him that the bathroom door had just opened. He pulled back the curtain, expecting to find Bruno or Milena on one of Ryker's errands. Instead he found himself looking into the tormented brown eyes of Suzanne Delar.

'I have to be at the club in half an hour,' she said nervously.

'So?' asked Lee, his expression revealing nothing of his disappointment at finding her in Ryker's house.

'I thought you might want to see me.' She hesitated, her eyes falling from his steady gaze, then lifting quickly as she became aware that he was standing naked in the shower. 'Do you?'

He nodded, stepping out of the cubicle and casually slipping on a heavy towel robe.

'I just didn't expect to find you back in the guest book.'

'That's what I want to talk to you about.' She paused struggling with an inner torment. 'I . . . I missed you.'

'Sure,' said Lee, drying his hair, then gazing at her with cold eyes. 'I don't need to ask if the same applies to Ryker.'

She went pale, the full mouth tightening into a thin, trembling line. For a moment it seemed as though she would turn and leave, but then her shoulders sagged and the small, delicate hands clasped before her in silent plea. He watched, wondering why even now in his stomach was an icy ball and every muscle cried out to take hold of her. Finally she let out a shaky breath and looked at him with a level gaze.

'There are things you don't know,' she said huskily. 'Things I can't talk about – not here. But if I'm to talk to anyone, it has to be you.' She looked at him beseechingly. 'Please, Lee.'

Suddenly she was in his arms, crying softly, clutching at him with desperate hands. He held her for a long moment, conscious of the soft fragrance of her hair, the wetness of her cheek and the full, vibrant warmth of her body.

'All right, Suzanne,' he said. 'I'll see you at the club.'

She looked up at him, a smile forcing its way through the tears.

'Try to understand me,' she said. 'I need someone so badly.'

He nodded again and with a tremulous smile she left, the aura of her perfume remaining long after she had gone. He told himself cynically that her problems couldn't hold a candle to his, that she was free, white and over twenty-one and nobody made her crawl into Ryker's bed. He told himself a good deal more in the same vein while he shaved and dressed in cool blue slacks and linen jacket, and then as he considered the effect in the mirror finally admitted that, no matter what, he was going to give her all the help he could.

During dinner Ryker revealed that they would be joined by a third member of the group the following day. His earlier expansive manner had now lapsed into an abrasive, sardonic mood, and even Milena was hard put to keep a smile on her face. Although the meal was a sumptuous affair of stuffed artichokes and a magnificent lobster thermidor, the conversation was depressing. Ryker's black mood persisted through the coffee and cognac, so when Lee announced his intention of taking a look at the night life Borsch was quick to make his own excuses. They left together, pausing in the cool, domed hallway. Lee nodded back towards the dining-room.

'What turned him off?'

'Who can tell?' said Borsch.

'Anything to do with this guy who's due tomorrow?'

'No. That's been laid on for weeks. It's more likely to be the girl.'

Lee looked mildly curious. 'Girl?'

'Don't get cute,' said Borsch. 'Just remember that nothing happens in this town that Ryker doesn't know about.'

'He didn't strike me as the jealous type,' Lee said idly.

'He isn't,' said Borsch. 'But this week she's special. Next

week he'll probably pass her over to Bruno.'

'That's what I like about you, Werner. Nothing ever gets to you.'

'Why should it?' He looked genuinely surprised.

'No reason,' said Lee. 'Except one of these days you may forget to breathe.'

The German gave him a thin, contemptuous smile and went on up to his room. Lee left the villa and turned north along the Bab-el-Ouad into the old town. The sun was setting behind the Atlas Mountains, picking out the domed and terraced rooftops in pinks and golds, and gilding the ancient towers of the Kasbah so that, briefly, it shone with the ancient splendour of the Turkish beys. It was the hour of prayer and from mosques that rose above the rooftops, muezzins sang their eternal call, echoing down to the narrow streets and alleys.

Lee wandered into a small square lined with ancient souks where young Arab boys vied with each other to entice the luckless tourist. Lee allowed himself to be led into one of the shops where he gazed with bored disinterest at cheap rugs and crude pottery. He moved to one of the narrow windows that allowed him a clear view of the square. After two minutes he had marked the man who was following him. Shaking his head at the plaintive entreaties of the proprietor, he strolled out and across the square, choosing the first narrow alley that cut its way down towards Bab-Azoun. Here tall, stained white walls leaned over him, the cobbled steps turning at right angles at regular intervals. Narrow doorways made black rectangles in the dim light, the still air heavy with pungent odours.

He turned the next corner, then quickly flattened himself against the wall, waiting. The soft pad of sandals came towards him, then the man rounded the corner, looking anxiously ahead. Lee hit him with a short, stabbing blow to the kidneys, then hooked an arm round his neck as he arched in agony. The man was Arab, dressed in dark slacks and a T-shirt. His hair was long and greasy, and from the gold chain at his neck and the ring on his finger he probably fancied himself. Right now he was gasping for breath, rolling terrified eyes to get a look at his attacker. Lee moved his free hand swiftly over his back and hips. He found the knife tucked into the waistband of his slacks, effectively concealed by the loose shirt.

The man was getting ideas, starting to balance himself for a backward kick. Lee tightened the hold on his neck and hit him again in the kidneys, just to let him know that this was not his lucky day, then pulled the knife from his waistband. The man went very still which simplified things. Reversing the knife, Lee rapped him behind the ear with the brass-bound hilt, then lowered the unconscious body to the cobbles. He tossed the knife over the nearest wall and quickly climbed the steps back to the square.

Hannigan was drinking Turkish coffee in the café facing the alley Lee had chosen. He crossed to the big American and sat down, ordering a beer from the beaming waiter. They waited until he had reached the fly-strewn counter at the rear of the café before speaking.

'Did you get rid of the boy-friend?'

'He decided it was time to crash out,' Lee said. 'But we'd better make this quick.'

'Suits me,' drawled Hannigan. 'I had a call from Max. He's putting the lid on everything.'

'Tell him to keep it on. The target is Rome, a shipment of bullion towards the end of the month. Ryker's planning to use a terrorist attack to divert airport security away from the gold.'

'Christ!' Hannigan said.

They leaned back and looked sleepy as the waiter returned with the beer. Lee put a small note on his tray and waved the change away. When he was out of ear-shot he spoke quietly, his glance sweeping the square.

'There's a lot I don't know yet, but I should have all the pieces in a week. You'll usually find me at the club around midnight, but don't try to make contact unless I go to the bar for cigarettes.'

'Check. How about Ryker? Can we get him involved?'

'We've got to, otherwise the whole business is a waste of time.'

'So?'

'So enjoy yourself until I come up with something.'

'That's not going to go down too well with Max,' said Hannigan, looking at him unhappily.

'All right, tell him that Borsch is the key man and once I know the timing of the operation we might be able to take him out. That puts Ryker on the spot.'

'You mean, he'd have to take over?'

'Either that, or write off the whole operation.'

Hannigan considered this, then nodded. 'I'll lay that on Max, it should keep him quiet for a day or two.'

Lee finished the beer and stood up. 'Do that, but stay

clear. Ryker wouldn't trust his own mother if she was tied to a wheelchair.'

'I'll keep it in mind. And by the way,' Hannigan said as Lee turned to leave, 'I picked up an interesting piece of information at the airport. Ryker has chartered an executive jet for one month from tomorrow.'

Lee paused, looking thoughtful. 'Do we have anyone who can bug it?'

'Already have,' said Hannigan, grinning. 'Hooked into the black box.'

'Where's the mike?'

'Directional mounted above the port side emergency hatch and a low impedance job on the flight deck.'

Lee nodded, then moved across the square towards the Kasbah. When he glanced back Hannigan was lighting a cigar and ordering more coffee. He smiled wryly at the big, ungainly American's casual indifference to the dangers around him. He looked the image of a loud American tourist absorbing the local scene, but Lee had a comforting feeling that when the chips were down he could swing into action with a cool efficiency.

He wandered into the Arabesque shortly before midnight, in time to catch Suzanne's final number. He pushed his way through the mass of locals around the bar and ordered a bourbon on the rocks. The gaggle of bar girls were grouped at the far end, either watching the dancer with frozen smiles of naked envy, or weighing up the locals with bored disinterest. Anyone who could afford anything more than the lukewarm beer was quickly whisked to a table, and equally quickly supplied with a limpid-eyed companion with an unquenchable thirst for champagne. Lee cut off the probing looks with an ice-cold stare and watched Suzanne finish her act, making her exit to prolonged applause. He turned back to his drink, and sipped it slowly, letting his gaze drift along the crowded length of the bar, stopping finally on a black, greasy head that had a familiar look about it. He smiled bleakly, wondering how much the Arab was being paid to follow him. He must have a lump the size of an egg behind his ear, and a headache to match, yet here he was setting himself up for an encore. The man turned, his inexperience showing as his eyes caught Lee's and dropped too quickly, too soon. Nevertheless, his presence created a problem. If Suzanne wanted a private talk, the less Ryker knew about it the better. The man lifted his eyes, clearly nervous now, so Lee smiled reassuringly at him and pushed his way along the bar.

The Arab stood his ground, although a thin film of perspiration on his upper lip suggested that he was already wishing he'd taken the night off. When Lee reached him he forced a tight smile, still nursing a faint hope that Allah would take care of his own. The hope vanished as Lee deliberately dropped a cigarette into his glass of beer.

'Now that was careless of me,' said Lee, conversationally.

The Arab swallowed his anger, remembering the iron arm around his throat and a fist with the kick of a mule in his kidneys. He looked at the sodden cigarette floating in his beer, glanced up at Lee and forgot what he was going to say as cold, blue eyes stabbed into him.

'Maybe you should get another drink,' Lee said helpfully. 'Somewhere else.'

The Arab forced a smile, teeth gleaming against the sallow tan of his skin. 'It does not matter, effendi. It was not a good beer.'

'Fine. Try next door. They could do with the business.'

The smile got tighter, but the initial fear was beginning to evaporate as he realized that Lee was the stranger here and he, Mohammed Hassan Alif Kazir, was alive and well and surrounded by his friends. He glanced pointedly at the locals who were beginning to pay attention.

'I prefer it here. There is no need to go next door.'

'Now that's a pity,' said Lee, putting his drink on the bar. 'For a while there I thought you weren't going to be any trouble at all.'

The tension came back into his eyes and he took a step back as Lee turned to face him. The American took a packet of cigarettes from his pocket, shook one out and put it between his lips. He lit it with a gold Dupont and blew smoke casually towards him.

'A friend of mine once told me of a time he kept bumping into the same character all over town. After a while it got so that he couldn't even go to the john without finding the same guy standing at the next stall. You know, he tried all kinds of ways to persuade this character to cut out and go home, but still he kept trailing around, sticking out his neck. This friend of mine reckoned that the guy could be one of three things. A police stooge, a private stooge, or a pimp.' Lee considered him thoughtfully. 'Now which one are you?'

'I don't know what you're talking about,' the Arab said, his thin face glistening with perspiration. 'I've never seen you before.'

'Is that a fact,' Lee said with mild surprise. He leaned forward to look at the ugly lump behind the man's ear. 'You ought to do something about that bump. It looks as though it might be infected.'

The Arab's eyes flashed angrily. 'It's nothing. Next time I'll watch where I'm going.'

'Fine. You do that.'

Across the room Suzanne had appeared and was looking anxiously towards the bar. Lee drained his glass and put it on the bar, turning to leave, then pausing to smile casually at him. 'Maybe I made a mistake,' he said.

'Maybe you did,' the Arab replied, a mocking smile appearing as confidence returned.

'No hard feelings?'

Lee held out his hand, smiling apologetically. The Arab shook his head, reaching instinctively for it. At the last moment Lee transferred his cigarette to the open hand, holding it inwards and grasping the Arab's in an iron grip. His eyes went wide, his mouth opened and he gasped in agony as the cigarette seared into the open palm. Desperately he tried to pull away, but Lee held him rigidly until perspiration began to run down the man's face. Then he released him, glancing down with surprised concern.

'Say, that's a nasty burn you've got there. If I were you I'd get something on it. You could see about that lump at the same time,' he added helpfully.

Clutching his hand, the Arab gave him a look of pure hatred and shouldered his way towards the exit. Lee watched him go with a twinge of sympathy. It just hadn't been his day – and he still had to report to Ryker.

Suzanne led the way to a secluded table at the rear of the club, ordering a Bacardi and Coke, then regarding Lee with wide, despairing eyes. He tried to look reassuring.

'Nothing's ever that bad.'

'You want to bet?' she said, forcing a tight smile.

'Okay.'

He waited while she scanned the smoke-laden room with nervous eyes. The waiter was returning with the drinks, so they waited until he had deposited them on the table and pocketed the change.

'I have to get away,' she said finally.

Lee shrugged. 'With your kind of talent you can pick your own spot.'

'I mean from Ryker,' she said, then tried to bite her way through her lower lip. 'I asked him to do me a favour, but . . . but I didn't realize what it involved.'

'What kind of favour?'

'My brother. He's . . . he's in prison.'

'In Algiers?'

'No.' She watched him nervously. 'In England. Ryker knows who could help.'

'Break him out?'

She nodded, relieved by his matter-of-fact approach. 'But that was two weeks ago and I don't think he's even got in touch with them yet.'

'Maybe he's been too busy,' Lee said laconically. 'How about your end of the deal?'

She gave him a long, steady look. 'Don't be stupid, Lee.'

'If you think you can play a fish like Ryker, you're the stupid one.'

Her mouth tightened angrily. 'I thought you'd understand.'

'Why? Because I know Ryker, or because I thought I knew you?'

Suzanne looked at him with helpless resignation. The eyes were cold, the mouth hard and unrelenting. She couldn't blame him. He couldn't know how long the days had been since he left, how many times she told herself that when he came back he would find a way, tell her what to do. She nodded sadly, pushed her drink away and started to get out of her chair.

'Sit down,' he said sharply.

'It doesn't matter,' she said flatly. 'I'll work something out.'

'Then start by cutting out the crap!'

'Watch your mouth!'

'The way Ryker watches his?' he asked bleakly. 'Listen, you knew what you were getting into the first time you saw Ryker. Maybe not the fine details, but you knew enough. So let's cut out the innocent sister act and get down to basics. If Ryker does get your brother out, then he'll own you. Permanently!'

She shook her head firmly. 'Never.'

'He'll have you cold. With your brother on the run he can put the finger on him any time he pleases. That means you'll do as you are told, when you're told, or your brother goes back inside with an extra sentence for breaking out.'

'He wouldn't. All right, he – he fancies me at the moment, but a man like Ryker can have any woman he wants. I'm just . . .' She hesitated, her mouth twitching bitterly. 'I'm just an easy lay!'

She watched him shake his head and smile the gentle smile

that was in such contrast to the quiet strength of the man. She wanted to tell him all of it, to purge herself of the guilt and loathing, but she knew that his disgust would be more than she could bear. Instead she reached out to him with a helpless despair, knowing so much of it was false, but feeling sure he would respond.

'You're more than that to Ryker,' said Lee. 'He's a manipulator, a man who gets his kicks by pushing people to the limits. You're important to him because you're fresh and new and clean. Stay with him and he'll destroy all that.'

'But if I try to leave he'll do something terrible. He'll take it out on me or Harry.'

'Harry's safer inside.'

'No.' She shook her head firmly. 'He's so young, so full of life. Ten years in prison will turn him into an old man.'

The tears welled up in her eyes as she looked at him beseechingly. Lee sighed and made a gesture of empty resignation. 'That's up to him.'

The silence grew between them while the light went out of her eyes and her shoulders sagged dejectedly. The group was playing a lazy Latin number, and beyond the bar the huge familiar figure of Bruno had appeared. He searched the room, then beckoned to a waiter.

'Bruno's here,' Lee said quietly.

'I'll have to go.' She forced a smile. 'Thank you, Lee.'

He gave her a twisted grin. 'For what?'

Bruno was moving across the club towards them.

'I keep forgetting that you work for him.' She hesitated. 'It's just that, when you took me home, I got the feeling that you didn't have much liking for him.'

'That's right,' said Lee. The huge frame of the chauffeur was trying to squeeze through an impossible gap between two tables. 'Do you think you can hang on for a couple of weeks?'

'Yes. Why?'

'Just a thought,' he said casually. 'I should be through here by then. Maybe we could work something out.'

Her eyes lit up and the smile was radiant. She reached out and pressed his hand, and then Bruno was beside them with his small, shiny eyes boring into Lee.

'The car is ready,' he grated.

'Fine,' said Lee, rising with Suzanne. 'You can take us both home.'

Bruno looked as though he was going to argue, but Lee didn't give him time to put words together. Taking a surprised

Suzanne by the arm he led the way across the room towards the exit.

The air was crisp and cool outside and as they moved towards the Cadillac Lee noted with amusement the group of young men lounging in the shadows. In their midst was a figure he recognized, now sporting an off-white bandage on his right hand. Even as they started to move towards him, Bruno stepped out of the club. There was an immediate halt and a shuffling of feet with laughable confusion until they all tried to stroll in different directions. The Arab had obviously planned a little private reprisal, but the formidable appearance of Bruno and the presence of the Cadillac, clearly placed Lee in a far more dangerous category. As he settled into the back seat with Suzanne, he could see them converging angrily on their leader. It really hadn't been his day at all.

Although it was almost one o'clock, Milena opened the door, her face impassive as Lee entered with Suzanne.

'Good evening, Mr Corey,' she said formally. 'Will you require anything before you retire?'

'You could talk me into a cognac,' he replied. 'Maybe you too, Suzanne?'

He didn't miss the quick glance that passed between the two women, then Suzanne smiled lightly and shook her head.

'No thank you, Lee. I think I'll go straight up.'

He looked at her steadily until her eyes fell. 'I'm sure Ryker wouldn't object.'

'Mister Ryker makes up his own mind, Mr Corey.' Milena spoke with polite control, but her mouth was a thin, hard line and her gaze imperative as she turned to Suzanne.

Lee shrugged and strolled into the lounge, dropping into one of the black leather chairs and lighting a cigarette. After a moment Milena entered, crossed to a cabinet inlaid with silver and ivory, and took out a decanter of brandy. She put it beside him with a crystal goblet, then considered him with a slightly puzzled expression.

'I wouldn't get too involved with Miss Delar,' she said, finally.

'Out of bounds to visitors, is she?'

Milena gave him a slow, mocking smile and turned to leave. 'The last man who got involved with one of our friends found it all too much for him. In fact, he lost all interest in women. Permanently!'

'Now that was careless of him,' Lee murmured, 'but don't you worry your pretty little head about me. The only thing I'm likely to lose around here is my patience.'

They exchanged looks of mutual dislike and she left, the silken swish of her kaftan suddenly a cold and sterile sound. The significance of her words had not escaped him. She had not said 'Ryker's friend', but 'our friend'. It explained many things, particularly Milena's strange lack of sexual attraction. Despite her slim, dark beauty, she failed to rouse the slightest response – a considerable achievement with a man whose hormones tended to jump to attention at the flicker of a thigh.

The suspicion that she might be a lesbian had previously crossed his mind as a vague possibility, but now it was back with conviction. So this was the *ménage* in which Suzanne had found herself. It made a great deal more sense than trying to believe that Ryker would go to all the trouble of setting up a prison break just to lay the local dancer. This was far more appealing to a man like Ryker, the kind of diversion he would find very hard to resist. First the conquest, then the corruption, finally the systematic destruction of mind and body. With grim repugnance he recalled Ryker's words at dinner. 'The days are gone when you could beat a woman half to death for the price of a good meal.'

Suppressing the cold anger inside, Lee considered the situation objectively. This new insight into Ryker's personality confirmed his view that, given the right circumstances, the man's ego would over-ride his logic. He had built himself into a master criminal without breaking a law or running the risk of conviction, but in the process he had become dissipated by power and his own sick fantasies. Logic would tell him never to break the cardinal rule, never to take an active role; but the sadistic streak that ruled his emotions would also rule his ego. At the right moment, with the right incentive, Ryker would step out of the shadows to become a pawn in his own game.

Eleven

The cry of a muezzin from a nearby mosque brought Lee out
of a restless sleep. A glance at his watch showed that it was
eight o'clock. He debated spending an extra hour in bed, but
as images of Suzanne, Ryker and Milena began to surface
in his mind he rose and took a cold shower. Donning
pale blue slacks and a dark blue cotton shirt, he went down
to the dining-room to find Ryker, Borsch and Milena already
taking breakfast.

'Ah, Lee, we were about to give you a call,' said Ryker
expansively. 'How did you sleep?'

There was a malicious gleam in the small dark eyes as he
waited for the answer. Lee helped himself to coffee and a
croissant before replying. 'Like a baby. It must be something
in the air.'

'Or the brandy,' suggested Milena, in a silky voice.

Lee ignored her and sipped his coffee. Borsch was tearing
a croissant apart and dipping it into his coffee with all the
delicacy of an elephant breaking wind. Bruno entered and
bent down to whisper briefly in Ryker's ear. He nodded, then
gestured his dismissal before turning to the others.

'We shall be leaving for the airport in one hour,' he
announced crisply. 'I trust that will be convenient.'

Borsch didn't bother to reply, contenting himself with a
nod as he mopped driblets of coffee off his chin with an
immaculate white linen napkin. Lee shrugged. 'Do I need my
passport?'

'No, but you'd better carry a gun.'

'Fine with me,' he said laconically. 'What have you got?'

'I think you'll find we can accommodate you,' said Ryker.
'We'll meet in the gun-room in thirty minutes.'

With that Ryker rose and went across the room into his
study. Lee noted with interest that he unlocked the door with a

91

Mills and Benson cylinder key, which made it just about un-pickable. Milena followed him into the study, taking the coffee with her.

'What gives?' he asked, giving Borsch an enquiring look.

The German grunted, selecting another croissant. 'Matheson arrived during the night.'

'Matheson?'

'Pilot. He'll get us out of Rome.'

'Ah,' said Lee sarcastically, 'then the package does include a return ticket.'

'First class. Providing this English prick doesn't screw himself stupid before we leave.'

'You're such a comfort, Werner,' said Lee drily. 'If you aren't saddling me with nutty broads with a fetish for guns, you're putting my fragile bones in the sweaty palms of a sex maniac!'

Borsch grimaced. 'He's all right. It's just that he's a bit bent.'

'You mean he's a bloody pouf.'

The German looked at him with pale, empty eyes. 'He was a top airline pilot until he got caught with a cabin steward. It doesn't make him any less of a pilot.'

'Christ,' said Lee. 'Off we go into the wild blue yonder with the flying queen!'

'It's not your problem,' Borsch said sharply. 'Ryker can keep him in line.'

'I might believe you if I thought Ryker was coming along, but we both know that isn't part of the plan.'

'Don't get carried away with yourself, American,' said Borsch, brusquely. 'We can always fill your seat on the day.'

'I'll bear that in mind,' said Lee, and pushed back his chair.

He left the German munching thoughtfully on a sodden croissant and climbed the cold, white stairs to the upper floor. He was about to enter his room when he saw the slim figure of Suzanne standing in an open doorway at the end of the passage. She looked at him for a long moment, then stepped back and closed the door. It took only five seconds to make up his mind, then he was moving swiftly down the passage and tapping on the door. It opened immediately and she looked up at him with wide, nervous eyes.

'I'm sorry, Lee,' she said simply.

He stepped into the room, taking in the wide vaulted ceiling and heavy ornate furnishings as she closed the door behind him. She was wearing a long, white robe in a soft towelling material that enhanced the golden tan of her skin and dark lustrous hair. She watched him, the large brown eyes still dulled by sleep.

'Never be sorry,' he said, lightly. 'Not when you know you're going to do it all over again.'

She shook her head, mouth pinched, tears welling up into her eyes. 'But I don't want to. I just can't . . . can't help it.'

He knew she meant it now, but the weakness in her would turn it into a lie whenever Ryker felt the need. He wondered at the savage, burning anger, the urge to risk everything by taking her out of here, out of Algiers, before it was too late. She was no more responsible for her actions than a junkie on a four-hour trip and it was going to get worse every time she came to this room. The tears were running down her cheeks, but she made no sound. It was all too much, and he took her in his arms and kissed her with a slow, gentle need that tightened her arms around him, pulled her with growing hunger against him.

The robe slid to the floor and her slim, full body pulled him down to the bed. Her eyes were closed, but her breasts rose and fell with quick, helpless passion. He let his lips move down to the smooth, taut stomach already pulsing with rising waves of desire, but as his mouth descended she gave a muffled moan and pulled his face back towards her.

'No,' she said huskily. 'You, Lee. I want you.'

A small, bitter voice inside him was telling him why, but it didn't matter any more as they moved with increasing tempo on the cool silk sheets. She came with a long, shuddering sigh, his own release prolonging it until every muscle in her was a hard, vibrating cord. And then she slid away to lie with her face in the pillow, the silken sheen of perspiration gleaming in the golden light. It was then he saw the thin red weals across her buttocks, the ugly bruises on her thighs. The rage made him pull her roughly on to her back, her eyes widening with shock at the anger in his face.

'I want you out of here, Suzanne. I want you out now, this morning.'

'It won't make any difference,' she said listlessly. 'It'll just mean I'll lose my job, my flat, even my passport. He's too strong.'

'Don't argue. Do it.'

She hesitated, a mixture of fear and hope in her eyes. 'There's still Harry.'

'All right, suppose he does get out. Suppose he comes here and finds out what kind of price you paid. If he's any kind of a man he'll take Ryker apart with his bare hands . . . and you know the end of that story!'

She shuddered. Lee rose from the bed, his eyes holding her, and this time she didn't look away. 'All right,' she said.

He nodded. 'We're leaving in half an hour. Don't give Milena any sign that you're not coming back – we'll deal with that tonight.'

'Yes.' She forced a nervous smile. 'I'll phone from the club.'

He left her then, pausing at his room to collect sunglasses and a light jacket, then making his way down to the lounge. Borsch was standing on the terrace, looking across the small garden with its profusion of crimson poinsettias and sweet-smelling gardenias. He turned as Lee entered, his face impassive.

'What took you so long?'

'My morning push-ups,' said Lee cheerfully. 'One might as well start the day right.'

Borsch gave him a sour look and led the way into the study and to what appeared to be a perfectly normal mahogany bookcase stocked with an impressive collection of leather-bound volumes. Removing the first volume on the fourth shelf, he pressed a button and with a soft hum of a powerful electric motor the entire section swung away from the wall to reveal an arched staircase leading down.

'Life is just full of surprises,' Lee commented drily.

At the foot of the stairs was a narrow hall, walls cut out of the sandstone foundations of the villa. A heavy steel door faced them and Borsch, who clearly knew his way around, pressed another switch that swung the door inwards to reveal a long, low gallery with two cut-out targets at the far end. Ryker, with Milena beside him, was standing at the firing line wearing heavy ear mufflers. In his hand was a long-barrelled Luger Parabellum P.08. As they entered he steadied the heavy gun in both hands and fired a burst of nine spaced shots into the target. Lee noted that he was using a 32-round snail drum magazine, a useful enough device if you were planning to take on a couple of divisions, but far too heavy and unwieldy for any normal confrontation.

Borsch had moved to the gunrack along the rear wall, so rather than spoil the morning by commenting on Ryker's lousy grouping, Lee wandered over and took down a neat little Mauser automatic. Borsch glanced at him critically, hefting a heavy Colt Python in his hand.

'Unless you're a crack shot with that, you might as well use a catapult.'

Lee checked the magazine, gave him a mocking grin, then turned and fired single-spaced shots from where he was standing. The six holes in the target could have been covered by a silver dollar. Ryker swung round, his eyes widening as he saw the pistol Lee had used.

'That's good,' he said. 'That's very good.'

Borsch grunted and raised the Python, blasting a tattered hole in the target with an arm as steady as a rock. As he swung the cylinder out to reload, Lee suggested drily that he'd missed the last shot. Ryker chuckled, moving to the gunrack and putting down the Luger. He selected a Mauser machine pistol, one of the old Bolo models that was still one of the world's most deadly hand weapons.

'How are you with one of these?' he asked.

'They are all right for people who need five shots instead of one, but unless you're planning a massacre I'll stick to a semi-automatic.'

Ryker nodded, accepting it. Borsch laid down the Python and began checking the magazine of an even heavier Colt Commander. He turned to the target, legs straddled, both hands gripping the butt. Lee winced at the thunderous explosions as Borsch put another ragged hole in the target, big enough to put a fist through, then turned back to consider the gun with a thoughtful expression. He glanced at Milena, who had remained completely unmoved by the thunderous echoes in the narrow confines of the gallery.

'Do you have a shoulder holster for this?'

She nodded, crossing to a drawer beneath the gunrack and producing a well-oiled leather holster with twin shoulder straps. Borsch gave a satisfied nod and removed his jacket to slip it on.

'Are you sure about that Mauser?' Ryker asked Lee.

'Is this for the big day, or are we starting a war this morning?'

'There probably won't be any trouble,' said Ryker smoothly, 'but as I'm going along I want you both armed and capable of dealing with any situation.'

Lee nodded, looking across at Borsch who was putting on his jacket and checking that it hung loose. It didn't and there was a conspicuous bulge under his armpit.

'Unless they're employing blind Customs Officers, you might as well stay at home,' said Lee.

'He's right, Werner,' said Ryker tersely. 'We can have that one taken out to the plane tonight.'

Borsch shrugged, handing the Commander to Milena and turning back to the gunrack. He took down a trim, double-action Walther PPK and checked the mechanism efficiently before turning to the target. He fired a number of single shots until he got the feel of it, then changed magazines and put a neat group into the target on automatic.

'They have a bad habit of jamming when you need them most,' said Lee helpfully.

The German gave him a contemptuous look. 'Listen, American, I've used more guns than you've used French letters!'

'Maybe,' Lee replied. 'But I'll bet I've had more fun!'

Ryker's amused chuckle didn't help Borsch at all. Dropping the gun into his pocket he went out of the gallery without a backward glance. Ryker indicated the Mauser. 'I still think it's a bit on the light side.'

'It'll do for now,' said Lee. 'But on the day I'll use the Walther P.38.'

Ryker nodded, satisfied with the choice, and they left the gallery, climbing the stairs to the lounge above. Borsch had gone out on to the terrace, but sprawled on the sofa with an expression of bored disinterest was a man he hadn't seen before. As Ryker entered he rose languidly and held out a well-manicured hand.

'Lovely to see you, Paul,' he murmured, taking Lee in with a glance. 'I gather we're going to see a man about a plane.'

Ryker nodded, shaking his hand. 'Lee, this is Jim Matheson. one of the best pilots you'll meet.'

Lee nodded coolly. The man looked as though he would be more at home flying a kite. He was tall, with wavy blond hair, narrow eyes and a pale, sallow complexion. He could have passed for thirty but was probably on the wrong side of forty. His pink shirt was carefully unbuttoned to a hairless chest, and his snug flared beige trousers impeccably tailored. He wore open sandals that showed off a perfect pedicure, and there was little doubt that the carefully shaped eyebrows owed much to a pair of tweezers.

Ryker was suggesting that they went out to the car, and as the pilot turned to leave, Lee was not at all surprised to see him collect a tooled leather shoulder bag from the chair by the door. He glanced at Ryker with wry amusement. 'You certainly can pick them.'

Ryker considered him bleakly. 'Sometimes, Lee. But don't make the mistake of thinking he's as easy as that inept fool you dealt with last night. Matheson spent the last three years

96

flying Mirages out of the Lebanon. He survived enough missile attacks for the Israelis to refer to him as the Black Shadow.'

'I think the Pink Panther would have been more appropriate,' drawled Lee.

Ryker gave him a wintry smile. 'Try telling him that.'

'No thanks,' said Lee, 'I'm all for one big happy family, And while we're on the subject, the next time you put a tail on me I won't screw around with cigarettes!'

'Then stay away from my property,' said Ryker, his eyes suddenly cold and deadly. 'I have plans for Suzanne – and they don't include the hired help.'

He stalked through the door, leaving Lee to follow. Across the room Milena was watching with a quiet, mocking smile. Lee produced a grin that gave no indication of the grim forebodings he felt. He could only hope that Suzanne followed his instructions, and Ryker was not prepared to jeopardize the operation at this stage. But it was with a feeling of helpless frustration that he left the villa. He realized now that his emotional involvement with Suzanne was creating a showdown with Ryker that could destroy his own value, and when it came to the crunch he knew there was only one course he could take.

Twelve

The dapper little man with horn-rimmed spectacles and crocodile shoes met them on the tarmac outside the private service hangar at the airport. He bobbed his sleek, perspiring head at least a dozen times as he shook Ryker's hand, introducing himself to the rest of the group as Henri Davereaux, the Algerian manager of Panatel Air Charters. Ryker finally disengaged his hand with barely concealed distaste and introduced Matheson as his chief pilot. Lee wondered drily where all the junior pilots were supposed to be, then fell in beside Borsch as Davereaux led them proudly towards a gleaming white Hawker Siddeley executive jet.

'You will note, gentlemen,' he burbled, 'that this is the Series 600 version of the now famous H.S. 125. It has a maximum cruising speed of 518 m.p.h. at an altitude of 27,000 feet with the necessary fuel reserve for 45 minutes, assuming an average payload of . . .'

Matheson interrupted him with a condescending look. 'I'm fully aware of the specifications, darling. Just show me the engineer's log and then we'll have a trot round and see if all the rubber bands are in place.'

Davereaux almost dropped his glasses as he snatched them off to damp down the perspiration with an already limp handkerchief. He gazed beseechingly at Ryker who stared back impassively. Without support from that quarter he managed only a rather shrill laugh, patting Matheson on the shoulder. 'We joke, eh? The English joke.'

Matheson had stopped beneath the twin jets mounted below the tail. He stared at them long enough to bring the perspiration out on Davereaux's face again, then shook his head in despair.

'Is . . . is something wrong, Monsieur?'

'It's greasy,' he said, with a grimace of distaste. 'I do hate greasy aeroplanes!'

'It will be cleaned tonight, I promise,' said Davereaux fervently. 'But the engines themselves – Rolls-Royce – superb.' He kissed his fingers in ecstasy.

'Let's hope so,' Matheson said with enough scepticism to bring a look of despair to the man's face. 'I don't suppose we can do anything about the colour? I mean – it doesn't exactly fill one with rapture.'

The Algerian was rapidly getting out of his depth. In desperation he led them to the companionway and into the main passenger cabin. Lee watched with amusement as the Englishman looked at the deep black leather armchairs with disdain, then moved on towards the flight deck. Davereaux turned to Ryker, pushing a number of forms at him.

'I'll need your signature, as the registered hirer, and the pilot's as Captain.'

'Of course,' said Ryker, signing the documents quickly with a gold pen. 'But you are aware that I requested seating for fourteen, not eight.'

Davereaux looked at him in horror, 'But I understood . . .' He stopped, then forced a desperate smile. 'It can, of course, be changed.'

'When?' asked Ryker bleakly.

'I would have to see the service manager,' he said weakly. 'Perhaps – two days?'

'Tonight,' said Ryker. 'Make sure it's done tonight.'

There was a shrill whine from the rear, then a full-throated roar as the Viper turbojets started up. Davereaux looked towards the flight deck in alarm.

'He mustn't do that. Not yet.'

'Why not?' Ryker asked patiently.

'He must sign the forms. I must see his registration, his pilot's log, there is a set procedure . . .'

Ryker took a folded cheque from an inside pocket and handed it to him silently. Davereaux opened it, studied the amount and nodded with some relief. 'Ah, yes,' he said. 'You're paying the full amount in advance.'

Ryker handed him a second cheque. 'Plus ten thousand deposit, just in case I need it for a second week.'

Davereaux beamed at him, his head bobbing at half-second intervals now. 'Splendid. I'm sure you'll be delighted, Mr Ryker. Now if we can just get on with the pre-flight check.'

Borsch and Lee took an armchair each and started to strap themselves in as Ryker and Davereaux went on to the flight deck.

'Are we taking him along?' Lee asked.

'After five minutes with Matheson he'll be begging to get off,' replied the German, with a rare display of humour.

On the flight deck Matheson was settled comfortably into the pilot's seat, his pink shirt and gleaming blond hair in stark contrast to the black Bakelite panels and rows of switches. Davereaux settled nervously into the co-pilot's seat, accepting the check-list Matheson handed him.

'I've gone through the pre-start checks,' he said casually. 'Port and starboard engines fired without too much bother.'

'Splendid,' said Davereaux.

'Let's get on with it then, darling,' Matheson said, and began flicking switches, checking gauges and dials, reading them off at machine-gun speed without once referring to the clipboard in front of him. Davereaux watched with growing relief, a look of incredulous delight breaking through the perspiration as he began to realize this was no two-bit flier he had on his hands.

'Excellent, excellent,' he burbled happily as Matheson dropped the clipboard into the slot beside him and eased the throttle forward. 'You may clear for take-off.'

'Already have, luvvy,' said Matheson, moving the mike on its flimsy boom in front of his mouth. 'Able Charlie to Algiers control. How are we for take-off, sweeties?'

The reply was brief and to the point. Matheson smiled and pushed the throttle levers forward, a quick glance at the dials as the engines rose to a high, throbbing roar, then he was releasing the brakes and they rolled forward on to the edge of the runway and made a graceful curve to face the long ribbon of concrete scarred with an arabesque of black rubber tyre burns.

'Able Charlie ready for take-off,' he murmured, his eyes sweeping the dials, his slender hands almost stroking the control column.

The response came and he pushed the throttles all the way forward. The Rolls-Royce 602 Vipers gave an answering roar and they began moving down the runway with rapidly increasing speed. Ryker had disappeared into the passenger cabin, leaving Davereaux buckled down tight with a man who looked as though he could fly but appeared to have very little respect for the half-million dollars worth of hardware at his fingertips. The runway was flashing beneath them now as the speed approached 180 m.p.h., the sleek jet eager to be away. Matheson eased back the control column and they leapt into a clear blue sky, the undercarriage retracting with smooth precision until a green light winked on the control panel and signified that the doors had locked beneath them.

'Able Charlie to Algiers control,' said Matheson crisply. 'Clear me for a double circuit.'

'You're clear,' answered the controller.

Matheson whistled tunelessly and wheeled the white jet against the sky, using full power to bring it round in a tight, crackling turn. He glanced at Davereaux, who managed to return a sickly smile, then snapped the throttles forward so that the roar died to a whisper and for a long breathless moment they hung a thousand feet above the gleaming white airport. The nose began to fall as their airspeed dropped sharply, but Matheson made no move towards the throttles, his expression one of languid disinterest as he watched the rows of dials. One after another the warning lights began to flash, then a persistent buzz from the stall indicator. Davereaux appeared to have stopped breathing, staring at the dials with mingled horror and disbelief.

The nose was trying to force itself up now, the wings wobbling, searching for the air pressures that would give them stability. They were falling at fifty feet per second, each beat of the stall indicator bringing them closer to the scarred tarmac of the airfield. Davereaux wiped a limp handkerchief across his face and opened his mouth to voice a desperate plea, but it froze as Matheson began to inch the throttles back and a soft rumble of power gradually built to a sighing roar as the warning lights flicked off one by one.

'Not bad,' said Matheson casually. 'But she's a teeny bit unsteady on full trim.'

Davereaux could only nod, gulping as Matheson stood the aircraft on a wing tip and turned it on to a perfect landing approach.

'Able Charlie to Control. Clear for landing?' Even before the answer came he was slapping the red handle of the landing gear, easing the throttles forward until they whispered over the strip of red and green lights to gently kiss the scarred runway. Davereaux relaxed visibly and, as Matheson put the powerful Vipers into reverse, found his equilibrium for the first time since they had taken off.

'Captain Matheson,' he began crisply, 'we strongly disapprove of activities which are outside the normal flight specifications of our aircraft. Your creation of stall conditions was well beyond the limits we allow. Furthermore,' he paused for effect, his small mouth pinched into a thin line, 'we insist that standard safety procedures be observed at all times.'

Matheson turned the jet off the runway and headed for the service apron, allowing Davereaux to continue in the same vein until he braked to a stop outside the maintenance hangars. The manager of Panatel finally ran out of steam and sat staring at him with prim disapproval.

'Is that all, sweetie?' Matheson asked mildly. Davereaux seethed, but managed a nod. 'Then let's get down to the nitty gritty. This lazy cow needs a full service and you'd better find a crew to do it tonight.'

'Nonsense,' spluttered Davereaux. 'It's fully serviced. We have a certified log and engineer's report.'

'I don't give a flying fuck what you have, it's got a ragged starboard engine, the hydraulics are soggy and the rudder is as stiff as an old boot. If you want me to sign your bloody piece of paper, you'd better get a night shift sorted out.'

Davereaux took all of ten seconds to consider the alternatives, then managed a tight smile and a bleak nod. 'Very well, Captain. It will be arranged.'

'Splendid. Now if you push off I'll take her up for an hour or so, just in case there's anything we've missed.'

The manager seemed about to argue, then sighed and gave another nod. He pushed the appropriate form towards him and held out a pen. 'You'll sign?'

'Of course, sweetie. But when I get back I'll expect to find a service crew waiting.'

Davereaux nodded as Matheson scribbled his name on the form, then clutching it to his briefcase clambered out of the seat and went back towards the main cabin. Matheson waited until he was clear of the plane, then eased the throttles back and taxied out towards the runway.

'Able Charlie to Algiers Control. Am I clear for take-off?'

'We have no flight plan on you,' said the Controller in a voice that suggested he couldn't really care less.

'That's all right, sweetie, we're just checking her out. I'll keep in radio contact.'

Matheson smiled bleakly as the Controller gave him clearance, then fed power to the Vipers and sent the sleek jet whining down the runway.

In the deep leather armchair Lee looked on an endless sea of sand etched with ragged wadis and occasional plateaux that looked little more than dark brown stains from this height, but could tower a thousand feet above the desert. They had crossed the ragged grey peaks of the Atlas Mountains fifteen minutes ago and were now deep into the heart of the

Sahara. Borsch had shown little interest in their destination, but Lee assumed this was because he had already been fully briefed by Ryker.

Below a small oasis drifted into view, a wide-based triangle of green speckled with a patchwork of buildings. The town was the largest they had seen, so Lee guessed it was El Golea. If Matheson turned east they would be making for Libya, if he went west then their destination was more likely to be Morocco. A moment later they banked steeply to the right, heading west, and almost immediately began to descend.

'Don't tell me we're going to land down there?' Lee asked, casually.

'I sincerely hope so,' Ryker replied drily, 'otherwise we've all been wasting our time.'

The shrill whine of the engines changed to a dull rumble and there was a thump beneath them as the undercarriage locked into place. Matheson's voice chuckled at them through the internal speakers.

'If I were you, sweeties, I'd buckle your seat belts and think beautiful thoughts.'

Borsch gave a quick, angry grimace towards the flight cabin and began to fasten his seat belt. Lee realized, with amusement, that the German was far from happy at the thought of landing.

'This I've got to see,' said Lee, rising and moving casually towards the flight cabin. For a moment Ryker seemed ready to argue about it, but contented himself with an irritated glance and began to fasten his own seat belt.

Matheson glanced round briefly as Lee entered and dropped into the seat beside him. He gestured negligently towards the barren surface rising towards them.

'A bitch of a place to build a runway.'

Lee nodded. 'Who had the idea?'

'One of the old wartime airfields. According to Paul it's been forgotten for about thirty years. Not even the camels know about it.'

'And you expect to land a jet like this?'

Matheson shrugged, his mouth creasing into a casual grin. 'Ryker's paying for it. Let him worry.'

He eased back on the controls and they sighed up over a low, rocky plateau to look down on a single finger of grey against the sand. A black Tuareg tent marked the beginning of the runway, and what looked like a truck was parked at the far end. It didn't look long enough to land a Cessna to Lee, and he gave Matheson a quick questioning look. He

103

was gently easing the throttle forward, almost floating the aircraft over the plateau so that it dropped sharply as it lost speed. At the last moment he fed full power to the engines and they surged forward, pulling out of the stall in time to sit squarely on the runway. Matheson chuckled softly, reversing the engine thrust and stamping on the brakes. With a shuddering roar and a protesting scream from the tyres, they hurtled down the short length of runway, bucking and jolting over the scarred and potholed surface. The truck shot towards them at an alarming rate as Matheson held the shuddering jet in a straight line down the centre of the runway. By the time they were halfway Lee was writing off the entire operation and trying to remember where the emergency exit was, but the two 3,750 lb. turbojets on full reverse thrust finally began to bite and the aircraft came to a shuddering stop less than fifty feet from the end of the cracked and cratered tarmac.

They sat looking at the truck for a full minute, before Matheson said softly: 'Christ!'

'If you think you can bring a Jumbo down on this you are out of your cotton-pickin' mind!' Lee said fervently.

Matheson grinned, eyes gleaming as though the idea actually appealed to him. 'It'll be fun.'

'Not for me it won't, so if you don't mind I'll try something else for a laugh!'

Ryker had appeared in the doorway behind them, his black eyes piercing into Matheson. 'Well?' he said sharply.

'If I can manage to reverse those bloody great Pratt and Witney's on time we'll have something like 200,000 lb. going for us. That should bring our speed down to about one hundred by the time we reach here.'

Lee gave him a disgusted look. 'In case you hadn't noticed, this is the end of the road!'

Matheson grinned. 'For the Jumbo, sweetie. Just for the Jumbo.' He gestured towards the desert ahead. 'If I fold the undercarriage here we'll need about a quarter of a mile of graded sand. That should be quite enough to stop us.'

'What about fire risk?' Ryker asked, his voice crackling with tension.

Matheson shrugged. 'I'll have jettisoned most of our fuel, and the 747 carries a pretty deep cargo hold for us to toboggan on. I don't think there's much risk.'

Ryker's eyes bored into the pilot for a long moment, then he nodded with satisfaction. 'All right, Matheson. A quarter of a mile?'

'Please. And if you can arrange to have it marked with the occasional splash of white, that would be lovely.'

Lee stared at them both in amazement. 'You don't seriously expect to get away with a stunt like this, do you?'

'If Matheson says it can be done, then it can,' Ryker replied bleakly.

'You're talking about one of the biggest pieces of hardware in the world. All you're going to do is make one bloody great hole just about there.' Lee stabbed a finger at the desert before them.

Matheson chuckled, completely unperturbed. 'It would be rather spectacular, but highly unlikely. On soft sand, belly down, she'll skate along quite comfortably.'

'It's settled then,' said Ryker with finality.

Matheson rose languidly from his seat, flashed Lee a silky smile and followed Ryker out of the aircraft. Lee sat at the controls for a long moment, repeatedly reassuring himself that it would never happen. Ryker and his group would never get off the ground in Rome, never get their hands on the controls of a Jumbo, much less get it this far. But a niggling thought kept surfacing. Rome's Leonardo da Vinci Airport was one of the largest and most complex in the world. He still didn't know the fine details of Ryker's plan, and if anything did go wrong he was going to be sitting in a million pound juggernaut which a pink-shirted nut blithely expected to plough across open desert at one hundred miles an hour.

It would be like going over Niagara Falls in a paper bag!

The gleaming white executive jet shimmered in the burning sun, the temperature a steady 135 degrees. Ryker and Borsch were waiting patiently for Matheson to explain to four Arabs the necessity of towing a grading bar backwards and forwards over a quarter of a mile of sand. The Arabs had emerged from the back of the truck with cheerful enthusiasm, but this quickly faded as Matheson explained what had to be done. Lee watched with interest as the pilot spoke to them in fluent Arabic, punctuating it with frequent affected gestures and persuasive smiles. The Arabs, for their part, contented themselves with sour looks and complaining gestures towards the sun.

'They're being just a teeny bit naughty about this,' the pilot said finally, moving back to Ryker. 'They insist that they were sent out here to clear the runway, and that's what they've done.'

'So how much more do they want?'

'As far as I can tell they're not frantically interested in more lolly. They've spent two days sweating their balls off and all they want to do is to get back to town and fill up on hash and Coke.'

Ryker looked towards the Arabs, who were huddled together in a disconsolate group. 'They have got the grading bar?'

'It's in the truck,' replied Matheson.

'Then tell them it's got to be done. If they can do it by tomorrow I'll pay them double.'

Matheson looked sceptical. 'A pound of hash might swing it, but then they'd never get round to doing the work.'

'Tell them,' said Ryker deliberately, 'that if they don't accept my offer Borsch will burn their truck and beat the four of them to a pulp!'

Matheson blinked, then beamed and moved back to the Arabs. He spoke quickly for a minute, during which their defiance changed to indignation and finally terror. In a moment they had the heavy grading bar out of the truck and were fixing it into place with heavy chains. Matheson strolled back, lighting a cigarette and giving Ryker a confident nod.

'They'll get on with it, but someone should stay.'

Ryker glanced briefly at Lee then moved on to Borsch. 'It'll have to be you, Werner.'

The German nodded, his face devoid of expression. Beyond them the truck started up with a grating roar. Ryker handed him a wad of money and turned back towards the aircraft, mopping perspiration off his face. They wasted no time entering the cool, air-conditioned comfort of the executive jet and Matheson soon had it turned round and taxiing back along the bumpy runway.

Lee sat beside Ryker, wondering at the look he had exchanged with Borsch. He had a feeling that the four Arabs had made the biggest mistake of their lives by not promising to get on with the work, then getting out when they had the chance. The shrill whine of the jets rose to a shuddering roar, then they were moving forward as Matheson released the brakes and sent them jolting down the runway. They reached airspeed a comfortable distance from the end and roared up over the desert. Below the truck was moving slowly across the sand, the solitary figure of Borsch a small, but strangely menacing figure in the sun.

Thirteen

They touched down at Algiers Airport as the sun was setting behind the Atlas Mountains. Ryker had maintained a stoical silence throughout the flight, despite Lee's efforts to get him talking about the hijack plan. After fifteen minutes he had given up and joined Matheson on the flight deck, putting up with the flier's gay chat for the remainder of the journey.

At the maintenance hangars Matheson handed the H.S.125 over to a surly chief engineer with polite instructions to strip the bitch down to her socks, then swayed back to Ryker and Corey with total indifference to the engineer's gaze of studied contempt. They moved past the huge hangars, across the short apron that provided free parking for a variety of small private planes, and out through the wire mesh gates towards the main terminal building.

Bruno was waiting beside the white Cadillac as they crossed the wide pavement. There were a few passengers moving in and out of the terminal and they were halfway to the car before Lee picked out the figure of Hannigan leaning casually beside the entrance. He paused in mid-stride, glancing at Ryker.

'Give me a couple of minutes, will you?'

'Why?' barked Ryker, who was clearly in a hurry to get under a cool shower.

'I need a pee.'

'What the hell was wrong with the plane?'

'Nothing,' said Lee mildly. 'I just prefer to do it with my feet on the ground.'

Ryker gave him a withering look and marched on towards the car. Lee smiled bleakly and entered the terminal, crossing the wide marbled concourse to the toilets. Inside Hannigan was already waiting, a small briefcase open on the washbasin.

'What's the panic?' asked Lee.

'No panic, just a slight change in plan. Max has managed to put pressure on the Italians to bring the shipment forward.'

'I don't see the percentage in that,' Lee said, frowning.

Hannigan shrugged. 'There's no point in making things too easy for Ryker. He was planning for the week after next. Now it's in three days' time.'

'Good old Max!'

Hannigan grinned. 'He's getting edgy. He wants a complete breakdown of Ryker's operation.'

'Don't we all,' said Lee drily. 'The Connector plays it very close to the chest. We've been told no more than we need to know.'

'How about the escape route?'

'A wartime airstrip about two hundred miles west of El Golea. And that's one part of the operation I'm going to have pleasure in cancelling.'

Hannigan nodded and took a miniature camera from the briefcase, passing it to him. It was one of the neat little Japanese models with automatic exposure setting and electronic shutter. Lee slipped it into his pocket, knowing what was coming next.

'A present from Max.'

'Now he wants pictures!'

'Ryker's blueprint. Max reckons that Rome is a security man's nightmare. He's got to know the precise moves you'll be making, and the target of the German group.'

'He ought to try my end for a while. He'd feel lucky if he found out what day it was!'

Hannigan gave him a sympathetic look and closed the briefcase, moving to the door.

'How about the tapes in the plane? Anything?'

Lee shook his head. 'Save yourself the trouble.'

'Okay. If you get a chance to use the camera call me at the hotel.'

Lee nodded and started to wash his hands. The big American paused, about to open the door. 'You realize this doesn't give you much time to take out Borsch?'

'There's never enough time to take out a man like that,' Lee said quickly. 'Just keep your fingers crossed that he doesn't take me out first!'

Ryker was waiting in the car with barely concealed impatience. Matheson had taken the seat next to Bruno in the front, so Lee settled down in the back and enjoyed a silent ride into the city. It gave him time to consider Max's decision with more care. On the face of it the new date for the bullion ship-ment served only to put pressure on Ryker, but there were other factors to take into account and these gave him some indication of what was going on in Max's mind.

The Ryker strategy had always been designed to trap a man who had consistenly planned ingenious and frequently brutal crimes throughout Europe. Over the years Ryker's organiza-tion had grown to the stage where he could command the respect of every professional crook in the world. A dozen major crimes in the past year had all carried his mark; brilliant timing and ruthless execution. With his kind of suc-cess it was only a short step to choosing one of the plum jobs for himself, and Ryker's ego guaranteed that would hap-pen. What Max had never envisaged was the scale of Ryker's plan. To hijack bullion was one thing. To do it under the cover of a fanatical terrorist raid on an international airport was another thing entirely.

No one who knew Max Weller for long could ever doubt his sincerity. He was a totally dedicated cop; a man who had fought for years to create a department within the FBI with the powers to operate in Europe as freely as the parent body could operate in the States. He achieved his ambition by ostensibly forming a group to liaise with Interpol, then promptly putting his key agents on undercover assignments throughout the world. But with Ryker he had bitten off a great deal more than he dared to chew. From the moment Stadelheim became a reality, C-2 was in up to the armpits and sinking fast. If Max withdrew Lee, he was going against everything he believed in; but if he carried on he was involv-ing a federal department in an international scandal . . . unless he won.

Lee could sympathize with the man's dilemma, but he could also appreciate that as long as he was part of Ryker's squad he represented a major threat to Max's own security. That was why Max had switched the bullion shipment. That was why he was asking the impossible. He wanted out, and if his panic measures meant that Lee Corey didn't get out too – who was going to point the finger? Lee sighed, touched the outline of the camera in his pocket. If he had any sense he'd toss it out with the garbage. But then, if he had any sense he would never have got involved with Suzanne Delar . . . And if Max knew about that angle he'd need oxygen.

Ryker remained in his abrasive mood throughout the dinner of cus-cus and succulent young lamb and so it became a stilted, sterile affair that defeated even Matheson's languid poise. By the time Milena was serving the thick Turkish coffee the pilot was clearly eager to be away. Pushing back his chair he dropped his napkin on the table and bowed mockingly to Ryker.

'I trust you'll excuse me, Paul, but it's time I trotted along to the Kasbah.'

Ryker considered him coldly, balancing the delicate porcelain coffee cup between his fingers. 'I don't want any problems, Matheson.'

'Problems?' The pilot's mocking smile grew tight around the edges. 'Why on earth should there be problems?'

'Don't get precious with me,' snarled Ryker. 'You know what I'm talking about!'

'My, we are in a bitchy mood,' murmured Matheson, but the smile had gone and there was an icy gleam in his eyes. 'From what I've heard you're about the last one to start laying down a code of conduct.'

'You're here to do a job, and that includes staying out of trouble.'

'I'm here to fly a bloody aeroplane, darling, and the rest of the time is my own.'

They stared at each other for a long moment. Ryker was in no mood for argument, but the pilot was equally determined to stand his ground. Once again Lee noted with surprise the edge of steel in the man. In so many ways Matheson was an enigma. From his mauve shirt, carefully unbuttoned to frame a small gold medallion, to his pale blue slacks and handmade shoes, he made a colourful figure. Yet there was far more to the man. It gleamed in the ice blue eyes that dared Ryker to go too far. It had been there in the slim, perfectly manicured hands that had clasped the controls of the 125 so gently, so effortlessly, to guide it firmly along the battered desert runway. Whatever tortuous path had led him to this villa in Algiers, it had not dulled his fire or blunted the spirit that had earned him the title of the Black Shadow.

Something of this thought communicated itself to Ryker as the tension built between them. The sheen of perspiration glowed on his dark features and the black marbles of his eyes suddenly dulled, as though a light had gone out. His thin mouth twisted into a cynical smile and he shook his head.

'Nobody's trying to tie you down, Matheson. I just don't want you to start making a name for yourself. Not when you can be traced back to me.'

110

'Chatting up a few boys at the bar isn't going to start an inquisition.'

'That's right,' agreed Ryker. 'But I know all about Beirut – and Athens.'

The pilot stiffened, his face flushing angrily. 'We all have to let our hair down now and then.'

'Not in this town. Not now.'

Matheson seemed ready to argue, but Ryker made a small, pacifying gesture. 'It doesn't matter. I know a place where you can relax. Bruno will take you.'

'What kind of place?'

'Your kind,' said Ryker wearily. 'Just stay off the hash. They mix it with any kind of shit they can find.'

The pilot hesitated, then nodded. 'All right. I'll give it a whirl.' He started towards the door, then paused to glance thoughtfully at Lee. 'How about you, darling?'

'No thanks,' drawled Lee. 'I'd probably cramp your style.'

Matheson grinned. 'I doubt it, but suit yourself.'

Milena followed him out into the hall, presumably to pass the instructions on to Bruno. Lee helped himself to cognac, watching Ryker. The man was fighting to suppress his anger. In spite of the arrogant façade, Lee was beginning to realize that Ryker was not half as strong as he pretended. The years in Algiers, surrounded by petty crooks, had dulled the edge of the man. There were flaws in his character, weaknesses which could warp his judgement under pressure.

Still simmering, Ryker waved a contemptuous hand after the departing flier. 'Unfortunately he's the best there is.'

'Maybe,' said Lee, 'but that doesn't mean to say he's good enough.'

Ryker bristled angrily. 'I said he's the best. The last thing I'm worried about is the landing.'

'Perhaps that's because you won't be sticking your neck out that far!'

The remark touched the right nerve and Ryker snapped at the bait. 'What's that supposed to mean?'

'Just that you seem to expect us to take a hell of a lot on trust. So far the plan you've told us has got enough holes in it to fly a dozen Jumbos through.'

'You'll be fully briefed when the time is right,' he said tightly.

'Sure, but I've got a nasty feeling that'll be far too late to pull out. I'll probably be on a plane coming in to land at Rome.'

Ryker fought to control his anger, his eyes burning into

111

Lee, probing for a motive behind the words. The American gazed back without expression, watching the indecision mount in the man as he debated whether to take a hard line and risk antagonizing a second member of the group, or to win his loyalty with a softer approach. The anger died as he chose the latter, rising from his chair and moving towards the study, indicating that Lee should follow.

The study was a long, dark, spacious room dominated by a black mahogany desk inlaid with ivory. Ryker crossed to it, gesturing to a deep leather armchair beside the desk.

'Sit down,' he said crisply, 'maybe it's time for you to get a closer look.'

Taking a key from the desk drawer, Ryker moved to what looked like an original Salvador Dali and swung it away from the wall to reveal a safe. Unlocking it he removed a dozen black folders, each marked with a serial number and the name of a city. Carrying them back to the desk he read off the names, dropping them beside the American.

'Paris, Naples, London, Hamburg, Oslo, New York, Beirut.' He tossed the last one at Lee. 'Rome.'

Lee opened it casually, finding a number of closely typed pages inside and two detailed plans. The first was a large scale map of Leonardo da Vinci Airport, the second what appeared to be a detailed plan of the cargo bay. A number of symbols were marked on the plans, and clipped to them was a schedule giving the time of every phase of the operation. With reluctant admiration Lee noted the complex pattern of movements that would start with Lodtz and the terrorists hijacking the Lufthansa flight 241 and its three hundred passengers and crew. The plans showed how, as Lodtz was holding the passengers as hostages for the release of Baader and Meinhof, Borsch and his group would be taking over the Pan American flight 394 with its cargo of gold.

According to the schedule the bullion would be loaded at 23.40 hours, some twenty minutes before the passengers were due to board. At that time, as the police assigned to guard the gold were rushing to deal with the terror on flight 241, they would enter the aircraft and dispose of the crew. They would be taxiing for take-off, with Matheson at the controls, before airport security even knew there had been a robbery.

Sheet after sheet listed equipment, the purpose and precise time it would be used. Every second was calculated, every move taken into account. It was a blueprint for chaos, a brilliantly conceived plan based on two factors. The airport security was designed to prevent people getting into prohibited areas, but no one would think of challenging a private executive jet making an unscheduled landing because of a faulty engine. While it taxied to the service area, Lodtz and his team would drop out into the darkness along the perimeter and move in without fear of detection to the Jumbo parked at Gate 17. By the time they launched their attack, Matheson would have booked the 125 in for an engine overhaul and, with bitter complaint, agreed to collect it two days later.

Lee put the file aside and looked across at Ryker, who was watching him with glowing eyes. 'Not bad,' he acknowledged. 'But suppose the guards don't rush off to deal with Lodtz?'

'You're big boys,' said Ryker smoothly. 'And you'll have help. There'll be three Italians with you, and two of them have worked in the cargo bay. That'll mean five of you to deal with anyone foolish enough to stay with the gold.'

Lee nodded, apparently satisfied, and casually indicated the other files. 'And those?'

'Current operations,' he replied smoothly. 'Robberies, smuggling operations, even a counterfeit deal in Beirut. Every one of them planned in detail to take place during the next few months, and every one foolproof providing my instructions are followed to the letter.'

Lee looked impressed. 'That's quite a string. You must have more contacts than the CIA.'

'An organization costs money. A great deal of money. But after Rome that will no longer be a problem.' He gestured at the files, his eyes gleaming. 'These will be the last operations I plan for a mere percentage. In future my terms will be slightly different. The only way to avail yourself of my services will be by joining my organization.'

Lee allowed himself to look mildly sceptical. 'Most of the outfits I know are pretty sharp when it comes to handing over control.'

'They'll have no alternative. Most of them are run by thick-skinned goons without an original idea in their tiny minds. They survive because they have a sufficient number of informants and a sufficient number of fools prepared to risk life imprisonment for a ridiculously small remuneration. By joining me they can take part in a wave of crime the like of which Europe has never known.'

Ryker finished, breathing hard, his eyes burning with the intensity of his passion. Watching him, Lee was reminded of Max Weller's words six months ago. 'Give him half a chance, and he'll organize western Europe – and once he's done that we'll never get close to him again.'

The phone rang and Ryker picked it up, his face still flushed with dreams of power. The voice at the other end spoke rapidly in Italian. It went on for a long time, then Ryker asked a number of questions, also in Italian. Lee understood enough to know that this was the call Hannigan had warned him about, but Ryker's expression gave nothing away as he put the phone down. Picking up the files, he carried them to the safe, put them in and locked it carefully before returning to the desk. His eyes were hooded, unreadable as he sat down, steepled his fingers and considered Lee thoughtfully.

'The test of any plan is its adaptability to a changing situation.'

'So?' Lee looked vaguely puzzled.

'So no matter what steps the Rome authorities take to protect their precious gold, we are in a position to take an equal number of steps.'

'You mean we've got problems?' Lee asked tonelessly.

Ryker's glance flicked at him, then he grinned wolfishly. 'Almost. Fortunately my informant in Rome is on his toes. Now the only difference it will make is that we will all be very much richer – very much sooner.'

'I'll buy that,' smiled Lee. 'How much sooner?'

'In three days' time.'

'That's pretty tight. Suppose your Germans aren't ready?'

'One thing you must admire in the Germans is their efficiency. They'll be ready now, and the sooner they go the less chance there is of Lodtz being discovered.' He chuckled to himself, warming to the idea. 'It changes nothing. Even the flight schedules are the same.'

Ryker picked up the phone and dialled the operator, dismissing the American with instructions to send in Milena. As he closed the door Ryker was asking for a number in Munich.

Lee spent the remainder of the evening sampling Ryker's excellent brandy and giving the impression that he felt like an early night. Ryker spent most of the time on the phone, rearranging his schedule. He appeared briefly at ten o'clock, looking surprised to see Lee, gesturing towards the city as he poured himself a large whisky.

'Don't tell me you've already lost interest in our local – amenities?'

Lee shrugged, ignoring the silky smile. 'I decided to get an early night.'

'Excellent,' said Ryker. He paused, splashing soda into his

114

whisky, his black eyes fixed intently on the American. 'It's such a pity that your interest in the attraction at the Club Arabesque was so – ah . . . futile.'

Lee grinned back. 'You can't win them all.'

'Indeed you can't,' chuckled Ryker.

A phone rang and Milena appeared, crossing swiftly and entering the study to take it. Ryker sampled his drink, nodded with satisfaction, then moved back towards the door as Milena appeared. She spoke to him briefly, her voice low and urgent. Twice they glanced towards Lee, Ryker's face darkening with suppressed anger, then he spoke in a quick, savage voice and went into the study, slamming the door. Lee gave an exaggerated yawn and finished his brandy. Milena watched him, and as he rose to leave moved to intercept him.

'Are you quite sure you're not going out, Mr Corey?'

Lee considered her with a mildly surprised expression. 'Sure I'm sure. What's it to you?'

'Nothing,' she said simply. 'But if you did decide to change your mind, some of us might get the wrong impression.'

Lee continued to look puzzled. 'What kind of impression?'

She hesitated, beginning to look doubtful. 'I warned you yesterday about our mutual friend. If you should decide to visit her tonight . . .?'

She left the question hanging. Lee let the puzzled expression change to irritation. He glanced towards the study, then back to her, his mouth tightening angrily.

'Why the hell should I visit her? She usually comes here after the show.'

Milena nodded, her dark eyes probing his face for some flaw in his expression, but finding none. She forced a small, cool smile. 'Of course. Have a pleasant night, Mr Corey.'

Lee gave her an irritated, baffled look, then moved on into the hall to climb the cool marble stairs to his room. The soft swish of the silken kaftan told him she had entered the hall and was watching him all the way up the stairs. He didn't look back, fully aware that they both suspected he was behind Suzanne's refusal to return to the villa that night. Not that it mattered. Ryker would have his hands full from now on, and it was unlikely that he would jeopardize the Rome operation for the sake of a girl.

In his room Lee stretched out on the bed and set the small travelling clock to wake him at 1 a.m. He went to sleep thinking of Suzanne in her small room surrounded by the collection of ornaments, so vulnerable, so helpless against the kind

115

of pressures Ryker would use when he found the time. Not for the first time, he doubted his wisdom in influencing her decision; doubted his own motives and his ability to provide any kind of protection when the chips were down. It was a troubled sleep, broken finally by the soft buzzing of the alarm. A glance at his watch showed that it was a minute after one. Moving swiftly and silently, he crossed to the balcony that led into the lounge. There were no lights, no sound of movement.

Satisfied, he removed his shoes and socks, then crossed to his suitcase. It had a battered, well-used look about it, the black leather carrying enough scuffs and scars to suggest it had seen many years' service. This was precisely what the FBI development laboratory had intended. Opening the case, Lee pressed the recessed stud in the bottom right-hand corner. With a click the side of the case fell open to reveal a long narrow compartment. Inside was a thin nylon rope, strengthened with copper wire, a selection of skeleton keys and a variety of tools that would have delighted any professional safe-cracker.

Lee took the rope with its collapsible grapple and the skeleton keys on to the balcony where he attached the rope to the main stanchion, then eased himself over and slid down to the balcony below. He stood for a full minute, listening for any sound of movement from the lounge, then quickly unlocked the doors with one of the skeleton keys and stepped into the room. His bare feet made no sound on the tiled floor as he crossed to the hall, listened again for any sound of movement, before moving back to Ryker's study. He knew the door was going to be a problem. The cylinder lock, requiring a double turn to release the locking bar, was one of the most difficult devices to pick. Using a fine steel probe with a herring-bone tip, he spent five tense minutes gently counting the teeth before he was satisfied that he had the right sequence. Reversing the probe to use the broad flange, he quickly pressed a series of points, each movement rewarded by a soft click. A moment later the door was unlocked and he stepped inside, closing the door and resetting the lock before switching on the light.

Ryker had taken the added precaution of locking his desk drawer, and a quick inspection showed it to be one of the awkward hand-cut variety. The skeleton keys were useless, but forcing it was out of the question. With a sigh of resignation Lee returned to the steel probe and settled down beside the lock. It took all of ten minutes to find the correct pressure point, but once it was located, a quick twist of the probe unlocked the drawer. The key to the safe had been dropped casually beside a bundle of correspondence and a small cassette recorder. Collecting it, he crossed to the Dali and pulled it aside to reveal the safe.

The villa breathed silently around him: the whisper of the air conditioning, the occasional throb of a deep freeze somewhere in the bowels of the house, the odd creaks and groans of stone and timber contracting in the cool night air. Every nerve was tuned to the sounds, ready to flash the signal that would pump adrenalin the moment an alien noise intruded.

He carried all the files to the desk, switching on the lamp and positioning the first page so that the automatic exposure could cope. Then he was working fast, clicking out each frame as quickly as he could turn the pages. After fourteen frames he had a complete record of the file, but there was time and sufficient film to give Max a little bonus. Turning to the other files, he photographed the contents of operations scheduled for New York, Paris and Beirut, before the camera was empty.

Switching off the lamp, Lee was carrying the files back to the safe when he heard the sound of the front door opening. It was followed almost immediately by voices. He could distinguish Ryker and the deeper voice of Bruno, also a woman. Cursing softly, he put the files into the safe, closed and locked it and returned the key to the desk drawer. The voices were entering the lounge now. There was no time to lock the desk drawer, barely time to run across the study to a shadowy recess beside the door. Flattening himself against the wall he tried to hear himself think above the pounding of the blood in his ears.

The door opened and Ryker entered, crossing to the desk. Lee waited with the copper taste of fear in his mouth, knowing that if Ryker tried to unlock the centre drawer he would realize immediately it had been opened. The door to the study had been pushed wide, almost shielding Lee, but also preventing him from seeing what Ryker was doing. Moving slowly, not even breathing, he leaned to look around the edge of the door. Ryker was opening the side drawer of his desk, taking out a small black book, then moving back towards the lounge. He passed within two feet of Lee, but he was already intent of the people in the room beyond.

'You think I'm giving you a load of crap? You think this whole thing is some kind of game?'

117

He snarled the questions as he went into the lounge, gesturing with the book in his hand. The next voice confirmed Lee's suspicions.

'I didn't say that.'

It was Suzanne, her voice thin, etched with fear. Lee moved again, turning so that he could look through the crack in the door, seeing Ryker staring at the frightened girl with contempt. Bruno loomed over her, a huge hand gripping her arm above the elbow. She seemed small and defenceless between them, her face white and strained. Ryker was flipping through the pages of the book, stopping now and reading from it.

'Delar, Harold. Age twenty-seven. Convicted of armed robbery January 9th, 1974. Sentenced to ten years at the Old Bailey on June 5th, 1974. Serving sentence at Wormwood Scrubs, Block D, Cell 243.' He pushed the book under her nose so that she flinched. 'It's there. Look at it. Now would I have that kind of information if I intended doing nothing?'

She shook her head wordlessly.

'All right then,' said Ryker, putting the book in his pocket. 'You better get one thing straight. Next time you try a trick like this with me I tear the page out, and all it means to your precious brother. Is that clear?'

Suzanne nodded miserably. Ryker looked at Bruno, who released her arm and stepped back. She rubbed it gently, her face pale, her eyes fixed on his as though expecting a command. He stepped closer, the anger vanishing to be replaced by a hot sadistic glow that suffused his features and twisted the thin mouth into a cynical smile.

'You've been a naughty girl, haven't you?' he said softly.

She looked up at him with a strangely eager expression. Although the face remained blank, frozen, the eyes burned with deep emotions; when she spoke her voice was low and submissive. 'Yes, Paul.'

'And naughty girls must be taught obedience, mustn't they?'

'Yes, Paul.'

'How must they be taught?'

The answer was a hushed whisper that barely reached Lee's ears. 'They must be . . . punished.'

Ryker chuckled softly and gestured imperiously towards the stairs. 'Then you'd better go and get ready.'

Lee watched her leave with mingled rage and frustration. Every nerve-end cried out for him to intervene, to take some positive action . . . to take Ryker by the throat and smash

118

some kind of comprehension into the man. Instead he stood behind the door, knowing with a sick futility that blowing his cover helped no one, least of all Suzanne.

Ryker was asking Bruno about Matheson, and from their conversation Lee realized that the pilot had not yet returned. The fact irritated Ryker and he muttered vague threats about what he would do if the flier came back high on hashish. They moved into the hall, switching out the lights in the lounge, and Lee allowed himself a small sigh of relief.

Crossing to the desk he quickly locked the drawer with the metal probe, then moved back to the door. Ryker was still in the hall, talking to Bruno, but after a moment he said good night and started up the stairs. Easing himself out of the study, Lee started across the darkened lounge towards the balcony. He was half-way across the room when the phone rang. For a split-second he froze, weighing the odds against reaching the balcony or getting behind the door. From the hall there was the slow tread of Bruno's footsteps as he moved towards the lounge, then the voice of Ryker calling down from the stairs.

Gratefully he lunged towards the balcony, snapping the door open and twisting out into the darkness, then pulling the door closed behind him even as the lights went on. Bruno appeared, moving towards the study, then pausing at the door as Ryker entered. They went into the study together, giving Lee enough time to lock the french windows, then climb on to the balcony. Quickly he pulled himself up to his room, hauling the rope up behind him, before leaning against the wall, letting the crisp night air dry the sweat on his face.

Stepping into his room, he stripped off his clothes, replacing the rope, keys and camera in the compartment of his suitcase. Below there were sounds of activity. Ryker bellowed up the stairs for Milena, then a moment later the front door slammed. From the garage outside came the throb of the car starting up. Lee slid between the cool, crisp sheets, feeling a deep sense of gratitude to whoever was responsible for the panic below. He assumed that the culprit was Matheson. He was probably making a name for himself at Ryker's expense, completely unaware that as a result at least two people would sleep well that night.

Lee drifted off to sleep, promising himself that he would be particularly pleasant to Matheson the following day.

Fourteen

Lee Corey awoke in the early hours of the morning with a nightmare vision of Suzanne being brutally tortured by Sigrid, watched by the grinning figures of Ryker, Borsch, Milena and Bruno. He glanced at his watch and saw that it was only five a.m. He lay back trying to relax, irritated by the dream. He could still hear the scream. A deep, sobbing cry of agony that seemed to echo throughout the house. Yet, strangely it had not been Suzanne's voice. It had been deeper, stronger, the voice of a man. As he drifted back to sleep a nagging thought kept telling him that it was a voice he should have known.

The next time he surfaced it was after nine o'clock and the sun was building a stifling heat in the room. He stumbled out of bed, opening the windows on the way to the bathroom. The memory of the nightmare had faded, but he could still remember the scream. It picked at the corners of his mind until he finally pushed it aside in exasperation. He rarely dreamed and the last time he had been woken by a nightmare was more than four years ago.

He relaxed in the hot bath and allowed himself to recall that episode of his life, finding with some relief that time had dulled the pain. Dallas, in the year after the Kennedy assassination, had been a city that seethed with hatred and repressed guilt. A tall, proud city bloated by power and wealth, where minds were bent and twisted until wrong became right and politics just a word that justified any means, any solution. Although the FBI had officially closed its files on the Kennedy assassination, following the death of Oswald and the imminent death from cancer of Jack Ruby, there were still a number of inexplicable aspects that had to be investigated. Rumours and counter-rumours flourished. A series of murders took place, violent shootings that appeared to have a pattern, a tenuous web of intrigue that seemed to emanate from some nameless cancer in the city.

Lee had been sent in to put the pieces together, to see if the pattern was real and sinister, or simply a savage manifestation of the guilt that ate at the soul of Texas. They had called it the psychological backlash, the need to justify violence with more violence, to bolster the defences with hate and prejudice. It was a city of over-indulgence, where everything had to be done twice just to show that it had been done at all. And the violence had to be twice as savage, twice as brutal.

For the first time in years Lee allowed the face of Paula to float up before him. The golden, laughing face with clear blue eyes and blonde hair swept back like a tawny mane. She had been twenty-four then, with all the arrogance of youth and the vitality of a woman sure of her destiny and her man. They had been married less than a year, and she had refused point-blank to sit in their apartment in Washington, while he enjoyed a month in Dallas. Somehow he had never found a way of changing her mind, and even after a week in the city she could only see the tall, clean buildings and the wide, golden streets. The hate and prejudice that seethed and smouldered in the night was an alien thing, an ugly blemish she was not equipped to see.

And so they struck her down one evening while he was busy on the case. They just blew her apart with a pound of gelignite as she turned the key in the car he should have driven himself. He remembered the shock and grief that had stayed with him for a long, empty year. The rage that became a cold and bitter hatred for the men who had planted the bomb, for his own department who took him off the case when he tried to take the city apart. It had been a year before he worked again, and then only because Max Weller offered him a more personal way of hitting back.

Lee stepped out of the bath and towelled himself vigorously, the stimulation driving the memories back and putting an edge on his appetite. Donning a pair of slacks and an open shirt, he slipped on sandals and went down to the coolness of the dining-room.

Matheson sat alone at one end of the long, heavy mahogany table. He looked like a cadaver after a bad night at the morgue. His face was puffy, his eyes bloodshot pools of misery, and the perfectly manicured hands could barely support a heavy earthenware mug of thick, black coffee.

Lee dropped into a chair beside him, pouring himself

coffee and reaching for the croissants before wishing him a cheerful good morning. Matheson glared at him with silent contempt.

'You look rough,' said Lee, sympathetically.

'Piss off,' he replied, with simple candour.

Lee was unable to restrain a grin. 'You should have stayed in bed.'

'Of course I should,' said Matheson, wincing at the effort, 'but Ryker has decreed that Borsch must be back in time for lunch.'

'In that condition?' Lee looked at him in astonishment. 'You'll be lucky if you hit the runway!'

Matheson's sagging features stiffened angrily. 'Listen, darling,' he snarled, 'I'm not a sodding bus driver! I've hit my share of runways with and without hangovers!'

Lee shrugged. 'It's not my neck. I just thought Ryker would have had more sense than to send you off looking like Peter Pan after a bad trip with the fairies!'

For a moment he thought Matheson was going to hurl the mug of coffee at him, but just as quickly his anger evaporated and he began to chuckle as he saw the funny side of the description. Admittedly it was more of a restrained giggle than a chuckle, but the cutting analogy obviously appealed to the flier's sense of humour and soon swept away his black depression.

'You must come to breakfast more often,' he said, then had another fit of the giggles. 'Peter Pan and the fairies!' He hugged himself in delight. 'God, you should have been there. It was more like Snow White and the Seven Dwarfs!'

He went off again into gales of laughter. Lee waited patiently for him to recover. 'Ryker seemed pretty mad when he went off to get you.'

Matheson stopped, looking at him in surprise. 'Ryker? Not me, darling. I flew home solo – suffering from a filthy trip on one of the worst loads of grass I've ever been passed. I think the bastards must have laced it with opium.'

'My mistake,' said Lee. 'I thought you were the reason he charged out at two o'clock this morning.'

'Not me. As a matter of fact it's all been quite bloody mysterious. I got a message from Milena to bring Borsch home, but when I asked to see Paul, she just said that he wasn't available.'

Lee gave a casual shrug and changed the subject, chatting amicably until the pilot finished his coffee and left for the airport. Milena appeared briefly, but when he asked where

Ryker was her expression became even more remote.

'Mr Ryker will be busy until later today,' she said. 'If it's anything urgent I may be able to get a message to him.'

Lee told her not to bother and went up to his room, pausing at the corridor leading to Ryker's bedroom. Suzanne would be there, perhaps with Ryker. There was nothing he could do about it, he decided. Not now. Not with the operation less than forty-eight hours away.

In his room he collected the small cassette of film from the camera, slipped it into his jacket and went down to the hall. Milena appeared as he crossed to the door.

'Lunch will be at one,' she said coolly.

'Fine with me,' he replied.

She watched him leave with her flat, empty eyes, then crossed to a phone as soon as the door had closed. She pressed a button connecting her to an extension, speaking softly as soon as Ryker answered.

'The American has left, also Mr Matheson.'

'And the girl?'

'She's still sleeping. I don't expect her to come down.'

'Very well,' said Ryker, his voice thick and heavy. 'You'd better join us.'

She put the phone down and moved into the lounge, crossing to the study, which was empty. She closed the door and went to the heavy bookcase on the far wall, feeling for the concealed catch that swung it out to reveal the stairs leading down to the gun-room. From below there was a sudden gasping moan, then a muffled cry of pain. She paused, listening, her eyes beginning to glow. The sound came again. A long, shuddering animal cry. Milena smiled and descended the stairs, the bookcase closing silently behind her.

Lee took his time moving through the old town, pausing occasionally in the colourful souks to check on any unhealthy interest in his progress. After an hour of strolling through a maze of steep arched alleys, he was sure that no one was following. He made his way to the Kasbah, descending the narrow street into the new town. He was soon in a busy area of French-style arcaded boulevards and shaded squares. Crossing Boulevard Che Guevara, he entered a quiet square where he knew there was a group of telephone kiosks. As a further precaution he stopped at a pavement café and spent five minutes watching the passers-by over a glass of mediocre wine before stepping into the phone kiosk to dial Hannigan's hotel. Reception answered and he gave the room number, waiting a full two minutes, before the disinterested voice returned to say that there was no reply.

Leaving the kiosk he went back along Che Guevara, losing himself in the throng of tourists and shoppers. After fifteen minutes he found another phone and tried again. Hannigan was still not in the hotel and according to the receptionist had been out all morning. Lee cursed with feeling, turning into the first bar he saw to kill a further fifteen minutes with a glass of tepid beer. It was now well past noon. Whatever had pulled Hannigan away from his hotel must be important, but the agent had to be back by now. Going out into the street he headed for the impressive five-domed Djamaa Djedid, reaching the mosque only to find all the phone kiosks busy. It took two impatient knocks and a menacing look to persuade a black-garbed woman to cut short the story of her life and let him get on with his.

'I'm sorry, sir, but Mr Hannigan is not answering his phone,' said the disinterested receptionist.

'Now what's that supposed to mean? Is he in the hotel or isn't he?'

'One moment, sir.'

The voice went away, leaving him hanging on to a vacuum. He waited with mounting frustration. The last thing he wanted to do was return to the villa carrying the film. It would mean going out again this afternoon, after Borsch had returned, then arranging a rendezvous that was risky at the best of times. The voice returned to inform him blandly that Mr Hannigan was not in the hotel.

'Did he leave any message?'

'No, sir. If you'd care to leave your name . . .?'

Lee put the receiver down and left the kiosk, flagging down a cruising taxi which took him back up the hill above the bay to Ryker's villa. He had no alternative but to try again after lunch, but he was already analysing the situation and coming up with a lot of disturbing answers. Hannigan would have expected him to try to use the camera last night, so it followed that Lee would have contacted him at the hotel that morning. Only an extreme emergency would have made the agent leave his room, but having done so he would have left some kind of message saying what time he expected to be back. No Hannigan and no message added up to a lot of trouble. He considered phoning the Embassy, then rejected the idea almost immediately.

The FBI had no permanent establishment at the Algiers Embassy and the diplomatic staff had probably never even

124

heard of C-2, let alone Lee Corey. He considered the situation with mounting concern as he neared the villa. About the only people he could trust with the film were the Ambassador or 1st Secretary, but the chances of getting through to either of them on the phone were small, unless he blew his cover and gave a C-2 classification and priority rating. Even if that worked the possibility of setting up a high level meeting was remote to say the least. They would insist he went to the Embassy, cover or no cover, and if Ryker didn't know within two minutes of his walking under the Stars and Stripes he wasn't half the man he thought he was.

Paying off the taxi outside the villa, Lee rang the bell and flashed Bruno a breezy smile that got absolutely nowhere. Matheson and Borsch were already eating when he entered the dining-room, the German attacking a mountain of rice and peppered beef with enough enthusiasm to suggest that his vigil in the desert had not been noted for its gastronomic delights. Lee accepted a plate of food from Milena, nodded cheerfully at Matheson, who was looking distinctly sulky.

'How did it go?'

Matheson said nothing, but looked at Borsch who lifted his head from its permanent position three inches above the plate and stared at Lee as though he couldn't even remember his name.

'We're back, aren't we,' the German said through a mouthful of rice.

'Have you seen Ryker?' he asked, ignoring the cold-eyed stare. The German nodded. 'Then you know about the panic?'

Borsch gave him an oddly startled look. 'Panic?'

'The new schedule,' Lee said patiently.

Borsch relaxed, strangely relieved, then gave a non-committal shrug. 'We're ready. The sooner the better.'

The German returned to his meal, showing no inclination to discuss it further. Matheson, a very subdued figure, quickly finished and announced that he was going to catch up his sleep. Lee watched him go, noting his sallow, strained features. Something had happened out in the desert that morning and he had the distinct feeling that Matheson didn't like it.

'Did you finish grading the landing strip?' he asked casually.

Borsch nodded, not bothering to look up.

'How about the Arabs?'

He stopped eating, staring at him deliberately for a moment before reaching for his glass of beer. He took a long drink,

125

his cold, unblinking gaze fixed on Lee.

'They're paid off,' he said finally.

'But will they talk?'

Borsch wiped his mouth on the back of his hand, then rose from his chair and started for the door. He had to pass Lee on the way and as he moved behind his chair, he reached out and grasped his wrist hard, staring up into the gaunt, empty face with tight anger.

'I asked you a question, Borsch!'

'Forget about the Arabs.'

Lee stared up at him, making no attempt to conceal his disgust. 'Was it Ryker's idea, or yours?'

The German reached across and twisted his hand off his wrist, the pale eyes burning with a brief anger. 'You're getting to be more trouble than you're worth, American.'

Lee rose to face him, certain now that he had shot down the Arab workers, probably the moment they finished the job. He let the rage course through him, hoping the man would give him some excuse to take him apart. Borsch's eyes widened with surprise as he recognized the eagerness in Lee's face, then his hand moved casually towards his left shoulder.

'Go on, Borsch,' Lee said softly. 'Try to get it out.'

The hand stopped. 'What's your game, Corey?' he asked with genuine bewilderment. 'What the hell are a few poxed-up Arabs to you?'

'They're people, not bloody camels.'

'So?'

The German was looking at him with a complete lack of comprehension. Lee controlled his anger with an effort, reminding himself where this was and whom he was dealing with. He gave a tight, cynical smile and shook his head in disgust.

'You're too stupid to understand. As far as you're concerned a bullet solves everything, but you're forgetting about tomorrow and the day after that. If you'd left them alone it would have taken three or four days for them to get back to Algiers, and by that time we would have been all through. Instead we've got four missing people, four bodies that can point a finger at that airstrip and tell any fool who passes by that something is going on – something that had to be covered up.'

'Don't give me that crap,' Borsch said thickly. 'It's the middle of nowhere. The chances of anyone passing are a million to one.'

'They were!' Lee said harshly. 'But even your poxed-up

Arabs have friends, maybe even wives and families. Maybe they know where they went. And maybe, just maybe, someone will go out to see what's keeping them!'

Borsch shook his head stubbornly. 'Why the hell should they?'

Lee gazed at him with utter contempt. 'You're dangerous, Borsch. You're just a walking zombie with a gun in your hand. If you dropped dead tomorrow the only person who would give a damn is your bank manager. The trouble is, you can't understand that the rest of the world doesn't work that way.'

The German looked at him silently for a moment, his face devoid of emotion, then he tapped the gun beneath his jacket with a deliberate finger. 'Just as long as you understand the way I work, Corey. That's all you need to worry about!'

With that he turned and walked out, leaving Lee with the chilling realization that the German had been completely unmoved. Despite the insults, he was perfectly calm and controlled. The knowledge brought a deep sense of foreboding. Somehow Borsch had to be removed if Max's plan was to have any chance of success, but the German's cool composure suggested that any attempt to provoke him would only have a reverse effect and serve to put him even more on his guard.

Lee took his time over the meal, reflecting on Borsch's strange reaction to his question about the change of plan. It was as though he had believed for a moment that Lee had been referring to something else. The more he thought about the German's startled expression, the more he was convinced that it had nothing to do with the robbery. Something was going on and if he knew the answer to that it would probably explain Ryker's absence. The realization brought a new and disturbing question. According to Matheson he had not seen Ryker the previous night, but Bruno and Ryker had gone somewhere – and in a 'hurry.

He was no closer to an answer by the time he had finished his meal. Leaving the dining-room he went into the hall, deciding to give Hannigan another try at the hotel. As he passed the lounge he saw Borsch and Milena in deep conversation by the door to the study. They were too intent on their discussion to notice him as he paused in the doorway. Milena was gesturing towards the study, showing Borsch something in her hand. The German glanced at it, then moved quickly into the study with Milena. Lee gave them a minute, then strolled casually into the room, the heavy fur rugs deadening his footsteps. Crossing to the study he paused beside the door, which was partially open, and listened for the sound of their voices. The room was silent. Frowning, he stepped forward and pushed the door open, glancing quickly inside. There was no sign of Milena or Borsch, so that could only mean they had gone down to the gun-room. It also meant that Ryker was probably down there too.

He left the villa and headed into the old town, a deep sense of urgency in him now as he found a phone kiosk and called the hotel. Hannigan had not returned, they said, and he had not called to see if there were any messages. The suspicion in Lee's mind was beginning to crystallize into conviction. Hannigan was in trouble and the more he considered the facts, the more he came to the conclusion that this was behind Ryker's preoccupation and the reason for Borsch's surprise. He spent an hour weaving his way through the crowded bazaars and smoke-laden coffee shops, calling the hotel three more times before dialling the number of the American Embassy.

A man answered with a clipped, Boston accent and he breathed a sigh of relief. 'This is a G-4 priority,' he said crisply. 'Let me speak to the Ambassador.'

'The United States' Ambassador is away for the day. If you'll give me your name and phone number I'll have him call you tomorrow.'

Lee stared at the phone in disbelief. 'Listen, Mr . . .?'

'Mitchell,' the voice supplied helpfully.

'Mr Mitchell, I just gave you an FBI priority, so let's not have any crap about names and phone numbers.'

There was a long pause at the other end of the line, long enough for Mitchell to log the time and start the tape. 'I need some identification, sir, before I can respond to a G-4 request.'

Lee controlled his anger with an effort. 'My authority is C-2, Washington, and I have a G-5 rating.'

'I'm sorry, sir, but I need proof of identity. If you call at the Embassy I will . . .'

'Are you out of your tiny mind?' Lee snarled. 'I'm sticking my neck out just to make this call. Put me through to the 1st Secretary.'

'I'm afraid he's engaged, sir,' Mitchell replied smoothly.

'I need a liaison officer. Now stop screwing around and find me one!'

'The Commercial Attaché is here. Perhaps he can help you.'

Lee hesitated, wondering how far he could go with the official. The chances were that the Commercial Attaché was a CIA man, just as the FBI used legal attachés for their cover in embassies abroad. He already knew that there was no legal attaché in Algiers and had assumed, with the emphasis here on political rather than criminal activity, that the CIA would have a strong establishment.

'No thanks,' he said finally. 'I've given you my priority and you know that entitles me to immediate assistance at 1st Secretary level.'

There was a click on the line, then a new voice. 'This is Roger Jefferson. Maybe I can help you if you tell me what kind of assistance you require?'

'What's your department, Jefferson?'

There was a brief pause, then the voice said smoothly: 'Commercial Attaché.'

Lee had expected as much. The fact that he could take over the conversation meant that he was either CIA or Embassy Security, which amounted to the same thing. He had problems enough without Central Intelligence breathing down his neck, wanting to know his authorization for being here, his purpose and jurisdiction. They wouldn't rest until they knew it all, and then they'd have Max Weller and C-2 by the short hairs for as long as it suited them.

'Okay, Mr Jefferson,' Lee said casually, 'but I'll have to check that out with my own people. What's the chance of you patching me into your Washington tie-line?'

'No chance, friend, it's a separate circuit. Tell you what, though. You give me a run-down on your situation and I'll flash it through on our telex.'

Lee smiled bleakly and hung up. The cassette of film was beginning to burn a hole in his pocket. He went into a souk and purchased envelopes and writing paper, then found himself a secluded table in a small bar across the street. The only way he could get the information to Max in time was through the Embassy, but the only man he dared trust with it was the Ambassador himself. On a sheet of paper he wrote his authority, the priority and classification – a triple red – then heavily underlined that it was for transmission to M. Weller, Department C-2, FBI, Washington. The G-4 priority would tell the Ambassador that the film had to be put on the next available flight to Washington, with a coded telex to Max informing him of its time of arrival. He wrapped the sheet of paper around the cassette, disguising its shape as much as possible, then put them in an envelope addressed to the

United States Ambassador, U.S. Embassy, Algiers, and marked it 'classified' in heavy letters. Slipping it into his pocket he left the bar and headed for the nearest phone.

It was four o'clock and he hadn't the faintest idea how he was going to get the envelope to the Ambassador. Mailing it was out of the question, for even if it arrived at the Embassy unopened the chances of it reaching the Ambassador in that condition were remote. The only way was by hand, tomorrow, but if he showed his face anywhere near the Embassy, Ryker would know.

The hotel receptionist was beginning to get bored with the same question and told him curtly that Hannigan had not been in all day. Without much hope he dialled the international operator and was told there was a three hour delay for the States and two hours for France. He stepped out of the kiosk and glared at the passing traffic. Unless he was going to abort the mission and catch the next flight out, he had to go back and gamble on coming up with some way of getting the film to the Ambassador the following day.

He caught a taxi to the villa where he had to ring the bell half a dozen times before Bruno finally opened the door. He stepped into the hall, turning to regard the chauffeur with an irritated expression.

'I was beginning to think you'd all left on vacation.'

'I was in the garage,' Bruno said, without much conviction.

'So where's everybody else? In the attic?'

Bruno stiffened angrily at the tone, his huge hands clenching in an unconscious reflex. Lee gave him a mocking grin, hoping to goad him into giving something away.

'You've really got a cushy number here, haven't you, Bruno? If you ever had to go back to doing a full day's work the shock would kill you!'

The effect was much better than he had hoped for. The chauffeur's thick neck bulged, the muscles standing out like ebony ropes, the fat round face glistening as naked anger burned in his eyes. When he spoke his voice grated with contempt.

'I don't have to take anything from you. Not anything.'

Lee shook his head with an expression of studied contempt. 'You'll take what you're given, Bruno, that's all you're here for. Now where the hell is Ryker?'

The wide nostrils seemed to flatten with the intensity of his anger. He stepped forward, his eyes burning into the American so that, for a moment, Lee thought he had gone too far. He was big enough, and mad enough, to snap his neck with one of the huge sweaty hands. Instead the anger vanished, to be replaced by a sly, gloating look.

'Mr Ryker is busy.' He paused, a pale tongue flicking out over thick dark lips. 'He's busy with a friend of yours.'

Tiny electric shocks arced across the back of his neck and every muscle went taut. It couldn't be Hannigan, otherwise he would have met a bullet the moment he stepped into the house. With a sinking feeling he realized who the friend must be.

'Is that a fact?' Lee drawled. 'Who would that be?'

'Suzanne Delar.'

Bruno watched his face hungrily, searching for some response. The disappointment showed as Lee shrugged and turned away.

'Big deal.'

He was about to enter the lounge when Bruno spoke harshly behind him, determined to wring some kind of response.

'He's screwing her, Corey. Him and Miss Milena. They're teaching her all the tricks they know – and they know plenty, both of them at the same time, and that toffee-nosed tart begging for more. They always beg for more!'

Lee turned and moved back to him, his face pale, but composed. He managed a gentle smile and said softly. 'What do they beg for, Bruno?'

The chauffeur grinned, opening his mouth to speak as Lee brought his knee up sharply into the groin. For a moment the man made no sound, his eyes bulged and whitened with shock, and then the breath was wooshing out of his mouth and he was bending forward, holding the pulsing centre of agony with both hands. Lee left him on his knees, head bent low, gasping out a stream of curses. If he'd been facing east you'd have thought he was calling to Mecca.

The lounge was silent and deserted, so Lee crossed to the leather sofa and sat down, lighting a cigarette and waiting. It was three minutes before Bruno appeared in the doorway, his face gleaming with perspiration. Lee considered him calmly as he came towards him, waiting until he reached the white llama skin rug before picking up the ornamental dagger from the table beside him. Slipping it out of its gold-inlaid sheath, he waved it casually towards Bruno.

'If I were you I'd get back to the garage. I don't think Ryker would appreciate the kind of mess you'll make around here . . . crawling about with your guts hanging out!'

Bruno looked at him with a deep, burning hatred, then finally turned away. Lee waited until he heard the door close

131

to the staff quarters, then moved quickly into the study. There was little chance of Bruno returning, and Matheson would probably sleep until dinner. That only left Borsch unaccounted for, but there was an even chance he was in his room. Releasing the catch on the bookcase, Lee swung it out and silently descended the steps to the room below. A single light glowed in the shooting range, building shadows at each end of the room and etching the blood-stained figure in the centre with horrifying detail.

Lee moved towards it, a cold sweat beginning to film his brow as he saw the extent of Hannigan's injuries. He had been brutally beaten, whipped and burned, but these were minor events compared to the series of knife wounds that covered the lower half of his naked body. Lee felt the vomit rise in his throat as he saw what they had done to him. For a moment a black nausea threatened to engulf him, but the agent's eyes flickered open and he quickly knelt beside him. He was too far gone to speak, blood welling slowly from a dozen wounds, his eyes glazed and only barely able to focus. His mouth opened, the breath rasping in his throat as he tried to speak, his eyes widening with a desperate urgency.

'Don't try to talk, Hannigan, just lay still.'

Hannigan shook his head weakly, eyes rolling back, the mouth moving soundlessly. Lee bent closer, trying to hear the words, but there was only a dry rattle in his throat and then the head lolled limply to one side. Lee stared down at the wide, dead eyes for a long moment, then slowly rose to his feet and moved back towards the stairs. He had only taken a couple of steps before he realized that he was not alone, that he had made the fatal mistake of not checking out the room when he entered. He turned to face the end of the shooting range as Borsch stepped out of the shadows with the heavy Colt Commander in his hand.

'I never felt right about you, Corey. There was always something that stuck in my throat.'

'The feeling was mutual,' Lee said bleakly.

Borsch stepped closer, gesturing at the still body of Hannigan. 'I'd never have known if you hadn't been careless. Ryker worked on him for twelve hours and got nothing at all.'

'Then you took over?'

Borsch nodded, his thin mouth twisting contemptuously. 'We had a little discussion. He knew he was never going to get out of here, so I had to show him a few of the alternatives!'

'You filthy bastard!'

Borsch smiled a rare smile and raised the gun. Even as his finger tightened on the trigger, Lee forced himself to relax and look distinctly relieved. Although every muscle was tensing for the numbing shock of the bullet, his face showed none of this. All Borsch could see was his obvious relief and a gentle almost serene smile of resignation. The German eased his pressure on the trigger, his eyes narrowing thoughtfully.

'Come on, Werner,' Lee said helpfully. 'Get it over with before Ryker spoils your fun.'

It took a few seconds, but then Borsch began to get the message. Slowly he nodded, putting it all together and realizing that Ryker's presence was the last thing the American wanted. The sadistic Connector would never be content with a bullet. He would want to play, taking Lee through a nightmare of torment before finally, reluctantly, allowing him oblivion. That was why Lee would welcome a bullet, why he was almost eager to receive it.

Borsch laughed softly and backed towards the phone that hung on the wall. Lee waited, knowing he would only get one chance. His eyes flicked to the gunracks, noting that the locking bar was leaning by the side. No one had bothered to replace it. The nearest weapon was the Mauser machine pistol, not the perfect choice, but more than adequate as long as one of the heavy .45 calibre bullets didn't find him first.

The German had backed up against the wall, his gun held steadily on Lee, his left hand reaching out to the phone. There were four extension buttons beneath it and Borsch would have to glance towards them, if only for a split second. Lee took a long, deep breath and held it, watching the German's pale eyes. Suddenly they flicked away to the side. Simultaneously Lee's hand lashed out above his head, smashing into the naked electric bulb that hung from the low ceiling. The bulb exploded, plunging the room into darkness, and even as Borsch fired Lee was lunging to the left, using the precious seconds of blindness that they would both suffer to take four loping strides and a shallow dive that brought him up against the wall beneath the gunrack.

Borsch, firing by instinct, sent four shots towards the rack, knowing that Lee would try for a gun. The heavy calibre bullets exploded amongst the assorted guns, the booming echoes reverberating around the room, covering the sound of Lee's movements as he reached up to the rack, grabbed the Mauser and then dived back across the room, rolling as he cocked the gun to come up on one knee with the weapon

133

cradled in both hands.

There was silence in the darkened room. Borsch knew that if he hadn't already been hit, Lee would have a gun and be waiting for the flash of his own. Neither of them moved, each man waiting for his eyes to adjust to the darkness. Borsch fired four shots, so he couldn't afford to waste any more. He was also in the open, vulnerable to any random pattern. He had to find cover, and so he had to move.

Lee waited, eyes straining, not even breathing as his ears tuned to the slightest sound. It came from the end of the gallery, a whisper of movement that told him Borsch was heading for the sandbags beyond the targets. He fired a single shot, hoping Borsch would fail to recognize it as the Mauser, rolling immediately as the heavy Commander boomed out, flame lancing from the barrel as Borsch tried to place the shot exactly where Lee's had been. But the American wasn't there any more. He was on one knee, pressing down on the trigger, firing a stream of bullets across the room. The flash of each shot lit the area between them like a stroboscope, revealing the German in a kind of grotesque animation as the bullets tore into him, hammering him back against the sandbags, twisting him one way and then the next, until finally the shooting ended and darkness fell on the broken, bloody figure on the floor.

Lee stood a full ten seconds after the echoes of the shots had faded away, listening for some activity above. He was fairly sure that the soundproofing would have muffled the Mauser, but the shots from Borsch's much heavier weapon might have filtered through to the rest of the house. There were no sounds of movement, so he went quickly to the body and used his cigarette lighter to make sure the bullets had done their job. A quick glance revealed that Borsch must have been dead before he hit the floor. The Commander was lying nearby, so picking it up he carried it across to the body of Hannigan. First he pulled the agent's body so that it was lying closer to the gunrack, then he placed the machine pistol firmly in his hand. Using the cigarette lighter again, he took three steps back and fired one shot from the heavy Colt into the dead agent's chest, then returned to Borsch and laid the gun beside him. Anyone who found them would now assume that Hannigan had somehow broken the light bulb, then managed to get his hands on the machine pistol before Borsch could put a bullet in him.

It wasn't as neat as he would have liked, it wasn't even logical if you took the agent's terrible wounds into account.

134

But Borsch's death represented such a disaster for Ryker that his emotions would take over. Rage would blunt logic; shock would dull his ability to sit down and calmly deduce what must have happened. As Lee climbed the stairs to the study a voice at the back of his mind was reminding him that Ryker had survived this long because he had a talent for analysing events and predicting their outcome.

The house was quiet as Lee made his way back to his room. Once inside he quickly stripped off his clothes, tearing his shirt into strips and flushing it down the toilet before soaping himself vigorously under the shower until he was sure that the smell of cordite had been removed. He dried himself, putting the towel on the balcony, where it would quickly dry in the late afternoon sun, then donned a clean shirt and a fresh pair of slacks.

There was nothing left to do now but wait. He stretched out on the bed, the tension draining out of him as he forced himself to relax. There was only one way to play this now, if the operation was to stand any chance of success – but the odds were formidable and the more he went over the scene in the gun-room, the more pessimistic he became.

Fifteen

It was six o'clock before sounds of activity echoed up from the hall below. Ryker bellowed for Bruno in a harsh, savage voice. Then light footsteps came to the door, paused a full ten seconds before going away again. He guessed that would be Milena. The voice of Ryker faded as he went back into the lounge, then there was silence for a while. He lit a cigarette, staring up at the ceiling, preparing himself for the confrontation he knew must come.

When it did, it came with a shocking ferocity.

Ryker entered, followed by an impassive Bruno, neither of them speaking until they reached his bed and looked down at him. Lee lifted an eyebrow, stubbing out his cigarette.

'Get up,' Ryker said thickly.

'What's the hurry?' said Lee, looking at them curiously.

'Up!' snarled Ryker, raising his right hand to reveal the snub-nosed Magnum he was holding.

Lee swung his feet off the bed, allowing the mild curiosity to harden into anger. 'Now look, Ryker . . .'

He got no further. Bruno hit him savagely in the stomach, then straightened him with a handful of hair which he used to slam his head against the wall.

'That's enough!' Ryker said sharply, pushing the gun into Lee's face as the fury took hold of him and he started to swing at the chauffeur. 'You stand and you listen, Corey. Anything else and I'll blow a hole in you!'

Lee stared at him in cold fury, then switched his gaze to Bruno, who was gesturing to Milena standing outside. She entered, considering Lee impassively, then moved close to him and took his right hand. Raising it to her nose, she began to sniff at the hand, wrist and forearm. After a moment she turned to his left hand, then to his chest and hair. Lee watched with a baffled expression, glancing over her head to Ryker

136

whose eyes glistened like ebony marbles.

'I've heard of some pretty kinky routines, but this is ridiculous.'

'Shut up!' Ryker said savagely.

Milena took her time, but finally stepped back and shook her head. Ryker relaxed slightly, then gestured at the room. She nodded and went to the wardrobe and chest of drawers, checking the clothes, holding some to her nose and smelling slowly. The last thing she checked was the shower, but when she returned she seemed to be satisfied.

'There's nothing here,' she said.

Ryker turned to Lee, his eyes boring into him with cold menace. 'How long have you been here?'

'Ever since I kicked Bruno in the balls.' He glanced at the chauffeur with a grin. 'What time would that be?'

Bruno's face tightened angrily, but he turned to Ryker and admitted it had been about two hours ago.

'Is that what this is all about?' Lee asked.

Ryker shook his head, his rage still seething below the surface, but at least no longer directed at Lee. 'We've lost Borsch,' he admitted harshly. 'He was killed in the gun-room.'

'Christ!' Lee stared at them in amazement. 'What the hell is going on? You mean someone just walked in and chopped him?'

'No.' Ryker shook his head. 'We picked up an FBI agent last night. Borsch was supposed to be questioning him.'

'Last night!' Lee stared at them in disbelief. 'You mean you stupid bastards have been keeping an FBI man here? Without saying a bloody word!'

Ryker glared at him, white-lipped, his fury so great he could barely speak. Bruno moved restlessly, just waiting for the word to take another swing. Lee turned, his hands stiffening, ready for him now.

'Leave it!' said Ryker, sharply. 'We had to check you out, but you're clean. If you'd been near a gun Milena would have known.'

Lee gazed at him with contempt. He was clean all right. So clean it would take a fluoroscope to detect traces of cordite from the shooting. Matheson appeared in the doorway and looked at them curiously.

'We're all a bit frantic, aren't we? Anything wrong?'

Ryker was silent for all of ten seconds, his eyes boring into the pilot's who failed to show the slightest concern.

'We have a problem,' he said finally.

'Haven't we all, darling. Mine is trying to get some shut-eye when everyone is charging about, bellowing like bloody dervishes!'

Ryker maintained his icy calm with a monumental effort. Milena had closed in on Matheson, looking towards Ryker for some signal. The pilot had clearly been elected as Suspect Number Two, but no one seemed quite sure how to go about it. Lee decided to solve it for them.

'Borsch has been shot,' he said.

'By anyone we know?' Matheson looked mildly interested.

'Possibly.'

Ryker wasn't giving anything away, but if he was waiting for a response from Matheson he was going to be disappointed. The pilot considered the information for a moment, then shrugged and turned to leave.

'Well I shan't shed any tears,' he said cheerfully. 'He wasn't my type at all.'

'He was vital for the operation!' snarled Ryker. 'Absolutely vital!'

'Aren't we all, dearie.'

Matheson waved a limp, mocking hand, and went back to his room. Ryker watched him go with impotent rage, then turned savagely on Bruno.

'Take the car into town. Talk to Nicky or Leroche and tell them I want a disposal job done within the next three hours.'

Bruno vanished, more than happy to be away. Lee had moved back to the bed, sitting down and massaging his bruised ribs. Milena glanced towards him without sympathy.

'Do you need anything?'

'I'll let you know,' he said bleakly, watching Ryker who was walking around with the expression of a man about to cut somebody's throat. Lee waited until he stopped in front of him. 'So what about Rome?'

'How good are you, Corey?' he said, spitting the words at him. 'Are you worth half a million?'

'My mother always told me I was a little treasure.'

'Could you handle Rome?'

Lee appeared to give it some thought, enjoying the tension that was etching hard lines into Ryker's face. The mere fact that he was prepared to ask the question showed how hard the German's death had hit him. The most rudimentary logic would tell him that Lee could never cope with the Germans, even if they were prepared to let him.

'Well?' barked Ryker.

'No chance,' said Lee. 'Unless you can put Lodtz and Carl in handcuffs, they'll take over the moment we hit Da Vinci

138

Airport.'

Ryker didn't argue. He just uttered a single, savage expletive and stormed out of the room. Milena remained for a moment, considering him with open dislike.

'You don't seem to be very concerned, Mr Corey. There aren't many people who would reject a fortune so lightly.'

'Maybe not, but the prisons are full of the ones who thought they were too good to be caught. The solution is simple, and Ryker knows it. He's the only one who can take over and make it work.'

'Paul would never do that,' she said with conviction. 'He doesn't need to.'

'He's got to. Otherwise none of us are going anywhere.'

She stared at him impassively for a moment, then turned and followed Ryker downstairs.

Lee lay back on his bed, wondering how long it would take Ryker to accept the inevitable. Either he went ahead as planned, taking Borsch's place himself, or he cancelled the operation and wrote off a million dollars he had invested so far. There were too many factors weighing against cancellation, not the least of which were Ryker's own greed and ambition.

The answer came shortly after dinner. It had been a subdued meal, relieved only by the appearance of Suzanne. She had taken the seat next to Ryker, studiously avoiding Lee's eyes whenever he glanced her way. From her lack of interest in the food he guessed that she had been forced to join them. Her presence made it impossible to discuss the Rome operation, but as soon as they had moved to the lounge for coffee, Ryker suggested casually that Lee and the pilot should join him in his study.

Closing the door he crossed to his desk and picked up the bulky file marked 'Rome'. He gazed at them for a moment with his small, unblinking eyes, tapping it against the fingertips of his left hand. 'We go,' he said. 'We go as planned.'

Lee and Matheson exchanged glances, waiting for Ryker to enlarge on the statement. He didn't, and the silence built in the room.

'Who leads?' asked Lee, finally.

'I do. You were quite right, without Borsch I'm the only man Lodtz will accept.'

'Suits me, sweetie,' murmured Matheson. 'I'm just a teeny bit worried about the FBI interest.'

'Don't be,' Ryker said with conviction. 'The man we are holding is dead. He was picked up by a couple of locals I had watching the plane. There's been no alarm by the Embassy or our own police so we can assume he was snooping about on his own. I'm not exactly unknown to the FBI, or half a dozen police agencies for that matter, but without proof they can't touch me. Not here.'

The pilot nodded, satisfied. Ryker opened the file and passed him two documents.

'These are your flight plans. We rendezvous at Tonder Airport in Southern Denmark, about ten kilometres from the German border. Our Germans are already on their way by road, the Italian end will fly into Flensburg on the early morning flight from Rome.'

'These are the heavies?' Lee asked.

'Good boys. Of the three, two have worked in the cargo bay at Rome Airport and know their way around. What's even more important, they're bringing sets of coveralls used by the Italian cargo handlers.'

'Why fly them into Flensburg?' Matheson asked, studying the flight plan with a puzzled expression. 'That means they'll have to cross the German border into Denmark.'

'Exactly,' Ryker said crisply. 'When they leave Flensburg they switch identities and cross the border with visas that cannot be traced back to them. That way, if anything goes wrong, no one is going to pin anything on you and your private jet.'

'Jolly nice of you,' murmured Matheson. 'But don't worry about me. I have no intention of being at all aggressive. I will park the 125 with maintenance and saunter over to whichever Jumbo you fancy. Nothing more.'

'There won't be any more. By the time you get on board it will all be over.'

'Let's hope so, sweetie. Otherwise I saunter in the opposite direction on maximum revs.'

Ryker allowed himself a small, bleak smile, and turned to Lee. 'Our operation will coincide with the attack made by Lodtz's group. When they go into action we move on the Jumbo. There shouldn't be any problems, not with all hell breaking loose on the other side of the terminal. We'll be dressed as cargo handlers and should be able to get in close to the security guards around the aircraft.'

'How many of them?' asked Lee.

'There are fifteen scheduled to cover the bullion aircraft until take-off, but when the shooting starts they're bound to send at least ten to help out. That leaves six of us, and five of them.'

'Six?' Lee said questioningly.

Ryker hesitated fractionally, his eyes flicking away. When they came back he said: 'I meant five. I was forgetting about Borsch!'

Lee nodded, but in his mind's eye he was going over the operation schedule. Ryker was too much of a perfectionist to make a simple mistake like that. The sixth man could be Bruno, but there was no provision for him in the plan he had read. The knowledge worried him, for it raised the ugly possibility that Ryker still had an ace up his sleeve.

'There's only one change in the schedule,' Ryker was saying. 'We leave at eight in the morning, instead of noon. So I suggest you both retire early – and sleep well.'

He beamed at them, then bent over the file with a gesture of dismissal. They rose and strolled out into the lounge, where Milena and Suzanne were talking together on the sofa. They stopped speaking as soon as they entered, Milena rising to offer them coffee and brandy. Matheson declined the thick black Turkish coffee on the grounds that it ruined his sleep and his arteries, but filled a large crystal goblet to the brim with a fine Napoleon before waving a limpid good night to them all.

Lee crossed casually to Suzanne, dropping into a chair and lighting a cigarette before speaking softly through the smoke. 'What happened?'

She looked at him with strained features. 'I can't talk about it.'

'Sure you can,' said Lee. 'I'm a big boy now.'

She glanced nervously towards Milena, who was moving towards Lee with brandy and coffee. 'Not now. Tomorrow.'

'No dice. Tomorrow is too late.'

Suzanne opened her mouth to speak, then closed it firmly as Milena reached Lee and pushed the beaten copper tray under his nose. Lee smiled up at her without any warmth, accepting the coffee and glass of brandy. Milena sat down between Suzanne and himself, smiling serenely at him.

'I suppose you'll want to retire early, Mr Corey.'

'Maybe,' he acknowledged.

'You appreciate that Bruno has instructions to allow no one to leave the house.'

'Does that include Miss Delar?' he asked, looking at Suzanne with a level gaze.

'Of course not,' said Milena, patting Suzanne on the thigh and almost purring the words. 'She only joined us for dinner, didn't you, my dear.'

141

Suzanne nodded, her face pinched and small. Lee swallowed his brandy and stood up, leaving his coffee untouched. 'Well it looks as though I won't be able to catch your act tonight,' he said lightly. 'Maybe some other time.'

She nodded, looking even more despondent, and as Lee went out into the hall he heard Milena speak to her in a low, sharp voice. He didn't catch the reply since he was already into the hall, where he noted with cynical amusement the impassive figure of Bruno wedged into a carved Moorish chair. They exchanged looks of mutual dislike as Lee climbed the stairs to his room, pausing at the top to look down on the chauffeur. He was still watching, as he would be all night, just hoping that someone would make a try for the door. Especially Lee Corey.

In his room Lee went immediately to the suitcase and took the envelope containing the microfilm from the concealed compartment. Ryker's change of plan presented him with a dilemma. If they were taking off at eight in the morning there would be no opportunity to deliver the package to the Embassy, and the chances of getting to a phone between Algiers and Rome were remote, to say the least. He sat staring at the envelope, debating whether to destroy it now, or somehow risk getting it across the city that night.

Max Weller would expect the attack to be scheduled for tomorrow night, but Lee had no way of knowing how much information Hannigan had been able to pass to Washington before he was taken. From Ryker's casual remark it looked as though the agent had been planning to collect the tapes from the plane, but there was no way of knowing whether this was before or after he had spoken to Max. Lee could only assume that Max did not know any details of Ryker's plan. Therefore he would be forced to stake out the bullion and the aircraft, using his own agents and the Italian police, and they would be completely unprepared for the simultaneous hijacking of the Lufthansa flight by Lodtz and his fanatics. There would be chaos . . . and Ryker thrived on chaos.

He began to wish he had used the CIA man at the Embassy, even though it would have exposed Weller's involvement in the Stadelheim affair. At least Rome would have been warned. At least Lodtz would have been stopped. The more he considered the situation, the grimmer it looked. Unless he did something tonight, the complex manœuvre to trap Ryker was going to turn into the biggest fiasco of all time. He went over the situation a number of times before accept-

ing the inevitable. Any attempt to get out of the villa un-
detected was bound to fail, thereby causing Ryker to cancel
the operation and devote his entire resources to making sure
that Lee never got out of Algiers alive. Faced with that prospect he had no hesitation in deciding to take his chances in
Rome. But there was one risk he was prepared to take. The
one that involved Suzanne Delar.

It was half an hour before he heard her saying good night
to Milena, coming out into the hall and pausing at the foot
of the stairs. Above, lost in the shadows of the landing, Lee
waited to see if she was going to collect her things from the
bedroom, hoping desperately that she hadn't already done so.
He breathed a sigh of relief as she asked Bruno to call a taxi,
telling him that she was going upstairs for a moment. Quickly
he moved along the corridor and into the bathroom, waiting
until she was about to pass before stepping out and taking
her arm.

She jumped nervously, opening her mouth to speak, then
pausing uncertainly as he gestured for silence. Her face was
pale, tense, and from the way her eyes moved nervously
towards the stairs, she seemed on the verge of running back
to Bruno. Lee put on his most reassuring smile and held
open the bathroom door. She hesitated for a long moment,
then reluctantly stepped inside. He followed, closing the
door and turning to her.

'I don't want to talk to you, Lee,' she said. 'I can't.'

'Then just listen. Ryker's got you on the hook, we both
know that, but if you do exactly what I say you can get out
of this mess once and for all.'

She looked at him with wide-eyed disbelief, her hands
twisting nervously in front of her. She wanted to believe
him, but it was too late for that now. There were so many
things he didn't know. She opened her mouth to tell him,
but Lee had taken the envelope from his pocket and was
holding it out to her.

'You're the only one who can deliver this for me. Do it
and you'll never see Ryker again, never need to be afraid
of his people again. I promise you that.'

She took the envelope, staring at the address with numbed
bewilderment. The words hit out at her with a shocking impact. 'The United States Ambassador'. She gazed up at him,
her mouth dry, her brain refusing to accept the shattering
truth. 'But, Lee . . .?' she began weakly. 'What's this for?'

'A way out. Take it to the Embassy and insist that you hand
it to the Ambassador or the 1st Secretary personally.'

'But why? What's it all about?'

'It would take too long to explain. Just do it, and by tomorrow night it'll all be over.'

He was about to say more when they both heard the footsteps outside the door. They froze, Suzanne's face going white with fear. There was a knock, then Milena's cool, impersonal voice.

'Suzanne? Are you in there?'

Lee nodded quickly for her to reply.

'Yes, Milena. Just getting some of my make-up.'

'Paul wants to see you before you leave.'

Suzanne stared helplessly at Lee, her brain still spinning with the shock of his revelation. He gestured quickly to her handbag, his steady gaze bringing an empty, hollow weakness. She couldn't tell him now. She couldn't tell him anything any more. Putting the envelope in her bag, she gave him a tremulous smile, turning to the door.

'I'm coming down now.'

'Very well.'

Footsteps moved away from the door and she started to open it. Lee took her firmly by the arm, turning her to him. He kissed her gently, his mouth relaxed and tender, and in a lonely corner of her mind she began to cry.

'Take care,' he said softly.

She nodded, forcing a shaky smile, and then she was hurrying away before the mask could crumble and he would see it all.

Lee gave her a full ten minutes to collect her things and go down to Ryker, then he moved silently back to his own room and lay on the bed until long after midnight with a gun in his hand. Eventually he put the gun away, undressed and went to bed, confident that nothing more would happen that night. But when he finally went to sleep, he was still telling himself that there had been no other way; that the girl's own actions justified his right to use her.

Sixteen

The African sun was already putting a liquid shimmer into the air as Matheson turned the Hawker Siddeley 125 to face the long strip of runway that ended a mile away. The aircraft shuddered as the Viper engines rose to maximum revs, shrieking out a song of power that echoed out across the shrub-covered plain to the tiered city of Algiers.

Lee gazed at the distant oasis of coloured rooftops and white domed buildings that rose in layers on the hills overlooking the bay, crowned by the fortified palace of the Kasbah. The aircraft began to move forward along the runway, rapidly picking up speed, and he turned from the window to Ryker, who was deeply engrossed in a mass of papers spread out on the seat beside him. The interior of the aircraft had been stripped of the heavy leather armchairs and replaced with four seats, with two more at the front and two at the rear. In twelve hours, he knew, most of them would be occupied and they would be on the last leg of their journey. The aircraft stood on its tail and there was a brief moment of weightlessness, then the crackle of power from the rear as Matheson pulled away from the runway.

'You can go forward and tell Matheson that as soon as he's able to put the plane on auto-pilot I want him back here,' Ryker said crisply, not even glancing up from the file.

Lee nodded and unfastened his seat belt, making his way along the steeply-sloping aisle into the flight cabin. Inside Matheson was draped negligently behind the control column, flicking one switch, then the next, whilst he chatted gaily with Algiers Control. From the sound of the conversation they would be glad to see the back of him.

Lee dropped into the seat beside him, waiting until he had levelled out and reduced power, before passing him Ryker's instructions. Matheson waved a limp but expressive hand

145

towards the rear.

'Tell the silly cow I'm busy.'

Lee grinned. 'Switch on the intercom and tell him your-self.'

'I've got to clear with Gibraltar Control, check with Paris and get up to twenty-three thousand feet on a flight path that will keep everybody happy.' Matheson glared at him, pushing the wavy blond hair from his forehead. 'And this bloody air conditioning still isn't working.'

'Life is tough.'

'How right you are, sweetie. I'll be an absolute rag by the time we cross Germany.'

Lee left him to it, returning to the main cabin to find Ryker stripping back the carpet and pulling open an inspection panel. He glanced up at him irritably.

'Well, give me a hand, Corey. We need the equipment un-packed and ready by the time we reach Tonder.'

Lee took over, pulling out six heavy canvas packs that had been neatly stowed in the inspection tunnel that ran beneath the centre of the passenger cabin. The first pack contained six pistols and two dozen assorted magazines of ammunition. Four were standard Walther P.38s with silencers, the other two Mauser machine pistols. Ryker took one of the machine pistols and two magazines, checking the heavy weapon critically before taking it back to his seat.

The second and third packs contained some thirty H.E. and incendiary grenades, all of them primed and sealed in plastic pouches. In addition there were three two-pound packs of plastic explosive with electronic detonators. He set these care-fully aside at the rear of the plane before turning to the remaining packs. There were two pairs of night binoculars, three walkie-talkies, six heavy-duty torches masked and blinkered for directional use, and a selection of black webbing and pouches.

The last two packs were by far the heaviest and as Lee un-wrapped the canvas covers Ryker moved back to watch him. The contents sent a cold shiver down his back. Each pack contained five of the new British Stirling 9 mm. sub-machine-guns, complete with deadly night-sights and silencers. Lee stared down at them for a long moment, fully aware of the havoc they could cause in a crowded airport. The night-sights were capable of amplifying available light some 5000 times and made it one of the most dangerous weapons in the world.

'That's a pretty high-powered armoury,' he said quietly.

'The best,' agreed Ryker. 'Each of those guns costs more than £2,000, and that doesn't include the price I paid to get hold of them.'

'Where from?' Lee asked casually.

Ryker hesitated briefly, then picked up one of the guns and slapped the heavy magazine into it. For a moment the short, stubby barrel swung and centred on the American. 'Why do you ask?'

Lee shrugged, ignoring the weapon. 'No reason.'

Ryker chuckled softly and tossed the gun to him. 'You'd be surprised how eager the British are to sell their latest little toy. These particular guns were sold to a firm specializing in airfield security. Rather appropriate, I thought.'

'Especially if the customs decide to board us at Tonder.'

Ryker shook his head contemptuously. 'They won't. We're discharging no cargo, just picking up a small party of business-men. Our flight plan routes us to a private airfield in Sweden where our arrival will be dutifully logged and recorded at 1.15 p.m. today.'

They placed a Stirling submachine-gun on each of the ten rear seats, together with two magazines and a pouch of grenades. The front seats were reserved for Carl and Lodtz, and in addition to the Stirlings these received a set of bi-noculars, walkie-talkie, and one of the torches. As they were completing the task Matheson appeared, strolling along the aisle and favouring the assorted weapons with vague dis-taste.

'My, we are having fun, aren't we?'

'You just get us there,' Ryker said bleakly.

'Whatever you say, sweetie. But from the look of that little lot, I'm surprised you didn't put in bomb doors and load up with napalm. We could have zoomed in and wiped out the whole bloody airport!'

'Maybe next time,' Ryker said carefully. 'We'll see how good you are on this one first.'

The pilot looked at the guns and grenades, his expression hardening. Lee watched him closely, wondering how far Matheson was prepared to go. The array of weapons left no room for doubt in his mind that Ryker intended giving no quarter, and once the Germans were on board they would be past the point of no return. He glanced at Lee, his eyes curious, calculating, searching for some indication of the American's feelings. He found nothing and turned back to Ryker.

'Pinching a planeful of gold is one thing, Ryker. This is

147

something else.'

'So?' Ryker asked softly, his eyes boring into him.

'So just how far are you planning to go?'

'All the way.'

The silence grew around them, the steady whistle of the jets the only sound as they cruised effortlessly at 23,000 feet. Ryker's eyes flicked briefly to Lee, a message in them. The American nodded, took a step to his left so that his hand was inches away from a Walther P.38. If the pilot saw the movement he gave no indication. Instead he slowly shook his head.

'I agreed to take part in a robbery, not a bloodbath.'

For the first time that day the tension began to show in Ryker. He had taken Borsch's place in a desperate attempt to salvage an operation that was vital to his future plans. For many men the gold itself would have been reason enough, but for the Connector it was also the power such a massive coup would bring him. He knew all too well what the price of failure would be, and as the pilot continued to regard him with cool distaste a black rage began to burn through his veins.

'Nobody ever backs out of a deal with me, Matheson,' he grated.

'I agreed to fly you in and to take your Jumbo out. You should have told me about the fun and games in between.'

'I operate on a need-to-know basis, and all you need to know is that when you step on board that 747 it will be fuelled and ready to go.'

'And if I don't?'

The question hung between them for a long moment. Lee reached down casually and came up with the gun, holding it lazily in his hand. Matheson flicked a glance at him, his mouth tightening.

'Use that gun in here and we're all finished.'

Lee moved the gun and pulled the trigger. The shot crashed out in the confined space, stunning the pilot, turning Ryker's dark features pale with shock. They stood, like abandoned puppets, their eyes glassy with fear as they waited for the air to explode out of the pressurized cabin. Lee smiled bleakly and pointed to the seat. He had fired at an angle so that the .38 calibre bullet tore through one seat, then the next, spending itself long before it reached the third row.

'You mad bastard!' Matheson exclaimed. 'If that had gone through the wall!'

'But it didn't. Now why don't you listen to what Mr Ryker has to say.'

Ryker was staring at Lee with a vaguely baffled expression. Matheson sat down, his eyes fixed malevolently on the American. Lee smiled, nodding to Ryker who took a handkerchief from his pocket and wiped it across his glistening forehead.

'The only thing we're concerned about is the gold,' he began. 'Our purpose is to take it over with the least amount of trouble, and that means no killing, no shooting, unless it's absolutely necessary. All this hardware is for Lodtz and his fanatics. What they do is no concern of ours. It just makes a very difficult robbery very simple.'

'We'll still be connected with the killings. Every policeman in Europe will be after our scalps.'

'You're wrong.' Ryker shook his head with conviction. 'All the Germans will have false papers when they board in Denmark. As far as the Danes are concerned we are taking them to a business conference in Sweden. Your flight plan says so, and Air Traffic Control will receive a routine notification of your arrival there. When you ask for emergency landing permission at Rome you will be on your way back to Algiers. Alone. The attack starts an hour after you have landed, long after you have handed the plane over to maintenance and apparently left the airport. There will be nothing to connect you with the terrorists, or the bullion robbery. Nothing.'

Ryker smiled bleakly, exuding confidence. 'It will be assumed that the terrorists came by car. Their vehicles will be found beside a section of fence on the far side of the airfield. Why should the authorities think of looking for a private jet arriving from Sweden, when the terrorists are German and came by car? The chances are that they'll never even know that you landed there.'

'They'll know when nobody goes back to collect the aircraft.'

Ryker gave him a condescending look. 'We're not fools, Matheson. Tomorrow morning I shall call our Mr Davereaux and complain bitterly about the serviceability of his aircraft. I shall claim a refund unless his own engineers carry out a full service and deliver it to us in Algiers.'

Matheson considered him quietly for a moment, then nodded slowly. 'It might work.'

'Might!' Ryker gave a short, barking laugh. 'Davereaux will panic. He'll phone head office and they'll have a crew at Rome before the day is out. They'll service it and fly it out, and

149

no one is even going to remember that you flew it in.'

'All right,' said Matheson, beginning to relax. 'But that still leaves your German friends?'

'They're on their own from the moment you drop them at the end of the runway. What they do is no concern of ours . . . just as long as they do it on schedule.'

The pilot rose to his feet, nodding slowly, but his eyes were guarded, his voice thin with tension. 'Very well, Mr Ryker, I'll fly your plane. But you're a cold-blooded bastard all the same!'

After Matheson had returned to the flight cabin, Ryker dropped into the seat beside Lee and regarded him curiously for a long moment. When he spoke his voice was tinged with a reluctant admiration.

'You have a useful knack of doing the right thing at the right time,' he said. 'If we'd lost Matheson, life could have become very difficult for us.'

'That's what I figured,' Lee replied casually, then indicated the small round hole in the seat in front of them. 'But we'll have to put some kind of patch over these holes at Tonder.'

'Carl will take care of it. He used to be in the furniture trade.'

Lee smiled cynically. When he fired the shot there had been the vague idea of using the holes as an excuse to go into the town, or at least the terminal building, to obtain repair materials. If he had managed to go alone it would have provided an opportunity to get to a phone. Instead the cold and ruthless Carl, a trained and fanatical killer, turned out to be a member of the furnishing trade. He fought back a feeling of gloom. So many things were going wrong and the closer they came to Rome the more he learned of Ryker's brilliant strategy. His only hope was Suzanne. Unless Weller received that microfilm in time, they were all lost . . . all the way down the line.

150

Seventeen

They landed at Tonder on the border of Denmark and Germany at 12.15 in driving rain and low, dark strato-cumulus clouds. Matheson taxied to the parking area beside the small terminal building, then went outside to supervise the refuelling. It took the best part of an hour, then as the tender drove away, a uniformed airport official hurried over from the terminal and spoke briefly to Matheson, before running back through the rain. A moment later a small group of figures detached themselves from the building and made their way to the aircraft in a straggling line. Ryker gave a grunt of satisfaction beside the window and Lee moved to the door, pulling the lever that swung it out and lowered the folding steps.

The Germans entered in a silent procession, their faces streaked with rain and the tension that had built in them during the past few hours. They filed past Lee with thin mouths and empty eyes, the dark and sinister forces that drove them painting their features with gaunt fingers of distrust. They moved stiffly, as though their minds had already rejected the bodies they served; as though the horrors that lay ahead were no longer part of their world. They entered the aircraft like the walking dead, waiting for the kiss of life that would come with the snarl of a submachine-gun.

The only member of the group who showed any animation at all was, predictably, Sigrid. She bounded up the steps, eyes glowing, kissing Lee with a blatant need before her eyes caught the blue-black gleam of the Stirlings. She left him then, grabbing the first empty seat and the weapon that lay there. In a moment she was totally absorbed in the gun, like a child with a new toy, checking the mechanism, trying the magazines, looking along the barrel with hungry eyes. She swung it, looking for targets, her pale tongue flicking

151

over dry lips. She found Lee and he stared for a long moment into eyes glazed with an insane need to kill, and then they cleared and she laughed softly, patting the seat beside her. He shook his head, covering his revulsion with an apologetic grin, then moved away towards Ryker before he forgot all about Weller and C-2 and put her out of her misery, the way he would a mad dog.

Ryker had risen to face the group, regarding them with a mildly benevolent expression, like Santa Claus with a sack full of goodies.

'As you can see, no expense has been spared to equip you with the finest weapons available.' There was a ripple of nodding heads and he beamed. 'Use them, Comrades. Use them well. I shall begin a general briefing in about four hours time, so until then I suggest you relax and familiarize yourselves with the equipment.'

Ryker joined Lodtz and Carl, speaking to them earnestly for a while, occasionally referring to his closely typed schedules. Lee took a seat by the window, watching the terminal. It was still raining heavily and he wondered what had happened to the Italians. Ryker's lack of concern suggested that they were not yet due. He glanced at his watch. Almost two o'clock. They would have to be airborne by three if they were going to make the detour over Sweden then lose themselves over the North Sea until dark. A small service van was moving across the tarmac towards them. He rose and moved back along the aisle to the door. Matheson came into view by the steps, nodding casually as the van came to a stop. A white-coated maintenance man got out, opened the rear door and began to lift out a number of meal containers. Lee went down the steps to give him a hand, noting with amusement how quickly Ryker came to the door.

They carried the containers into the aircraft and stowed them in the small galley at the rear. There were two packs, each containing twenty foil-covered trays that needed only to be placed in the infra-red oven for thirty seconds. Matheson paid the delivery man in dollars, assuring him that the containers would be returned to one of the central depots during the next few days, then remained by the steps until the man had climbed back into his van and driven away.

By two thirty Ryker was beginning to show visible signs of impatience. Matheson spoke to traffic control, revising his take-off schedule for three o'clock. Above the clouds were black and thundery, visibility down to five hundred yards on the runway and getting worse. Matheson returned from the flight cabin, unable to hide his mocking delight at these un-expected obstacles.

'Air Traffic say that unless we get off in the next twenty minutes, we may find ourselves grounded.'

A sheen of perspiration glowed like a silver mask on Ryker's saturnine features, the muscles along his jaw tying themselves in knots as he fought to control his rising fury.

'Who the hell do they think they are?' he rasped savagely.

'They think they're in charge, sweetie. That's why they're called controllers!'

Ryker gave him a venomous look and went back to the door, staring across the water-logged tarmac to the terminal where lights glowed dimly through the rain.

'We'll eat,' he said, as though that was going to solve some-thing, and shouldered roughly past Matheson.

They were half-way through a hot, tasteless meal of chicken and french beans when Passenger Control informed them that Signors Girondi, Lassane and Verreti were clearing immigra-tion. Matheson immediately contacted the Control Tower and received reluctant permission to take off. The twin Vipers rumbled to life as the three Italians, clutching canvas holdalls, ran through the rain and panted up the steps into the air-craft. With mixed emotions, Lee closed and locked the door, then signalled Matheson that they were ready to go.

The flight across Denmark and over Sweden was uneventful, and after climbing to 33,000 feet they turned out over the North Sea and began the long, curving approach that would bring them over the European air lanes some time after ten o'clock. At this height, and in this region, they were effectively lost to radar, and Matheson had received confirmation from the Scandinavian controllers that their flight plan was now closed.

Ryker produced his detailed plan of the Leonardo Da Vinci Airport, indicating the runway Matheson expected to use and the point along the slipway where he would slow to allow them to drop out. After he had briefed them on the time and method of their approach, he handed over to Lodtz, who took even less time.

'Lufthansa Flight 241 will be parked at this gate,' he said, indicating the third leading pier at the northern end of the terminal. 'The passengers will board the aircraft, a Boeing 747, at 11.45. We move in across the service apron to the air-craft stand at 11.50, or sooner if Ryker's assessment indicates that we should do so.'

One of his team, a squat, heavy-browed Bavarian named

Seegal, rose to ask with deliberate stubbornness why their plans should be arranged to suit Ryker. Lodtz shrugged, his pale eyes flicking over the rest of the faces, then returning to Seegal with icy contempt.

'The answer is simple enough for even you to understand,' he replied bleakly. 'We will be flat on our faces in the darkness beyond the service apron. Ryker and his team will be across by the cargo bay, and from that position they can assess the best time for our attack. It is also useful to both sides if our attacks coincide, creating as much confusion as possible.'

There were no more questions, so Ryker suggested that it was time for them to get changed. Sigrid moved along the aisle, handing out tins of dark stain which the Germans proceeded to rub into their faces and hands. Lee had joined the Italians for the briefing, trying unsuccessfully to start up a conversation. It appeared that none of them spoke English, and Lee's knowledge of Italian left too many holes to warrant an attempt at communication. They were all heavily-built men in their late twenties or early thirties, and from their frequent glances towards Lodtz and his team of terrorists, suitably impressed by the company they found themselves in. Each man had selected a Walther P.38 and, from their rapid working of the guns, were quite capable of using them. Beyond that Lee was not too sure. They had the look of second-rate goons about them. All muscle and bone with nothing in the 'think' department.

Sigrid was stripping down to bra and pants, giving him a sullen glance as he went by. The effect was destroyed by the black stain covering her face, making her look more like something out of a Black and White Minstrel Show. He flashed her a promising grin before moving to the front of the aircraft and entering the flight cabin. The moment he stepped in he knew they had trouble. The cabin reeked of pot.

'Take a pew, sweetie,' said Matheson, waving a limp hand at the seat beside him.

'Are you out of your mind? If Ryker comes in here he'll go berserk.'

'I don't care if the silly cow has galloping thrombosis. As long as we're doing our thing at thirty-three thou, you do it my way or not at all.'

Lee looked at him in disgust. The pilot was so high he couldn't even focus. Lee pulled the thin reefer from between his fingers and ground it on the floor, then searched his pockets for the rest of it. Matheson made a weak attempt to stop him, but he slapped his hand aside and slammed him back in the seat, when he tried to get up.

'Is this thing on auto-pilot?' he asked, finally locating the pouch of tobacco and packet of finely-ground hash.

'It's totally controlled by my super-conscious mind,' Matheson informed him loftily. 'The all-seeing eye is in command, moving us through space and time as I ordain.'

Lee slapped him twice across the face, watching the eyes focus and a dull anger tighten the mouth.

'Do you feel that?'

'Do it again and I'll bloody kill you!'

'Fine, now how many joints did you take?'

Matheson grinned stupidly, his eyes starting to go again. Lee grabbed his wavy blond hair and lifted him to his feet, noting with some satisfaction that when the eyes focused again they had tears in them.

'How many?'

'Two,' said Matheson, and swung wildly at his jaw.

Lee avoided the blow easily, then stepped in to hold the pilot up before he collapsed over the controls.

'So how long will it last?'

'Not long enough, sweetie. Not long enough.'

Just as quickly Matheson was on the way down, his face sagging with dejection, his eyes clouding with misery. Lee lowered him into his seat, hoping that the auto-pilot was at least taking them in the right direction.

Matheson started to hold a conversation with himself. 'It's a lousy bloody scene, darling. No honour left, no cause, no purpose. Here we are, crawling about like maggots in a tin can, carrying a plague of evil to some other heap of maggots. Just a plague of bloody maggots, that's all we are, darling.'

'How long will it last?'

Matheson closed one eye and considered him through the other. 'How long is life? How fast is a bullet? How short is . . .?'

Lee pulled him to his feet again, slapping him deliberately for a full minute. When he stopped the pilot took a long, shuddering breath and groped for his tobacco. He didn't find it and looked reproachfully at Lee.

'Get me one of those crappy chicken dinners, will you?'

Lee considered him dubiously. 'Are we on the right course?'

Matheson glanced at the instruments, then shrugged. 'More or less. I don't need to set a flight path for Italy until ten. By then I'll be my own worst enemy again!'

Lee went out into the passenger cabin, ignoring Ryker's

155

questioning look and making his way to the galley at the rear. He loaded half a dozen trays into the oven, set the bell to go. The Germans had all changed into black sweaters and slacks, many of them already buckling on the webbing and filling the pouches with grenades and ammunition. Rimmer had joined Sigrid and they were in deep conversation, the girl frequently referring to a plan of the airport and stabbing a finger at the position she clearly wanted to hold. Rimmer was politely shaking his head, occasionally pointing towards Lodtz and indicating that she take it up with him. The bell went and Lee took out a tray, passing Sigrid as she pushed the plan aside with a sulky expression. She caught his arm, her grip tight and demanding.

'I hope that's for me?'

'Not unless you want to take it up to the pilot.'

She pouted, the pressure on his arm growing more persistent. 'I haven't seen much of you at all.'

'Later,' said Lee. 'When you've had a chance to clean up!'

Her mouth twisted angrily against the dark stain of her face and she quickly let go of his arm. He moved on, feeling her malevolent gaze all the way into the flight cabin.

Matheson was leaning back in his seat, his feet propped on the instrument panel, dreamily contemplating the universe. Lee dropped the tray on his lap and took the seat beside him.

'Eat.'

'You are a darling,' he murmured, 'I just don't know what I'd do without you.'

They went into the approach circuit for the Leonardo Da Vinci Airport at 22.45, Air Traffic Control quickly dropping them through the landing stack when Matheson reported overheating in the starboard engine, coupled with falling oil pressure. In less than five minutes they had him on his final approach coming in low over the suburbs of Rome.

In the main cabin the air crackled with an electric tension as the last minute preparations were made. Lee, together with Ryker and the Italians, had changed into dark green coveralls with the insignia of the Rome Airport Authority. The loose-fitting garments easily concealed the small amount of equipment they needed, the only bulky object being the walkie-talkie. Ryker had elected to carry this openly on the assumption that anyone who saw it would think he was using it to contact his dispatch office.

Lee occupied the seat by the door, ready to pull the lever the moment Matheson turned off the runway and dimmed the cabin lights. He looked down the aisle towards the flight deck, wondering why Ryker was spending so long in there. Matheson had almost recovered from the effects of the pot, but if Ryker expected any kind of intelligent conversation he was in for a disappointment. Nevertheless a small note of alarm was beginning to sound in the corner of his mind. Ryker had waited until they were on the final approach before going to see Matheson, and he had made sure that Lee took up his station by the door before doing so. He wondered what was so important at this late stage.

There was a squeal from the tyres as they touched down on the runway, then the rising roar of power as the engines were reversed to reduce speed. The cabin lights flickered and Lee rose to stand beside the door, the black-clad Germans rising simultaneously and moving down the aisle towards him, like a well-drilled team. The aircraft braked and began to turn off the runway, slowing to a crawl as it moved on to the slipway. The lights went out and Lee pulled the lever by the door, feeling the cold night air rush in as it lifted outwards. Lodtz stepped into the opening, his face so black it was indistinguishable from the night outside. Only the eyes gleamed, staring at him, and then he was gone into the night. The next figure to leave was slim and managed to leave a faint aura of perfume before she, too, was gone. One after the other they dropped into the night until there was no one else waiting beside him. Lee pulled the lever, closing the door, then buzzed Matheson on the flight deck.

The lights went on and they began to move forward again, around the perimeter towards the maintenance hangars. Ryker appeared, walking down the aisle towards Lee, the Italians falling in behind him.

'The next time the lights go,' he said tightly.

Lee nodded. 'You want me out last?'

'First,' said Ryker. 'You can leave the door to me.'

Lee shrugged, hiding a sudden alarm. The previous day Ryker had made a point of telling him he would go last, pulling the lever to close the door a split-second before he jumped. The lights blinked out and there was no more time to think. He pulled the lever and stepped out into the night, hitting the cold damp tarmac and rolling to cushion the shock. The aircraft moved slowly over him, the hot blast of jets burning at him as he rolled clear of the runway on to the grass. As his eyes adjusted to the darkness he made out other figures rolling away from the plane, then a last bulky shape that dropped heavily a second before the door swung down.

Ahead lay the terminal complex, bathed in brilliant light, and all around was the noise of jets coming and going in the night. Along the loading piers a line of aircraft were parked, the service vehicles scurrying between them. He wondered if Max was in one of them, supervising the stake-out that would already be waiting in the target aircraft. And then he wondered if Suzanne had gone to the Embassy at all; if the microfilm had been dispatched in time or diverted by some over-enthusiastic official. And then he stopped worrying. There was no more time.

Eighteen

Ryker lowered the nightglasses and spoke softly into the walkie-talkie set.

'Ready Black Leader.'

There was a hiss of static, then Carl's voice came through clear and precise. 'Standing by.'

It was 11.42 p.m. and they were sprawled on the cold wet grass some six feet from the concrete apron, the brilliant lights which illuminated the entire area fading into deepening shadows along the perimeter. To their left a couple of Boeing 727s and a VC 10 were parked by loading bays, and to their right the long concrete building that housed the freight offices, dispatch departments and bonded warehouses. The terminal building lay before them, dominated by the glass-walled concourse which separated them from the main aircraft stands that stretched the length of the building. The Jumbo piers were at each end of the huge building, the Lufthansa Flight 241 already boarding, unaware that in the darkness lay ten fanatical killers determined to use any means to achieve their ends.

Lee glanced towards the north end of the terminal, unable to see the Jumbo stands, feeling the tension build in him as the seconds ticked by. If Max had received the information in time there would be a hundred gun-sights already scouring the darkness for them. For the hundredth time, Lee told himself that the air of normality was nothing to go by. The very nature of a stake-out meant that everything should appear to be normal. A hand tapped him on the shoulder and he turned to see Ryker pointing towards the main doors of the cargo bay. Two uniformed policemen carrying stubby sub-machine-guns had appeared, taking up positions on either side of the door.

'Any minute now,' Ryker whispered, 'they'll start moving

the bullion.'

Lee nodded, glancing at his watch. They were on schedule, the loading was due to begin in three minutes. Beside him, Ryker clicked on the walkie-talkie.

'Go, Black Leader. Go.'

Lee swung round, staring at him in amazement. The Germans weren't supposed to go until the gold was actually loaded on to the aircraft. Ryker was watching him in the darkness, his teeth gleaming in a mocking smile.

'Don't look so surprised, Corey. It's better this way.'

Lee was suddenly aware of the Italians around him. One on each side, slightly to his rear, the third lost in the darkness behind him. He could feel their eyes, could feel the wall of tension between them.

'What the hell are you playing at?' he said tightly. 'It's too soon.'

'On the contrary, my timing is always perfect.'

Lee lay in the darkness, seething, knowing that any sudden move would be all the proof Ryker needed. Somehow the Connector had begun to suspect and somewhere along the line he had begun to make alternative plans. But what those plans were, only he knew. Lee cursed silently, feeling the move behind him as Ryker laughed softly in the night. The cold steel barrel of a silencer came to rest behind his ear, then a hand groped round to his waist and removed the Walther P.38.

'You're out of your mind, Ryker! What kind of double-cross is this?'

'Let's just say that your motives are suspect. You go in with us, carry out my orders. If you fail at any stage, one of us will kill you.' He leaned close to him, his breath rasping in his ear. 'It's a very simple choice, is it not?'

A white flare exploded in the sky above the north end of the terminal and simultaneously a siren howled up into the night. Lee was suddenly aware that no aircraft had taken off or landed for the past five minutes. The entire terminal was strangely silent. So Max had been prepared, but the knowledge only served to fill him with bewilderment. He had begun to believe that Suzanne had been caught with the microfilm, but the only way Max could have set the trap at the north pier was by having that film. It didn't make sense. He looked towards the brilliantly-lit north pier, watching the small dark figures converging on the area. A voice was echoing across the service area, amplified from a dozen speakers. Significantly it was in German.

'Achtung! Achtung! Aufgeben – die Waffen strecken.'

The message was repeated twice – and then the shooting started.

Sigrid was halfway across the tarmac, close behind Lodtz and Carl, when the flare exploded above them and the sirens began. There was a frozen moment of numbed disbelief, then Lodtz was snarling and diving to the ground. Sigrid slid the breech back smoothly, cocking it, lifting the nightsight and swinging it round in a half circle that scanned the airfield behind them. A cordon of dark figures were moving through the night. She turned back, feeling a black despair. 'All over. Before it even started.' The voice was ordering them to put down their weapons. Around her the group were crouching or lying on the ground, their dark faces glistening with fear. Carl was facing the terminal, staring straight into the spotlight that had stabbed out to envelop them the moment the flare had shown their position. He didn't move, just stood with the gun at his side, staring into the light. Behind her, Heinz was cursing in a flat, empty voice. There was a clatter as one of the group threw down his gun. Then the rage came. A shivering, shuddering, incandescent rage. Without even being aware of it she found a fragmentation grenade in her hands. The pin slid out, the detonator popped, and then she was running, screaming *'Scheisse'* at the blazing lights.

The first shots took Carl as he stood in the light, tearing into his body, turning him and lifting him clear of the ground so that the sky seemed full of the blood that sprayed out of a dozen wounds. His body fell beside Lodtz, a lifeless, broken thing. Bullets were exploding on the concrete all around them, but Lodtz didn't move. He stared into the dead face of his friend, then slowly and carefully picked up his gun. The first burst extinguished the battery of spotlights, the second burst caught a maintenance van as it raced towards them from the shadows beside the pier. The bullets must have killed the driver instantly, because he had no time to brake. The vehicle spun out of control, smashed into the side of the building and overturned, spilling out uniformed security guards who lay where they fell. Lodtz reloaded, then gestured savagely to the rest of the group. They began to run, crouching, weaving, searching for cover, And then the night erupted as Sigrid's grenade exploded beneath the fuel tanker parked beside the towering 747.

With the explosion Sigrid left the shelter of the generator truck she had reached, miraculously unscathed, and ran for the Jumbo. Ahead the fuel tanker was expanding into a ball of liquid fire, effectively shielding her from the rows of marksmen on the roof of the terminal. There was a flicker of movement to her left and she spun, crouching low, firing from the waist and moaning with delight as the bullets tore into the two security men who had stepped forward from beneath the plane. She reached the huge set of eight wheels, wedging herself between the front and rear pairs. Now she could cover the rest of the group.

Swinging up the night-sight, she scanned the darkness beyond them. More than twenty men, either police or soldiers, were running towards the service apron. She pressed the trigger, swinging the gun in a steady arc, watching men spin and fall as the murderously accurate burst of 9 mm. bullets ripped into them. The silencer was magnificent, she decided, the only sound a gentle thudding of air, the only vibration a steady pressure on the shoulder. She pulled out the empty magazine and clipped a fresh one into place.

Lodtz and Seegal had reached the cover of the generator truck and from this position could sweep the area behind them. Seegal took care of this whilst Lodtz pulled the pins from two grenades and tossed them towards the terminal. The first shattered windows the length of the building, the second showered white-hot magnesium into the departure lounge. In seconds the room was blazing and the marksmen crouching behind the windows were staggering back. Lodtz leaned out to beckon to Rimmer and two other men who were lying flat on the concrete, firing at the men on the roof. Nearby were two still bodies, Lintner and Felderstein, and beyond was Jorgen, twisted in helpless agony near the darkness he had tried to reach. Rimmer waved acknowledgement and slapped his companions. They began a low, weaving run towards the generator truck, only halfway across when two armour-plated riot trucks roared around the corner of the terminal.

Lodtz watched helplessly as the three men turned to face the new threat. Gunfire opened up from the roof again, high velocity bullets shrieking off the concrete all around them. One man went down, his mouth gaping, his strangled cry of agony lost in the uproar around them. The riot trucks drove straight at them, submachine-guns opening up, chopping Rimmer across the legs as he lobbed a grenade towards the first vehicle. It detonated seconds after the driver wrenched over the wheel, but in doing so he collided with the second vehicle coming up behind. The exploding grenade shredded the front tyres and both vehicles came to a grinding stop. The third man fired a final burst, then tried to run towards Lodtz. He managed only three steps before nickel-plated bullets tore into him, turning him round, then slamming him down on the cold wet concrete.

There was a brief moment of silence as the security forces assessed the damage. The riot trucks were immobilized, the blazing tanker was perilously close to the 747 . . . and if that went up, the terminal would be in danger. In the departure lounge asbestos-suited firemen were spraying chemical foam over the blaze. At least a dozen men lay dead or wounded, excluding the seven dead terrorists.

In a small room high up in the control tower, Max Weller stared with tight features at the bloody chaos on the TV monitor. The attack had come too soon, another five minutes and the trap would have been complete. He found it difficult to understand what had gone wrong, why Ryker had moved so early. His own men were still waiting on board Flight 394 and the bullion had not yet left the cargo bay. He switched on the radio link with Faulkner on board the 747.

'Gerry?'

'Yes, chief.'

'Anything moving?'

'Not a thing.'

'Is the bullion cleared from cargo yet?'

'I checked a minute ago. It was still inside, waiting for clearance.'

Max hesitated. If he held up the gold, Ryker wouldn't wait for long. He would pull out, using the darkness, perhaps even get clear of the airfield. They had to catch him in the act. There was no other way.

'Okay, Gerry. I'm authorizing clearance now.'

'Right, chief. We're ready for them.'

Max flicked another switch and spoke briefly to the Director of Security. The man was more than reluctant to go ahead, but Max pointed out that the sooner the gold was on the 747, the sooner he could release his guard detail to reinforce the men at the north pier. Switching off he stared once again at the photo-copies of Ryker's plan. It was all there. The timing, the method, the attack on the 747 as the last of the gold was loaded. He turned back to the intercom, pressing the switch.

'Gerry?'

'Yes, chief?'

'According to our information, Ryker and his team are wearing airport security uniforms. Don't let it put blinkers on you. They could be wearing something else.'

He switched off and turned back to the TV monitor. The men from the riot truck were crouched behind the stationary vehicles, pouring rapid fire into the shadows of the generator truck. Even as he watched a grenade exploded, wounding two of the men and sending the rest running for the cover of the terminal. He shook his head, baffled. If this part of the plan was wrong, could he trust the remainder? He pressed the switch on the intercom.

'Gerry?'

'Yes, chief?'

'Detach five men from the stake-out and get them over to the cargo bay.'

'Trouble?'

'Maybe. I'd just feel happier if some of our own men are around when it leaves there.'

In the cargo bay Lee watched with numbed disbelief as the Italians finished gagging the six security guards beside the baggage trolley. Ryker stood covering the men, his face distorted by the nylon stocking, but his wolfish grin was unmistakeable. It had all been so ridiculously easy. The Italians had strolled across the service apron, talking casually until they reached the doors to the cargo bay. The guards had suddenly found themselves facing three menacing guns and had quietly stepped back inside. After the guards had been knocked unconscious, Ryker and Lee had crossed the wide tarmac and joined the Italians. They knew their way through the cargo bays, choosing a route that bypassed the main freight counter, passing behind rows of freight containers to the edge of the bonded warehouse. Here the bullion was waiting on three trolleys connected to a single tractor. The guards had been beside it, listening to the distant gunfire. The sight of three cargo handlers crossing the open bay did not alarm them at all. By the time Ryker and Lee stepped out, wearing the nylon masks, there were three guns at their backs and a stream of rapid Italian informing them that the slightest move would earn them a bullet and their wives a pension.

'You drive,' Ryker said crisply, gesturing to the tractor.

Lee shrugged and climbed on to it. 'Where to?'

'The east exit. We're going out on to the main aircraft

stands, along the loading gates to a 747 you'll find beyond the east pier.'

'You play things pretty close to your chest, Ryker,' Lee said bitterly.

Ryker chuckled. 'That's part of my charm. Lodtz was always meant to be a diversion, just as you became a decoy. Make the slightest move and I will kill you. Do it right and you may convince me that Flight 394 is not full of policemen.'

Lee started the tractor and turned it towards the ramp leading down to the east door. Ryker jumped on to the trolley behind, stripping off his mask a moment before they emerged in front of the main passenger gates. There was no activity here. The aircraft were empty, all passengers safely inside the terminal. There were also no guards, for the battle was taking place at the north end of the building . . . and Weller's men were waiting on an empty 747 on the opposite side of the terminal.

Sigrid had one grenade left. A large, grey canister marked incendiary. She placed it beside her, strangely empty of sensation now. The battle had become a boring game of firing at blurred figures as they showed briefly at a window or along the edge of the roof. She could be sure of only three, and it was not enough. Not if this was to be the last time. She looked back towards the generator truck. Lodtz was between the wheels, the Stirling across his arms, a small heap of cartridges in front of him which he was pushing into an empty magazine. He was doing it slowly, with difficulty, and she lifted the night-sight to confirm that he was wounded. Blood glistened the length of his left arm, putting a gleaming satin finish on the black woollen sweater. She swung the sight to Seegal, finding him beside the rear offside wheel. He lay on his back, the Stirling still clutched in his hand, his head turned at an odd angle, the eyes glistening in the drizzle of rain that had begun to fall. There was movement on both sides of the pier now. Dark, uniformed figures were advancing behind a heavy fire tender beyond the 747, and on the other side figures sprinted from the corner of the building to the riot trucks. Wedged between the wheels she made a difficult target, but not for long. With a sigh she picked up the incendiary grenade and backed slowly towards the nose of the plane. In the deep shadows beneath the fuselage she went unnoticed. Across the concrete apron two figures appeared, running lightly forward, then crouching down and firing long steady bursts towards the generator truck. The second burst found the petrol tank and the vehicle exploded with a dull roar, the flames funnelling out between the front wheels, engulfing Lodtz as he tried to fit a fresh magazine into the Stirling. With a long, keening cry of agony, he rolled into the open, his clothes blazing, still clutching the gun in his hands. No one moved. A hundred pairs of eyes watched in fascination as he tottered forward, a slowly moving pillar of fire. Then Sigrid shot him.

It was the only time it failed to give her pleasure. She did it with contempt. She had never thought she would hear Janos Lodtz moan and whimper like an animal. Seconds later the bullets came searching for her beneath the plane. They sang off the concrete like a thousand angry bees, whispering in the darkness round her face, finding her as she knew they would. A bullet tore through her left side, another plucked at her shoulder, a third slammed like a hammer into her back. But they didn't hurt. She sat down on the concrete beneath the nose, unable to understand why they didn't hurt. There was only a dull, cold ache. Nothing more. It was the greatest disappointment of her life. All the time she had believed they tore and burned and racked the body with the fires of torment. But they didn't hurt at all. Hysterically she began to cry.

The soldiers and security guards began moving cautiously across the open ground. Sigrid saw them, lifted her arm awkwardly to wipe tears from her eyes, then pulled the tape of the grenade and tossed it into the gaping mouth of the huge Pratt and Witney turbofan engine. The blast singed her hair and plucked at her clothes, and then she was staggering away into the darkness as men ran for their lives and the gigantic 747 slowly, majestically, blew itself apart.

Max was waiting impatiently in the room below the Control Tower when Faulkner finally buzzed him from the plane.

·'Harry just called from the cargo bay, chief. The guards are on their faces and the gold has gone.'

'Christ! When?'

'Hang on, Harry's still talking to them.' There was a brief pause then Faulkener again with a baffled tone in his voice. 'They didn't come this way, chief. They took the east door.'

'East!' Max pressed two switches on the intercom. 'Security, full alert on the main loading area. East door. Check every plane on the apron.'

There was no time for the reply. The building shook and he turned in time to see the 747 on the monitor explode with

166

shattering ferocity, and then the remote TV camera cut out.

The 747B was parked beyond the main terminal departure gates, a generator truck hooked into the fuselage power points. The aircraft had bold scarlet livery proclaiming it to be a Sun Charters flight and Lee noted with bitter disappointment that the slim figure of Matheson, wearing a smart blue Captain's uniform, was already talking to the ground maintenance man. It couldn't really go this far, he told himself. Unless Max had gone to sleep and the stake-out aboard flight 394 believed they were actually coming, someone must realize the bullion was on its way to another plane. Behind them there was a dull, reverberating roar that shattered windows along the concourse. There were screams from passengers milling about at the windows, then the sky was bathed in a crimson glow. He didn't need to guess the cause.

He drove the tractor beneath the 747, stopping beside the open cargo hatch. The Italians jumped off and quickly began to load the small flat boxes into the aircraft. Matheson had climbed the steps into the plane and now appeared on the flight deck high up above the nose. He waved to the man beside the generator and with a long, groaning whine, the first of the gigantic engines rumbled into life. Ryker stood beside him, his eyes shining with unholy delight, as he watched the sky turn crimson beyond the terminal.

'Time to go on board, Corey,' he said softly, nudging him towards the steps.

Lee went slowly to the foot of the stairs, pausing briefly to look back along the line of parked aircraft. There was no fleet of cars, no swarm of policemen. The Italians had already cleared the first trolley and were starting on the second. Bitterly he went up the steps and into the passenger cabin. The first person he met was Milena, wearing a crisp, pale blue stewardess's uniform. The second was Suzanne.

He stared at her for a long, frozen moment, before speaking with icy contempt. 'You bitch! You silly bloody bitch!'

And then Bruno stepped forward to hit him with the barrel of a Luger and there was only darkness and a dull, red pain.

Nineteen

Matheson let the fourth engine warm up, then pulled the throttle back to idle. Ryker stood beside him, peering tensely through the canopy towards the far end of the terminal. Two security cars had appeared, moving along the line of parked aircraft.

'Time to go,' he said, his voice crackling with tension. 'They'll see us in about one minute.'

A green light winked on among the mass of dials and instruments that covered every available space before him. Matheson began to relax.

'The cargo's on board.'

'Then let's move.'

The pilot leaned over and looked out of the window to the maintenance man below. He was holding his earphones, still plugged into the plane, looking up at the flight deck. 'Thank you, ground,' he said calmly. 'Disconnect please.'

The Italian stared up at him with a baffled expression. He spoke quickly into his microphone, the broken English still managing to convey his bewilderment.

'*Por favor*, Capitan . . . you do not have the-ah . . . the passengers?'

'That's all right, sweetie. We're just moving the old girl over to maintenance.'

The figure below scratched his head and looked anxiously towards the terminal, clearly out of his depth and hoping for help from that quarter.

'Never mind him. Move it,' snarled Ryker.

'Towing a generator truck behind us is going to be just a teeny bit conspicuous.'

Halfway along the parking area one of the security vehicles had stopped beside a VC.10. The other was moving on to the next aircraft. The moment it cleared the fat bulk of a Lockheed Tristar, they would see the generator truck and know it was starting the engines. Below one of the Italians had moved up to the maintenance man, tapping him on the shoulder. As the man turned the Italian pulled off his head-set and stuck a pistol in his face. They vanished under the belly of the aircraft and Matheson breathed a sigh of relief.

'Here we go,' he said softly.

Ryker grunted and moved back towards the body of the aircraft, crossing the first-class cocktail bar, then descending the spiral staircase to the huge connecting cabins that carried seating for more than four hundred passengers. The size and scale of the aircraft never ceased to amaze him. The empty seats stretched away in endless procession, the high ceiling making it more like a small theatre than a flying machine.

He reached Bruno and Milena as the first two Italians came on board. Their faces were running with perspiration, the green coveralls saturated with the effort of loading the bullion.

'Where's Mario?' barked Ryker.

They pointed to the steps leading down into the darkness. Bruno looked out, turned back and shook his head. Ryker cursed, snatching the internal phone from the wall.

'Matheson. Are they close?'

'They're boarding the Tristar, but the other car is on the move.'

Ryker hesitated, the blood pounding in his temples, his mouth parched with the hot, blinding tensions that were beginning to block out all thought, all logic. He gestured savagely to the steps as he spoke into the phone.

'Now, Matheson. All the power you've got!' There was an immediate answering roar from the engines. At the same moment Milena gestured quickly.

'He's coming.'

A figure appeared in the darkness, lurching through the open door. Only then did they recognize the blood-stained features of Sigrid. There was a moment of shocked silence. Ryker stepped forward, forcing a twisted smile to his lips, but stopped when she lifted the Stirling submachine-gun and waved it unsteadily at him. Suzanne, sitting beside the un-conscious figure of Lee Corey, could only stare at the bloody figure incredulously. She was more dead than alive.

'The door,' Sigrid gasped hoarsely. 'Close the door.'

Milena stepped into the open doorway to push the steps clear before pulling the lever that activated the hydraulics and slowly sealed the door. Immediately the aircraft began to move, the engines thundering out over the terminal as almost two million pounds thrust them with increasing speed across the loading apron towards the slipway.

The security car containing two Italian policemen and one of Max's FBI squad was just clearing the tail of a VC 10 when the 747 began to move. Together with the other car they had spent ten minutes checking out the line of twenty-six aircraft, assuming that only aircraft beside loading gates would be ready to leave. The simple fact that a charter aircraft, well clear of the loading area, was a sitting target for Ryker was a point which had so far escaped Air Traffic Control. In fairness to the harassed Italians perched high above the terminal, they were far too busy coping with the scene of total devastation below. Some twenty fire appliances were spraying foam over the blazing wreckage of the 747, whilst a further six were at work on the wing of the terminal itself. The situation was further complicated by a fleet of ambulances and auxiliary vehicles ferrying wounded security men out of the danger zone. There simply wasn't time to consider Ryker or the gold, much less the 747B which was thundering down a slipway towards the main runway.

The phone in front of the Senior Controller had been buzzing persistently for three minutes. In exasperation he snatched it up.

'*Momento! Momento!*' he shouted.

'Never mind your bloody *momentos*,' bellowed Max Weller. 'You're about to lose a 747 and half a ton of gold!'

The Controller blinked, then half rose from his seat to look out over the airfield. In the distance the aircraft was making a wide turn, ignoring the warning signs along the slipway, cutting directly towards the departure point. The two security cars were racing towards the runway to intercept.

'Well?' shouted Max. 'What are you going to do?'

'Signor,' he said regretfully. 'There is absolutely nothing we can do.'

'We can block the runway,' Max said savagely. 'I can get those two cars right in the middle and tell the men to get clear.'

'No. No, I cannot allow that. If the aircraft failed to stop, there would be another disaster.'

'That's their problem!'

'No, Signor, it is mine. I have thirty-three aircraft stacked up to twenty-two thousand feet, waiting to land. If the 747 were to crash this airfield would be out of commission for the rest of the night.'

Max slammed down the phone and went to the window,

chewing savagely on a cold cigar. Across the airfield the Jumbo was lining up for take-off, the security cars already on the runway about a quarter of a mile ahead. The radio phone was bleeping and the Italian Director of Security, looking like a man who has just taken a stroll through hell, was anxiously waiting for him to answer it. The mighty engines of the 747 rose to a thundering roar and it began to move forward. They were going for broke, he realized. It was the only thing they could do. He turned wearily to the phone and picked it up.

'Chief?' It was Harry, his slow drawl unusually quick and sharp. 'You've got about thirty seconds.'

'Okay, Harry. Let it go.'

He put down the phone and went back to the window, watching as the cars drew back to the edge of the runway, allowing the mighty jet to roar past, lumbering up into the night like a Brontosaurus with wings. He wondered if Lee Corey was on board and had to suppress a burning anger at the thought. Although, logically, he knew that Hannigan's disappearance had complicated matters for the agent, he had still managed to get the microfilm to the Embassy. But somewhere along the line Ryker had known, and then he'd used the situation to his own advantage. They had expected four terrorists, not ten. An attack on the bullion aircraft, not in the cargo bay. And according to the plan he had received from Algiers, both groups were arriving by car on the south side of the airfield. He knew now that this had been totally false. He also knew now that he could never show sufficient proof to extradite Ryker from Algeria.

Staring up into the night sky, he cursed Corey with a bitter finality. Tonight Ryker had started a new kind of war. A strategy of terror where even the authorities would be forced to accept that the price of law and order was too high – too painful. He turned away from the window and picked up his hat and coat. The security man stared at him with haggard features.

'We could call the air base and have them send up a couple of fighters.'

'What's the point,' Max said wearily. 'That baby can cruise at 45,000 feet for the best part of 7,000 miles. And you can't have fighters searching international airlines in the middle of the bloody night.'

He stepped out into the cold night air that reeked of burning kerosene and chemical foam. He began to walk slowly away from the terminal, trying to come to terms with the one unpalatable fact. Paul Ryker had won.

At that precise moment the Connector was facing Sigrid across the wide centre aisle of the 747 with a growing sense of desperation. The woman was almost out on her feet, a steady stream of blood oozing from her side and shoulder. Her face was chalk white, twisted into a grotesque grin, and the eyes never left him, burning into him with a savage intensity.

'How could we have known?' Ryker asked for the third time. 'The leak must have come from your people.'

'Impossible,' she rasped. 'Only Carl and Janos knew the details.'

The gun never moved from its line on his stomach, her finger white with the tension on the trigger. He licked dry lips, feeling the sweat running down his face like warm rain.

'Look,' he said placatingly, 'let us take care of those wounds. You're bleeding to death. We can talk about it all later.'

'Now,' she said. 'I want to know who set us up and why.'

There was a movement across the aisle and his eyes flicked towards it, seeing Corey begin to stir. Suzanne, her face a white mask of misery, stared back at him helplessly.

'All right, Sigrid,' said Ryker, trying to hide the fear in his voice. 'You might as well know. I discovered that Corey is working for the FBI. He set us all up.'

Lee was trying to sit up, wincing with the pain and holding the back of his head. He glanced round slowly, taking in the scene with glazed eyes, then quickly looking at Ryker as memory flooded back.

'When did you know?' Sigrid asked, her breath shallow, the slim body beginning to sway unsteadily.

He watched her hungrily, willing her to die. In any other situation the sight of this bloody, pain-racked figure would have been a supremely sensual moment. But he was on the other end of her torment and the knowledge filled him with terror. They were too alike, they had the same warped passions and he knew that the end would be savagely brutal.

'The attack,' he said hoarsely. 'When you started the attack.'

'He's lying, Sigrid,' said Lee, turning towards her in his seat. 'He's known since yesterday. He just used you all to give himself a better chance.'

Sigrid stared at him with glassy eyes, trying to comprehend the words. What little life was left in her was contained in the hands which held the submachine-gun. She was completely unaware that Milena had stepped silently back to a

172

position out of her line of vision.

'He knew?' she asked, desperately trying to absorb the information.

'The bastard's lying,' snarled Ryker. 'Don't listen to him.'

Lee rose to his feet, facing her. 'All right, I was working against you, but Ryker knew and that's why he changed his plan.'

The words finally penetrated, making sense. She found a last reservoir of strength and straightened, the gun steadying on his chest, the finger tightening on the trigger.

'Wait! Listen to me!' cried Ryker. 'I can explain . . .'

'*Stirb!*' she gasped, her face contorting into a twisted mask of pain and hate.

Milena stepped forward, a thin knife held expertly in her hand, to slip it smoothly between the fourth and fifth ribs, angled at forty-five degrees for the heart. Sigrid's breath left her in a small sigh – a second after she pulled the trigger. The breech slammed forward, the firing pin finding nothing more lethal than an empty magazine. For a long moment they stood· in frozen attitudes, their minds numbed by images of bullets shattering the pressurized skin, of air screaming out into the night, sucking their bodies with it to a high oblivion. Sigrid crumpled slowly to the floor, Milena unmoved behind her, the knife in her hand gleaming redly in the light. Then Ryker turned with blazing fury and smashed his fist into the American's face.

Lee tried to come back at him, still dazed from the concussion, but Ryker was like a madman. Totally oblivious of the white-faced girl between them, he rained blows into his face. Lee grabbed a wrist and pulled him forward, but Bruno had stepped behind the seat and now clubbed him down with an iron hard fist. Ryker finally stepped back, breathing heavily, then turned and walked unsteadily down the deserted aircraft.

Suzanne watched him go, only dimly aware of the man slumped beside her, his face a mass of ugly cuts and bruises. With a sudden, shocking clarity, she was aware of the changes that had occurred in her. There had been no revulsion when Sigrid appeared, no horrified protest when Ryker had launched his vicious attack on Lee. There had been only a detached interest, an empty void where concern and horror should have been. And gradually there had been something else. A sense of excitement; a warm, pervading glow that came from nowhere and drank up the violent passions around her. She had been like the spectator at a bullfight, knowing that the bloody spectacle should only provoke disgust, but finding instead the fierce thrill of primitive passions. Only this had been no corrida. Ryker had been no matador. She had become the victim of her own fantasies, the willing pupil of Ryker's twisted desires. 'Oh dear God,' she thought. 'I enjoyed it. I actually enjoyed it.'

For Suzanne Delar, today had been graduation day.

The sun rose, tipping the edge of the blanket of cloud some thirty thousand feet below, when they were a silver speck in the sky above the endless wastes of the Sahara Desert. Matheson had made a long, sweeping arc across Libya and the nomadic lands of Chad and Niger, before turning north across the two thousand miles of desert towards Algeria. He knew that at this height, in this region, they were clear of radar and virtually undetectable. He wondered idly about the American, feeling a grudging respect for the way he had almost brought Ryker down. He shook his head, smiling, as he recalled the way Corey had forced him to go to Denmark. If he had only known then that Suzanne had taken the microfilm to Ryker, who had sat up all night preparing a false plan before photographing it so that she could get it to the Ambassador, Corey would not have been quite so eager to get to Rome.

As it was, Ryker had kept even Matheson in the dark until they were on the final approach to the Da Vinci airfield. His instructions had been simplicity itself. After handing the jet over to maintenance, he had only to cross to the departure lounge where Milena was waiting with a holdall containing a captain's uniform. He changed in the toilets, then joined Milena with Suzanne and Bruno, all now wearing Sun Charter uniforms. Long before the attack started they had been on board the plane, checking it out, the airport authority oblivious to the fact that the real crew had received a message at their hotel informing them that the flight was postponed until the following day. He grinned maliciously as he thought of the 380 Italian holiday tour operators still waiting for their trip to the Seychelles. They were never going to forgive Sun Charters.

Ryker entered, standing on the raised deck behind the triple flight seats, staring out of the canopy at the deep blue sky that seemed to be nothing more than another crystal canopy holding back the airless void of space. Some of the stars were still visible and he appeared to enjoy the moment, gazing out until Matheson turned and raised an enquiring eyebrow.

'How long?' asked Ryker.

174

'On automatic for an hour, then we start our descent.'

He nodded, then managed a grudging compliment. 'This is a lot of aircraft to handle.'

'I'm not handling it, sweetie. As long as nothing goes wrong, it flies itself. But if we get problems, we need a crew of three – and even they would be pushed.'

Ryker gave him a baffled look and waved at the million dials. 'You know what's happening.'

'Vaguely,' said Matheson, without much conviction. 'I suppose I can understand about twenty per cent of it. The rest tell me things I wouldn't want to know about anyway.'

'But can you bring us down?'

Matheson laughed softly. 'You haven't read your Newton, sweetie. What goes up, must come down!'

Ryker gave him a disgusted look and went back into the passenger cabin, telling him there was coffee when he felt like it. Matheson yawned, checked the auto-pilot and climbed out of the seat.

Lee was sitting beside a window halfway down the main cabin, Suzanne four seats away, looking small and dejected. The pilot collected a cup of coffee from Milena at the centre galley, passing Bruno and the two Italians and taking the seat next to Corey.

'In a bit of a spot, aren't you?'

'It happens to all of us at one time or another.'

'True,' murmured Matheson. 'But the result isn't usually quite so drastic.'

Lee smiled drily. 'It hasn't happened yet.'

'That's what worries me, sweetie. I have such a weak stomach and I get the feeling that dear Paul is saving you for something rather nasty.'

Suzanne glanced at them quickly, her face tight. Lee stared back coldly, directing his words at her.

'Then he's wasting his time. The worst is over.'

Matheson laughed, his eyes on the girl, amused by the situation. She was half turned towards them, her cheeks burning.

'You had no right to use me like that.'

'Sure,' Lee replied with icy contempt. 'I should have known better. Any girl who ties herself up with a couple of kinks like that is on a one-way trip to nowhere.'

'You know why I did it,' she said, biting her lip.

'I know why you think you did it. But by the time he's through with you I'll bet you won't even remember you've got a brother!'

She flinched at the words, but before she could make an

angry retort, Ryker was beside her. He glanced at Lee, his hand moving to her shoulder and massaging it gently as he spoke.

'Don't worry, my dear, there'll be plenty of time for Mr Corey. More time than he would ever dare to imagine.'

Lee stared back at him without expression, but there was an icy knot in his stomach as he saw the sadistic gleam in the man's eyes.

'How long has she known?' he asked, nodding at Suzanne.

'Since I had her brought back to the villa,' Ryker revealed mockingly. 'She was given a simple choice. Either she walked out and said goodbye to many things, including her brother, or carried out a simple task that would guarantee a future for both of them.'

'Hijacking has never been simple.'

Ryker shrugged. 'I needed a crew to walk out to the plane with Matheson. Without a steward and stewardesses people might have got suspicious. It was the simplest part of my plan, but the most crucial. They had to be waiting in the main concourse when we arrived with a set of Sun Charter uniforms. I'm sure Suzanne feels that the trip was well worth two tickets to South America, plus a little something for a rainy day.'

His hand was squeezing her shoulder with rhythmic movements. She stared straight ahead, her face pale and taut. Lee watched her sadly, knowing he couldn't help her any more. She had made the only kind of choice she was capable of making, and had yet to pay the price.

'You'll never let her out of Algiers, Ryker. We both know that.'

The hand stopped moving on her shoulder and his mouth tightened angrily. He gave a short, barking laugh, then turned and strode away towards the rear of the plane. Suzanne glanced briefly at Lee, her eyes clouded with doubt, then she rose and walked listlessly towards Milena.

'That's the trouble with birds,' mused Matheson. 'They never know what they want until they haven't got it.' He grimaced wryly. 'I never could stand them.'

Lee grinned and reached into his pocket, taking out the small leather pouch of special tobacco. He passed it over to the pilot.

'How about rolling us a smoke.'

Matheson beamed with delight. 'What a lovely idea.'

He quickly shook tobacco into the palm of his hand, then a small amount of the finely ground pot, passing the pouch to Lee so that he could roll the mixture in a thin brown rice paper. With a speed that only comes with years of practice, he fashioned two narrow reefers and passed one to Lee. He glanced back towards the rear of the aircraft before holding out a light.

'Do you think Ryker will be back?'

'I doubt it,' Lee reassured him. 'But just to be on the safe side . . .'

He reached up and turned the ventilator on full. Matheson chuckled, sucking the hash-laden smoke into his lungs and holding it there, eyes closed, for a full thirty seconds. Lee smoked carefully, taking only short puffs and blowing it out almost immediately. Even so the mixture was strong and by the time he was halfway through the reefer, a tell-tale lightness was coming into his arms and legs. Matheson was staring up at the ceiling with a contented expression, letting smoke trickle slowly from his nostrils.

'Why don't you finish it on the flight deck?' Lee suggested, passing him the rest of the tobacco. 'No one is going to bother you up there.'

'Good idea,' he agreed. 'You're such a sweetie really. I wish there was something I could do.'

With a regretful look he made his way unsteadily up the aisle, but fortunately no one paid him much attention. Lee didn't relax until he had vanished up the stairs, then stubbed out the reefer and settled back to wait. Landing the 747 was going to be tricky enough with a clear head, but with double vision and delayed reactions it would be about as easy as doing handstands in a hurricane. He smiled wryly, reminding himself that he didn't like landing at the best of times.

177

Twenty

The ungainly bulk of the 747 thundered over the plateau two hundred miles west of El Golea at 7.15 a.m. The sun was already scorching the sand, putting a shimmering haze in the still air. The shattering roar of the huge engines seemed to echo from horizon to horizon, disturbing nothing but the blind horned vipers that lazed among the rocks.

Lee pulled the seat belt tight across his stomach, making sure that the seat was as far forward as it would go. Ryker had gone up to the flight deck whilst the Italians were wedging themselves in the rear beside Milena and Suzanne. Only Bruno remained, strapping himself in at the opposite end of the row to Lee, a pistol tucked into his belt. The aircraft banked unsteadily and through the window he watched the rippled sand dunes turn beneath them. As they straightened up, the aircraft lurched again and he smiled bleakly. There had been a distinct sloppiness in the controls ever since they had begun to descend towards the desert floor.

On the flight deck Ryker was staring at Matheson, speechless with rage. The pilot was lolling in his seat, grinning inanely, as the distant plateau rushed towards them.

'You stupid bastard!' choked Ryker. 'You'll kill us all.'

'Oh piss off, you silly cow,' Matheson replied, waving a limp hand towards the door. 'I don't know what you're bothered about. I'm too pretty to die!'

'Take her up again,' he hissed. 'Take her up and stay up until you're sober!'

Matheson considered the suggestion for a long moment, then shook his head. 'No chance, sweetie.'

'Why not?' Ryker asked hoarsely. 'Why the hell not?'

'Well for one thing we haven't got the fuel, and for another . . . I couldn't stand the suspense!'

They had passed over the plateau and were now banking

steeply into a full 180 degree turn that would line them up with the runway. The aircraft shuddered, buffeted by the hot air currents, causing Ryker to clutch at the side of the cabin. Matheson lazily moved the controls, flicked at switches with bland indifference. The cold sweat of fear ran down Ryker's face as he stared at the desert floor a thousand feet below. He still could not believe this was happening. The landing had always been the most dangerous part of the operation, an experience he never expected to share. Desperately he took the only course left open to him. He jammed his pistol into the back of Matheson's neck.

'If you don't climb immediately,' he snarled, 'I'm going to blow your head off.'

Matheson chuckled and blew him a kiss. 'Better strap yourself in, sweetie. Here we go.'

He snapped down a lever beside the seat and there was a rumble far below as the heavy undercarriage unfolded and locked into place. The 747 yawed wildly and Matheson was suddenly very busy, feeding more power to the engines and notching up more flap. Ryker stared at him with impotent rage, then suddenly turned and hurried back towards the main cabin. When he had gone the pilot straightened, leaned forward in his seat and began whistling softly. He had enjoyed his little game with Ryker, but although the pot had put a singing in his ears and a lightness in his limbs, he was in full control of his senses. The plateau was lined up ahead and he eased back the throttles, letting the huge aircraft settle belly-down towards the sand, notching up full flap as the rim of the plateau raced towards them.

There were only seconds left now and he began to laugh softly, feeling the fire in his veins, the throbbing surge of excitement as the monstrous machine hung in the sky a mere hundred feet above the plateau. This was what it was all about. This was the only reality he had ever valued. The pulsing vertigo of mind that stretched the nerve-ends to every vibrating component of the machine. The endless moment in time when all had been done, when the brain began to split each optic pulse into a frozen frame of crystal clarity, so that the desert floor and battered runway came up at him in a steady procession of sharply defined pictures. A thousand of these pictures had flashed into the recesses of his brain before the warning sounded and he became aware of the high sand drifts across the runway.

He cursed bitterly. There was no going back. Some time during the past twenty-four hours a sandstorm had passed this way, building ragged banks of sand across the runway at regular intervals. He should have seen them on the first pass, but with Ryker breathing down his neck and the heady arrogance that always came with pot, he had failed to notice. With a rueful grin he pulled the throttles back and they slammed down on to the battered runway.

Almost immediately Matheson reversed the giant turbofans and slammed the throttles forward, the brief silence quickly shattered by the awesome howl of two million pounds of instant energy. But they were already on to the first drift of sand, lurching through it with spinning tyres and screaming metal. At the controls Matheson fought desperately to keep them on a straight line, one hand gripping the undercarriage lever, ready to snatch it up the moment they left the runway. The first sand drift slewed them round and he only had time to partially correct before they hit the second. The mighty aircraft shuddered as it swung broadside, the forward motion immediately causing the tyres, now at a completely wrong angle, to burst into flame. They were in that position, sliding sideways on blazing tyres, when they hit the third, and heaviest, drift of sand.

The starboard undercarriage was torn away from the fuselage and the aircraft heeled over, bringing the giant engines into shrieking contact with the runway. The impact ripped away the entire wing, spinning the aircraft round so that the second undercarriage collapsed, slamming the port engines against the tarmac. The speed was still close to a hundred miles an hour as the shattered 747 left the runway, hurtling across the desert with a savage violence, the scream of tortured metal filling the sky as the second wing sheared away and the wide, fat hull ploughed on through the sand.

Matheson watched from his canopy high on the nose of the hull. Ahead was a long broken plateau, no more than fifty feet high, surrounded by boulders. They were bouncing and wallowing towards it, the interior of the aircraft a wailing wall of sound as impact after impact detonated against the hull. With a weary sigh of resignation Matheson realized that they were going to reach the rocks. He also realized that the bulging overhang at the top of the cliff was about thirty feet above the ground. Unless he was very much mistaken, that was about the height of the flight deck. A second later he knew he was right. The last frozen image to reach his brain was the canopy shattering around him as a wall of rock descended on the flight deck.

Someone was screaming in the passenger cabin and it took a

full ten seconds for Lee to absorb the fact that it was Suzanne. He unfastened his seat belt, pulling himself up the steeply angled line of seats to the centre aisle. On the other side was Bruno, beginning to fumble for the release mechanism of his belt. With dazed eyes he saw Lee reach the aisle and tried to grab his pistol, wasting three attempts before it penetrated that the pistol was no longer there. He stared stupidly at the floor, whilst Lee looked down the aircraft to the rear, noting only slight damage and no apparent injuries. Bruno was cursing viciously, trying to free his jammed belt release. It was too good an opportunity. He moved quickly along the aisle to the centre section where a huge hole gaped in the hull. Avoiding jagged shards of metal, he stepped out into the blinding sun and began to run unsteadily for the rocks.

It was at least two minutes before anyone else appeared from the aircraft. One of the Italians stumbled out, helping Suzanne and Milena through the rear escape hatch. A moment later Ryker followed, a gun glinting in his hand, scanning the desert around them. Bruno appeared finally with the last of the Italians and they stood in a group beside the broken fuselage, arguing about something. At last Ryker seemed to take control, handing his pistol to Bruno who moved towards the rocks. The Italians began to open the cargo hold whilst Milena made her way back along the track gouged in the sand. In the distance, at the end of the runway, stood the truck which the Arabs had used.

From his vantage point at the top of the plateau, Lee could look down on Bruno as he picked his way through the scattered boulders at the foot of the precipitous slope. He could also look down on the crushed canopy of the 747, accepting sadly that no one in there could be alive. Behind him, stretching for at least half a mile, was a mass of boulders and ravines. It would take a hundred men a week to search the area. He grinned with satisfaction as Bruno began to grunt and sweat his way up the slope. Slipping quietly back from the escarpment, he moved swiftly into the barren area of rocks and found a dark crevice no more than two hundred yards away. Settling himself into the shadows he prepared to wait, wishing he could see Bruno's face when he reached the top of the escarpment and saw the futility of his task.

There was considerable activity around the shattered 747 for the remainder of the morning. The truck had moved up to the cargo hold and, with frequent rests in the blazing sun, the Italians together with Bruno and Ryker, loaded the cases of gold into the vehicle. The heat among the rocks was intense and by noon Lee was parched with thirst. He made a brief trip to the outcrop, looking down on the activity beside the wrecked aircraft. Milena and Suzanne sat miserably in the shade, the others continuing to load the bullion. Ryker dare not risk spending any more time here than necessary, so Lee assumed that they had abandoned any idea of searching for him. He returned to the stifling heat of the crevice and must have dozed off, for he was jerked awake by the harsh sound of Ryker's voice.

He was standing some two hundred yards away on the top of the rocky outcrop, bellowing across the jungle of boulders and ravines.

'It's a pity I can't accommodate you personally, Corey, but the outcome will be the same. You're two hundred miles from nowhere and the temperature is 135 degrees. We're setting fire to the aircraft so don't expect to find anything there.'

He paused, scanning the area as though he expected Lee to give him a wave. When he continued he could not fail to conceal the angry frustration in his voice.

'You're a dead man, Corey. Without food and water you'll last maybe a day, and then the sun will fry the brains in your skull. I'm only sorry I won't be around to see it.'

And then he was gone and a moment later the truck started up moving slowly across the desert towards the north. At the same time there was a dull explosion beyond the rocks and black smoke curled into the sky as the fuel ignited. For the next fifteen minutes there was only the roar of flames and the occasional explosion of containers in the aircraft, but when silence finally descended he could no longer hear the truck. He was in a world of silence . . . and heat.

Twenty-One

The sun was low on the horizon, painting the desert in harsh reds and browns, before Lee ventured out of his crevice again. The blistering heat of the afternoon had begun to subside, but the air was still a hot, stifling blanket that sucked the moisture from every pore. Already his lips were dry and cracked, his mouth beginning to burn with the craving for water. Picking his way through the rocks to the edge of the escarpment, he considered his position with a grim awareness of the odds against survival.

He realized now that Hannigan must have been taken at the airport before he had had an opportunity to call Washington. That meant that the location of the desert airstrip had never been passed to C-2. The Sahara was about one of the most desolate spots on earth and even if Max guessed they would use the desert, it could take months to locate the wreckage. His only chance lay in reaching one of the wells to the north, but it was a daunting prospect. Without food or water he must somehow find the strength to walk more than a hundred miles, the only alternative being a slow, painful death without hope, and ultimately, without sanity.

All that remained of the fuselage was a charred and twisted ruin. He surveyed it dejectedly, feeling his last hope fade as he saw that nothing could be salvaged from the wreckage. With a black despair he sat down on a rock and tried to come to terms with the reality which faced him. By morning he would have a raging thirst and very little reserve of strength to combat the full heat of the sun. With a bitter resignation he finally accepted what, in his heart, he had known all afternoon. The odds against survival were too high.

Lee rose to his feet and started to move back towards the meagre sanctuary of the rocks, when a flash of blue caught his eye. Crossing to a boulder some yards from the twisted tail section, he found a flimsy blue scarf that had been caught between two stones. He recognized it as part of the stewardess's uniform worn by Suzanne and Milena, but as he tugged at it with casual curiosity he began to realize that something was tied to one end. Quickly pulling away some loose stones he uncovered a black plastic waste disposal bag from the plane. Inside was a single can of beer, two packets of biscuits and a Luger.

He stared at them for a long moment, knowing before he unfolded the small sheet of paper, how they had got there. The note was brief, hurriedly scrawled: 'I'm sorry, Lee. I wish I could do more. God bless. Suzanne.' He read it at least a dozen times, then folded it carefully and placed it in the pocket of his shirt. She must have found the Luger after Bruno dropped it in the crash. The rest she could have obtained from the galley, running the risk of being caught by Ryker or Milena whose revenge would have been swift and merciless. Opening the can, he took a long drink of the warm beer, his spirits rising as he contemplated this unexpected development. Without realizing it, Suzanne had given him a far better chance than she imagined. The black plastic would enable him to condense water each morning, as the cold night air was warmed by the sun.

With mounting enthusiasm he headed for the broken wings that lay a quarter of a mile from the fuselage. One of the engines was still in place, although half the casing had been shorn away by the impact. Lee spent the next ten minutes working on the engine, bending a narrow gauge fuel pipe backwards and forwards until it finally broke under the pressure. Repeating the process at the other end, he was rewarded with a two-foot length of thin steel tube which he then proceeded to clean thoroughly with sand. As darkness fell he was ready to leave the wreckage. The can of beer and biscuits he carried inside his shirt, the steel tube in his belt along with the plastic bag and under his arm a curved section of steel casing he had found beside the wing. Locating the Pole Star he struck off across the desert, heading north.

The moon rose after an hour and from then on he made good time, walking across an endless expanse of flat, hard-packed sand. By counting his strides he soon established that he was covering four miles an hour and, allowing for a five-minute rest period each hour, had covered some forty miles by dawn. Even at this rate it would take at least five days to reach El Golea, but if he cut due north instead of north-east he could reach the low range of foothills that extended some three hundred miles into the Sahara from the Atlas Mountains. Lee estimated that this should only take him three days and as the foothills were dotted with wells frequently used by the camel caravans en route for Laghouat, it was a risk worth taking.

By the time the sky had begun to pale in the east he was totally exhausted, but in spite of the fatigue that racked his body, he set about his preparations to survive that merciless heat of the Saharan day. He had accepted from the start that in the open, with temperatures around 135 degrees, he could not expect to last more than a few hours. But if he was able to shelter from the heat, perhaps even sleep, then he could survive to walk a further forty miles the following night. Taking the plastic bag he split it carefully down two sides and placed it in a shallow hole he had scooped in the sand. He next chose a site some yards away and began to dig with the piece of metal casing. It took thirty minutes to make a hole six feet long and three feet deep, and by the time he was finished the sun was beginning to warm the cold dawn air. Moving back to the sheet of plastic, he was delighted to find a respectable amount of condensed water at the bottom. With extreme care he lifted the plastic and poured the precious liquid into the beer can, estimating that he had collected four large teaspoonfuls. During the night he had drunk twice this amount, but calculated that with his reserves, and assuming he could obtain the same amount each morning, his supply should see him through two more nights. It meant, however, that he could not afford to drink during the day. He ate two of the biscuits, washing them down with a mouthful of the diluted beer, then wrapping the remainder in the plastic he climbed into his shallow grave and began shovelling the loose sand over his body. The final, and most difficult task, was to hold the steel tube between his teeth with the scarf covering his face as he pulled the last of the sand over his head. His theory was that the sand would insulate him from the intense heat, but breathing through the tube soon proved to be a problem. Sand began to work its way through the scarf and, the moment he relaxed his lips, into his mouth. He was on the verge of abandoning the plan, deciding that he preferred dehydration to suffocation, when he discovered that by turning his head to one side and holding the tube in the corner of his mouth, he could relax sufficiently without getting a mouthful of sand. After an hour he became quite accustomed to the claustrophobic effect of being buried alive, but sleeping was a fitful nightmarish business. By noon the sand was growing hot as the temperature above began to soar, but what was even more disturbing was the fact that the steel tube was heating up and causing each breath to parch his mouth. Resolutely he forced himself to endure the agony of thirst, knowing that without his self-made tomb he would soon be suffering from burns and sunstroke. Mercifully exhaustion sent him into a deep sleep and when he awoke the air from the tube was cold again.

He dug himself out in a world of darkness, his eyes red and swollen from the abrasive effects of the sand. Surprisingly he felt refreshed and after a small drink and two more biscuits, set off briskly towards the north. By midnight he was crossing a region of majestic sand dunes that took almost as much energy to descend as they did to ascend. The constant drag of sand quickly cut his speed by half and when the sky began to pale again he estimated that he had made no more than twenty miles during the night. In addition he was weakening, the pangs of hunger and constant craving for water beginning to take their toll. This time he ate half the remaining biscuits and drank all the water he was able to condense in the precious minutes of sunrise. As he began to pull the sand down on top of him he knew that, even if he made good time the following night, he would find himself without food or water on the third day. He slept badly, dreaming of an endless line of cars and a girl with golden hair who was trying to turn an ignition key somewhere. He found himself running from car to car, always finding the wrong one, always hearing the distant whirring of a starter motor. A chorus of echoes, but nothing more. He awoke with a blinding headache and a mouthful of sand, and found it was night again.

He had no clear memory of digging himself in on the third morning, but by noon he felt as though he was being roasted alive and came out of a delirious sleep to find that he was barely covered by sand. The beer can was empty, either through evaporation or carelessness or his own desperate thirst. It didn't matter. With swollen tongue and blistered features he stubbornly dug himself in deeper, no longer caring if his mouth filled with sand, just as long as he was able to breathe. But the day was a pain-racked torment, waiting for a night he knew would be his last.

The foothills of the Atlas Mountains reach out into the Sahara in a series of rocky gullies and volcanic slopes, descending gradually from the high escarpment that marks the end of the desert and the beginning of the mountains. Lee

186

stumbled into the gully in the last hour before dawn, his eyes so swollen he was barely able to see. But it was clearly a gully, with boulder-strewn slopes and hard rock bottom. On either side sand had drifted into tall dunes, sometimes running across the gully to block it completely. With mounting excitement he stumbled through the darkness, knowing that at least there would be no need to dig himself in after dawn, that this was the region of wells and wadis. But when the sun rose he found that the gully faded away into a sea of sand and low on the horizon, at least a million miles away, was the grey outline of hills. He swayed on rubbery legs, trying to estimate the distance and coming up with figures that brought only frustration and despair. He knew he could not walk a mile, let alone ten or twenty, so he found a shaded rock and slipped into a fever-ridden sleep. When he awoke the sun was an incandescent furnace in the sky, the world a shimmering blanket of heat. He felt no pain, just a numb and weary resignation, a calm relief that the long walk was over. In the distance, between the end of the gully and the distant foothills, a line of camels were moving slowly through the sand. He had been watching them for a full five minutes before his numbed senses began to comprehend that where there were camels there were usually people.

With cracked and blistered hand he pulled the Luger from his belt and fired three spaced shots into the air, then walked slowly out across the sand to meet the tall, blue-robed Tuareg who rode towards him. The last thing he remembered was the gurgle of water from a goatskin bag, smelling like sour hay and tasting like the finest wine.

The journey to Laghouat was a blurred procession of sounds and images. He remembered sitting by a fire in the desert, eating a thick, spicy, cus-cus with three tall figures in the blue robes of the Tuareg. He remembered the long, groaning call of the camels and the clicking commands of the riders. He remembered Laghouat with its noise and teeming herds of camels and goats. But most of all he remembered Ryker and all that he had done.

Lee stepped off the battered mountain bus in the centre of Algiers two days after the Tuareg first found him in the desert. His face was still cracked and swollen, but the fever had gone and his steps were sure as he approached Ryker's villa along the darkened street. Walking silently up the short drive to the garage he quickly forced the lock and eased the cantilever door upwards. The Cadillac was inside and from the coldness of the radiator had not been used for some hours

187

at least. He went around it and opened the door into the rear of the villa.

Although it was no more than ten o'clock the house was strangely silent. There was a light in the hall, but a quick check of the lounge and dining-room showed them to be deserted. With sinking spirits he climbed the stairs, beginning to believe that Ryker was not in the house. He was halfway down the hall when he heard the sobbing moan of pain. Slowly he moved forward, the Luger in his hand, pausing at the door to the bedroom, wanting to be sure. The certainty came with the harsh, grating laugh that could only be Ryker. It was answered almost immediately by a gasping sob of fear.

He opened the door without a sound, slipping inside to stand a full ten seconds before his presence was noticed. Images pulled at the dark corners of his mind during those seconds, rage blurring his senses as he took in the revolting tableau. Ryker stood back from the bed, his black eyes gleaming, his face contorted with a sadistic delight as the grotesque bulk of Bruno cruelly twisted Suzanne across the bed. Beside her was Milena, leaning forward with a wide rubber gag which she was trying to fit over the terrified girl's face. The sweat gleamed on their bodies in the dim light and the air reeked with the acrid odours of fear and lust.

For a long, frozen moment, Lee's finger hung on the trigger, every fibre urging the last milligram of pressure that would send the bullets smashing into the Connector. From Suzanne's abject terror and the ugly bruises across her back and thighs, she had learned the final lesson. She had discovered too late that the essence of sadism is pain, and ultimately that the pain will transcend all pleasure. There could be no prize of gold with a man like Ryker. Not when he could find too many interesting ways of ensuring her silence.

The gag was in place and Milena was leaning back, stroking the girl and laughing softly. She glanced round at Ryker, only then seeing his fear. Slowly she turned, her face stiffening with shock as she saw the American.

'Ryker,' Lee said bleakly, 'turn round and put your hands against the wall.'

Nobody had moved whilst he spoke, but now Bruno rolled away from Suzanne, releasing her hands. She stared at Lee with wide, beseeching eyes, but he ignored her, watching Ryker carefully as he turned towards the wall. On the bed Bruno waited patiently, his eyes fixed on the gun.

'You can name your price, Corey,' Ryker said hoarsely. 'All

188

you want. Anywhere in the world.'

'Right now the thing I want most of all is a small excuse to put a bullet in you. So don't tempt me!'

Ryker spun round, his eyes glassy with fear. Lee levelled the gun, freezing him. From the corner of his eye he saw Bruno's hand appear from below the bed, realizing too late that his clothes would be there and with them his gun. He dropped into a crouch, turning fast, but the Browning automatic in the chauffeur's hand was already centring on him. A bitter rage roared through his veins as he saw that he would not be in time. Then Suzanne was lunging at Bruno, grabbing the pistol in both hands, tearing at it to give Lee the vital second he needed. Lee fired once, the bullet taking Bruno high in the chest, but even as it threw him back he was pulling the trigger of the automatic, firing point-blank into the girl.

Before the echoes had faded, Ryker and Milena were on the move. Seizing a chair from the corner of the bedroom, Ryker swung it towards Lee as he turned back to cover him. It was a wide, heavy chair, and there was no time to avoid it. There was barely time to shield his face before it smashed him to the floor. Ryker didn't pause in his stride, running all the time for the door. Lee was rolling towards him, coming up with the gun in both hands, tracking him and finding, instead, Milena with a knife in her hand. She was drawing her arm back to throw it and there was no time for niceties. He had seen her with a knife once before. He fired as her arm swept forward, the bullet shattering the bone and knocking her back across the room with a cry of agony. He rolled again, knowing Ryker was somewhere behind him, but all he found was an open door. Getting weakly to his feet he crossed to it, looking out, but there was no sign of Ryker. Only the hollow echo of his steps on the stairs.

Wearily he turned back. Milena, her face a marble mask, was staring at Bruno who was sliding gently down the wall, his face blank and uncomprehending as the life ran out of him. Lee crossed to the bed, reaching for the gag on Suzanne's mouth before seeing the hole in her breast. Her eyes were already glazing, the breath a whisper in her throat as he tore off the gag and lifted her head from the pillow. She saw him then and tried to speak.

'Easy,' he said softly.

Suzanne gazed up at him, recognizing the fear in his face as he worked to staunch the flow of blood. There were so many things she wanted to say, so many things she wanted to explain, not just to him but to herself. The thoughts

189

whirled in her mind like butterflies, refusing to connect or relate to one another, and her head felt like a balloon as the room began to grow dim around her. So instead she said: 'Ryker. The gold. Oasis Brezina.'

'Don't worry,' began Lee, then stopped as he saw that she had finally fainted.

He finished bandaging the wound with strips torn from one of the white silk sheets, then crossed to the telephone and called an ambulance. After that he dialled the American Embassy and asked for Max Weller.

'Where the hell are you, Lee?'

'Ryker's.'

'Dammit, why didn't you come to us. You're the only bloody witness we have!'

'He's all yours, Max. You'll find him on the mountain road heading for the Oasis Brezina . . . and the gold.'

He put down the phone before Max could reply, returning to sit by the still figure on the bed. Milena spoke plaintively twice, but he was not interested in her problems. He was looking at a beautiful girl and trying to understand the motives which had brought her to this room.

She came round briefly as they lifted her into the ambulance and her eyes glistened as she saw the concern in his face. The need to go after Ryker, to end it now with a savage finality, was a biting hunger, but he pushed it to the back of his mind and stepped into the ambulance. Max would already have his quota of cold, efficient agents on the road to Brezina.

It was almost midnight before Suzanne came out of the operating theatre, looking like a small wax doll as they wheeled her into the recovery room, and it seemed an age before the green-gowned surgeon appeared.

'The young lady should be all right,' he said, with a reassuring smile. 'The bullet missed everything vital. There will be a scar, of course, but . . .'

Lee nodded, thinking of other scars that would never heal. He walked out of the hospital into the cool night air and found a bartender who looked as though he might be prepared to sit up all night with him. Four hours and a full bottle of bourbon later, his thoughts about Suzanne were just as confused and uncertain as they had been during the long walk out of the desert. Leaving the bar he made his way back to the hospital to find three messages from Max, all marked urgent. He ignored them and asked to see Suzanne.

She was awake, but lethargic with the effects of sedation.

'Ryker?' she asked.

'They'll have him by now, thanks to you.'

She smiled weakly and shook her head. 'No, not me.'

They sat for a while, searching for truth and finding only inanities. It was as though the shadow of Ryker lay across the room, clouding their minds with all the wrong images. 'What will you do?' Lee asked her, finally.

She gazed at him with a gentle sadness. 'Don't worry about me, I'll cope.'

A nurse came in and told him it was time to leave, but still he hesitated, trying to find the right words. Finally she found them for him. 'We can never go back, Lee. People never can. You make a choice and in making it you change a part of yourself. It would never be the same again.'

The cry of a muezzin was lifting up over the mottled rooftops of Algiers as he left the hospital. He bought a morning paper from a kiosk, laboriously translating the French report of the arrest of an international criminal and the recovery of fifty million dollars in gold bullion. According to the report the operation had been carried out by Algerian police following an intensive investigation which had led them to the cache of gold at Brezina. There was no mention of the shootings at the villa, nor of any accomplices.

With a bleak smile, Lee called a cab and told the driver to find him a small, quiet, very discreet hotel.

Twenty-Two

A blazing African sun was scorching the tarmac as the Trident thundered along the runway and lifted up towards the Atlas Mountains. Lee gazed out of the window, knowing they would turn north before he saw the desert and not at all sorry. There was a movement beside him as someone sat down and he turned to find Max Weller leaning back with a satisfied expression.

'You were supposed to report to the Embassy,' he said in a conversational tone.

'Maybe next week,' Lee replied.

'As a matter of interest, how did you know I was going to be there?'

'I knew you wouldn't be far from Ryker, just hoping that something would turn up.'

'Like a bent nickel,' he said, admiring Lee's battered features. 'You're due for a spot of leave.'

'I'll buy that,' said Lee, 'providing it isn't less than twenty years!'

Max smiled a wintry smile and considered the clean white tips of his fingernails. 'About the girl,' he said with subtle menace. 'I gather she'll be out of hospital in a couple of weeks.'

'So?'

'So your report on her part in the operation was rather vague.'

Lee gazed at him with quiet contempt. 'You got the gold, Ryker, and a presidential commendation. What more do you want?'

'I want you to go to Brazil in one month's time.'

'I want you to go to hell,' Lee replied fervently, 'but they probably wouldn't have you!'

Max Weller smiled benignly. He never could resist a compliment.

192

DATE DUE